Five Days in October

Judson B. Emens

© 2008 Judson B. Emens
All Rights Reserved.

No part of this publication may be reproduced, stored in a retrieval system, or transmitted, in any form or by any means, electronic, mechanical, photocopying, recording, or otherwise, without the written permission of the author.

First published by Dog Ear Publishing
4010 W. 86th Street, Ste H
Indianapolis, IN 46268
www.dogearpublishing.net

dog ear
PUBLISHING

ISBN: 978-159858-849-1

This book is printed on acid-free paper.
This book is a work of Fiction. Places, events, and situations in this book are purely Fictional and any resemblance to actual persons, living or dead, is coincidental.

Printed in the United States of America

To Donna,
A loving wife and mother,
My best friend,
The light of my life.

ONE

The room was dark. Not coal black but murky, deep-river dark with slivers of light stretching across the bed from an early morning half-moon. Abi was asleep, dreaming of thousands of monarchs fluttering over a sunny meadow when a small sound slid underneath her door and chased them away. She found herself deep in the fog of uncertainty, that time between dreaming and awakening. Listening. Not breathing. Her weighted eyelids parted as seconds crept. Nothing. Then, an almost imperceptible creak from the hallway. It was thunder to frightened ears. It thundered again. Two creaks were all there ever were. Then, the doorknob turned.

Moon slivers shook from her pounding heart. She stiffened; her stomach; her arms; her fists. The bed caved on the left as he raised the covers. Dread, a precursor of evil, consumed every fiber of her being. She could feel his heat. He pulled her to him, kissed her face and whispered, "I love you," as his hot, night-breath came at her faster, now. She wanted to cry, but remembered he had told her how it made him feel bad when she cried. So, she didn't.

The oldest daughter of The Honorable Jonathan Bankston Morgan and Rebecca Sullivan Morgan was, again, suffering the malicious depravity imposed on her for the past two years of her young life. The still darkness of her bedroom on this October morning shielded her from having to witness the revulsion. Fall and winter were kind in this respect. Spring and summer cruel, dispatching early dawns that forced her to witness her father's crime.

This morning he finished quickly; told her he loved her and closed the door behind him as quietly as he had entered. Then the bathroom door closed and the shower splashed in rhythm with his usual mindless humming.

Abi stared into the darkness feeling nothing. She rolled over, reached for her teddy bear, clutched him to her breast and began the prayer she always said after her father left the room. "Dear God… please… tell daddy to stop. Tell him I love him… but I want him… to leave me alone. I'm sorry I have been bad. Please help me." As always at this point in her prayer, the tears come and she and Teddy cried themselves back to sleep in the warm, cozy confines of her sanctuary, immune from further awakenings.

For too long, thirteen-year-old Virginia Abigail Morgan had served her father in a manner she had never before known. A way that she hated and wanted to stop. Today, it would.

TWO

The heavily starched, white, size seventeen, pin-point buttoned-down hugged the well-tanned, Giorgio-cologned neck of his honor, Judge Jonathan B. Morgan, Circuit Court Judge of the Thirty-first Judicial Circuit of Rutherford County, Alabama.

The lazy spin of the overhead fan cooled the back of his moist neck, still warm from his hot shower. He would be early, this Saturday, for his ten o'clock meeting at the Willow Creek Country Club for coffee with Rutherford County's social elite. But, he wouldn't be able to join them for the regular Saturday morning 'Bloody-Mary' golf tournament because civic duty beckoned. As this year's Chair of the United Way, Judge Morgan's time wasn't as free as it once was, and today's meeting, although image-necessary was a resounding pain in the ass. Nonetheless, he would persevere, for his reputation, for the family, for the good Morgan name, which he almost sullied last year in the Democratic primary. Jonathan Morgan almost became the first Morgan in three generations to lose a bid to be elected Circuit Court Judge of Rutherford County. Had it not been for the black vote, he would have. The embarrassment to his father and his grandfather would have been irrevocable.

The stage was set last year by his father and grandfather orchestrating the announcement of Jonathan's candidacy. With the help and chicanery of his family, countless friends and paid volunteers who stole his opponent's flyers, spread outright lies and blackmailed influential politicians, Jonathan out mud-slung his worthy but under-financed opponent in a hotly-contested election to become what Rutherford County couldn't do without… a Thirty-first Judicial Circuit Court judge by the name of Morgan.

Jonathan slid manicured thumbs underneath maroon and gray, striped suspenders giving them a quick pop signifying reverent admiration of his mirror's work. At thirty-eight, he knew that the looks were still there. His hair was full and dark, more pepper than salt. His complexion was smooth and naturally tanned, the teeth dazzling and the smile, a killer. He touched the twenty-year-old, inch-long scar on his right cheek and smiled. He wore this badge of courage proudly because it was a constant reminder to the townsfolk that he had laid it on the line for Lincoln High School as one of Alabama's most prolific quarterbacks. Some said he would have been better than Richard Todd, the gangly right-hander from Mobile, who starred at Bama and later, with the New York Jets. But it wasn't to be. He never played a down of college ball, disappointing dozens of colleges. Instead, he'd followed his father's dictate, just as his father had before him. *"The law should be your passion, your only obsession."* And so it was.

He straightened his tie and grabbed his gold, engraved money clip as he caught Rebecca's reflection out of the corner of his eye. Still smelling of last night's Jack Daniels, she moaned and rolled over, wrapping her escaped leg in a tourniquet of sheets and blankets. If there's a God, she won't wake up, he thought. He didn't need a continuation of last night's lunacy.

Rebecca Sullivan Morgan was aging quickly at thirty-six. Most thought it was the three kids taking their toll. Only a select few knew it was the liquor.

Jonathan's revulsion of his wife was exceeded only by self-adoration. Willow Creek awaited.

THREE

Poolie, thinking that his mother was watching the boxcars pass while they were stopped at the railroad crossing, summoned up enough nerve to punch the button of his favorite radio station. He had heard enough gospel singing. A young man in his prime can only stomach so much of the good-book's rhythm and blues. He turned down the volume, punched the button, turned the volume back up to where it had been and sat back before she even noticed. The clackety-clack of the train tracks prevented detection of the deed. After the train passed and the radio commercial concluded, the provocative, guttural utterances of a young female rapper regaled Poolie and his mother with suggestive lyrics aimed squarely at young, red-blooded, swiveled-hipped twenty-year-olds like Poolie Buford. In a heartbeat, Hattie Mae spun around, aimed a big fat forefinger between his frozen wide eyes and dared him to draw air.

"Poolie! How many times am I gonna hafta be tellin' you? I ain't gonna be listenin' to no such trash as this in my car or in my house. You wanna be listenin' to trash tellin' you how to be trash, get yo' ownself a car!" The deep vertical line between Hattie's wide-set eyes was a warning. "Now, don't be messin' with that radio no more. The good Lord sho'nuff got His work cut out helpin' me raise you."

Poolie didn't say word one. Just stared straight ahead. He'd heard all this before. The caboose passed and the white 1977 Buick Regal, with a red Landau top and just a few rust spots, eased over the tracks and pointed towards downtown Lincoln, the county seat. The only municipality in the state of Alabama that dared to have the name of the country's sixteenth president.

After passing the courthouse, Hattie slowly turned right on to Forrest Drive, in order to enjoy the beauty of this part of town. The homes were grand, old, sprawling relics of a time gone by, shaded by massive, ancient oaks and hackberries, over a hundred years old and a hundred feet tall. Most of the owners maintained well-manicured lawns in the finest tradition of southern plantation landowners, from whom they claimed they descended. The Morgan home came into view after Hattie turned on to Hickory Street. Dappled shade blanketed the front lawn and the north and east sections of the ornately carved wrap-around porch.

Nestled amongst the manicured boxwoods, grew vivid reddish-purple crepe myrtles and mimosas. The home, built in 1851, was a most dignified aristocratic and truly striking example of Victorian architecture. It had been placed on the National Register of Historic Places in 1973, much to the Morgans' delight. Hattie's grin was as big as a crescent moon as she remembered sittin' down and peckin' out some two-fingered blues on the 1876 rosewood Steinway last Christmas after havin' just enough of the judge's apple wine.

As the big Buick turned into the wide, segmented driveway, Hattie stopped. Poolie opened his door, leaned out and grabbed the dew-drenched newspaper that the no-count paperboy had thrown in the grass instead of the paper-box. Poolie laid a quick cussin' on him, requiring swift admonition from Hattie. Easing down the driveway that Hattie called her own, she swelled with pride as she reflected on her history here with the Morgans. When her husband, Roosevelt, died twenty years ago, she learned hard how difficult it was for a colored widow in a small southern town to find gainful employment. The Morgans were an answer to her prayers.

Hattie didn't have no problem cookin' and cleanin' and raisin' other folk's young'uns. Her momma had always told her that's what a woman was put on this earth to do. 'Yessir,' she always said, 'it's the closest thing to godliness they is.' Hattie remembered how all the townsfolk, colored and white, spoke high of her momma and it was simply 'cause she took and raised her chill'un proper'. Hattie figured she could carry on that tradition and it would give proper respect to her momma's memory.

***

The popping sounds of hot grease in a black skillet and the aroma of coffee percolatin' announced that Hattie had arrived and breakfast was soon to be had. As she set the breakfast table, the twins, Thomas and Sara Beth, knocked over a glass of fresh-squeezed orange juice, running after Boomer, their Boston Terrier. Two fat black hands grabbed two skinny, white necks and sat their bony rear-ends down with a thud on solid pine chairs. Nine-year-old ears listened as Hattie explained the difference between heathen behavior and proper chillun's behavior and that sometimes the only difference is a hickory-tanned hide. They caught her drift. She concluded her scolding with a warning. "If'n you two think you can jest run wild in this house and not pay no mind to what ole Hattie's a'tellin' ya', then I guess all that's left for ole Hattie to do is go on up those stairs and wake yo' momma and tell her I done lost control and that she's gonna hafta' gimme a helpin' hand." With that, Hattie turned as though she was going upstairs.

Thomas and Sara Beth turned, wide-eyed, looking at one another, fearing what was to come if Hattie woke their mother. "No, Hattie, we'll be good. We'll stop running. Please, please don't wake her up," Thomas Matthew hollered, pleading their case. Sara Beth ran into Hattie's skirt and hugged hard. "Hattie, you know she'll whip us, if she thinks we've been bad. We'll mind. Just give us one more chance. Okay?" her freckled, angelic face smiling up at Hattie.

"Well, y'all sho' are convincin'," Hattie said, strokin' her chin, givin' the impression of serious thought. "Tell ya' what I'll do. If both of ya' don't get in no more trouble in the next half hour, I won't tell yo' momma. How's that?" She stepped back; hands on hips, watching smiles crease both faces.

"Thank you, Hattie, thank you," the twins squealed in unison, clapping their hands. And the remainder of their Saturday morning was spent keeping their promise.

Unable to fight off the aroma of fried bacon and the worrisome racket emanating from Boomer and the twins, Abi crawled out of bed knowing more sleep was wishful thinking. She made her bed and as always, crowned her pillows with Teddy, perfectly in the crease at his lookout post. Flattening her hand, she smoothed out the last wrinkle, stood up, took a step back and stared. Stared at the bed that once held only good memories. So many that she couldn't possibly remember them all. She felt the corners of her mouth turn up as one popped into her mind, suddenly chased away by another and another.

A minute passed. Then two. Her eyes glassed and her jaw hung heavy, as a medicinal trance took hold. Breathing slowly, she came back to herself, turned and walked, slapping bare feet on hardwood then tile. She needed to feel hot water beating soap-lathered skin. And she needed to see it slither down the drain.

Well-scrubbed, Abi caught crimson fuzz on her damp hair as she pulled her Alabama sweatshirt over her head, jumped into her fuzzy Garfield house shoes and shimmied down the plush turquoise-carpeted stairs. She had a stomach full of empty that was dying for Hattie's special Saturday morning breakfast. Turning to go through the dining room, Abi felt relief seeing her father's black BMW gone. Feeling a bit giddy, she tapped a forefinger on the dining room window, waving at Poolie who was closing the backyard gate with one hand while holding a squirming Boomer in the other. Boomer was bad to bolt from time to time, prone to running with the big dogs when opportunity knocked.

Light yellow kitchen walls pitched the melodic refrains of Hattie's 'Amazing Grace', a sound so rich and full, it was worthy of Jesus himself. Bursting into the kitchen, Abi caught her foot on the kitchen chair making a chalk-on-blackboard sound across the tile floor. Hattie, who had just stuck her head in a just-turned-on oven, snapped straight up grazing the edge of the oven with her just-bought, plastic guardian angel barrette.

"Lawd have mercy, chile. You almost sent me to the promised land," Hattie blurted, clutching her chest. Hattie's big brown eyes always lit up when they looked at Abi. "Give me a big ole hug, sweetheart. Did you get a good night's sleep?"

Abi nodded, not wanting to give thought to last night.

"Me too, honey. I believe it must be this time a' year. I always sleep best in the fall when I can raise my window and let in some a 'that fresh, nippy air. Sit yo'self down, darlin'. We gonna have ourselves a powerful-good breakfast this mornin'." Hattie was in her element and lovin' it. Oven to table. Table to fridge. Fridge to sink. Repeated over and over.

As Hattie deftly tossed Abi's fried eggs, Abi grabbed a glass of fresh-squeezed and pulled up a chair, letting the morning sun warm her face.

"Ya' know what we're havin' this mornin', Abi?" Hattie asked, smiling into the grease-poppin' skillet.

"Well, it's no secret we're having bacon, I could smell it all the way up to my room," Abi said.

"We're havin' fried eggs, just like you like 'em, with the yellow runnin' and the white cooked, fried bacon and cinnamon toast with sugar, oatmeal swimmin' in butter'n sugar and hot chocolate with those itty-bitty marshmallows you like. Don't that sound good, baby?"

Turning off the oven with her left hand, Hattie plucked crimson fuzz from Abi's sun-bathed, honeyed locks with her right. "Looks to me like somebody was in such a giddy-up hurry, they plumb forgot to mirror theyself," Hattie grinned. Abi looked up as Hattie plucked two more pieces and floated them into the garbage can, the sun striking one, missing the other.

Thick black hands pressed both sides of Abi's face like coal bookends. Bending low from her waist, brown eyes into blue-greens, Hattie's heart warmed, drenching itself in mother-daughter love. "Honey, you always the tonic for whatever's ailin' me. You know that? Any time I got the blues, all I gotta do is see yo' pretty face and I lose those blues just like that," snapping her fingers.

Abi, looked up and smiled, her eyes moistening. "Hattie, I love you. I can't imagine what it would be like around here if you weren't here. Promise me you'll never leave."

"Don't you fret, honey, Hattie's not goin' anywhere. Not me, no sir." Hattie sensed that Abi might have something on her mind. A serious something. There seemed to be more here than words were sayin'. Although the words were sayin' a lot and they was makin' their points, there seemed to be another something out there that no word was touchin'. "Honey, anything you wanna talk about? Anything weighin' heavy on yo' mind?" Hattie probed gently.

Abi stood and hugged Hattie. A good, long hug, with arms too short to meet. Each sensed in the other a need to comfort and soothe. Eggs cooled. Hattie began to softly hum, almost rocking Abi to sleep on her feet, gently swaying. Left then right. Left then right. Two hearts beating as one. Abi wanted to confide in Hattie, like she had many times before. Then, like the other times, she couldn't. It was such a terrible thing to tell. Maybe another time, she thought.

Feeling that the temptation to divulge her secret had passed but still feeling the need to respond to Hattie's perception that something was bothering her, Abi broke the silence by offering a substitute. "Hattie, may I ask you something?" Abi's head rested on Hattie's warm, massive, blue and gray flannelled shoulder.

"Anything, honey," Hattie purred behind heavy-lidded, almost closed eyes.

"Some of my friends make fun of me because I like you so much. They call me names and well, they call both of us names." She hoped Hattie wouldn't ask what those names were.

Hattie opened her eyes. "Baby, what chillun' says and what chillun' knows, is two different things. They ain't old enough to know much a'nuthin' but they's always spittin' out hard words tryin' to make fun of anybody that ain't them. It's their nature, bein' teenagers. That's all. They think they's funny and that they's lookin' like 'big-Ike's' in front of their friends. Don't you pay 'em no mind. Most of 'em will outgrow it in time. Hattie paused in thought. "So you been talkin' 'bout us?" Hattie mused, raisin' a crooked eyebrow, realizin' how proud she was beginnin' to feel 'bout this revelation.

"Well, you know, in class. When we talk about family and that kind of stuff. When I talk about my family, I almost always talk about, you know, how much our family loves yours," Abi explained. She grabbed the forks out of the drawer and without realizing it slammed one down hard on the round oak table. The loud pop startled Hattie, who turned her head and attention to Abi, who was now wearing a scowl and gritting her teeth, her mouth a straight line across her face. "They think because you're black and I'm white that we shouldn't like each other so much," Abi retorted, slamming tines. "Why do people care so much about the color of a person's skin?"

Her dark brown face against the backdrop of the yellow walls, Hattie wanted to give this question some thought. Stroking warm butter on wheat toast, Hattie spoke. "It seems to me that some folks always got to have somebody to look down on. Long as I can recollect it's been that way. Folks puttin' other folks down for bein' black or white, fat or skinny, poor or rich, this religion or that religion. It don't make no never-mind to good, kind folks like you and your family, though."

Abi listened hard to Hattie's perception of the matter and thought, maybe Hattie was right. Maybe some people just have to have somebody to kick around. But, the why of it bothered her.

Grabbing her juice and feeling newly educated on the matter, she concurred, "Hattie, you're right. The more I think about it, you're right as rain." After a pause to swallow, Abi continued. "Now, why do you think it is that these people feel that they have to have folks to kick around?" she inquired, proud of herself for this probing question.

While she was laying the last piece of toast on the server, Hattie responded, " 'Cause they've been told to be this way, honey. Mostly by their mommas and daddies and other kin. Just raised that way, as I sees it. Just a bad habit for hundreds a' years." Hattie thought she'd lay down one more piece of wisdom just for emphasis. "If they was no folks on this whole earth and one day God put you and me here and we was the only folks around… do you think we would tear into each other 'cause God made you light and me dark? I don't think so. We'd be gettin' along jest fine 'cause we'd know we'd be needin' each other. Not to mention we'd be scared to death of the whuppin' the good Lord would lay on us if'n we was to hurt the other'n."

Abi choked a laugh at the thought of God bending big Hattie over his knee for a good whipping.

"So," Hattie concluded, "I love you and you love me, no matter what kinda' skin we wrapped in. Ain't that right, sweetie?"

Abi nodded with a mouthful of toast.

"So, just don't pay no attention to those makin' fun of you. Be above it all, honey. Be above it."

There was a definite, touchable goodness about listening to Hattie that drew Abi like a moth to a flame. Abi thirsted for these moments, committing Hattie's pearls to memory for later use when they would be used to slay other dragons.

"You be 'bout to starve, ain't ya', baby?" Hattie winked. "Sorry I went on so", and then chuckled, "I'm worse than that money-grubbin' preacher a' mine who starves us past dinnertime every Sunday, tryin' to squeeze another drop a' blood out all us turnips."

After the twins had eaten, Hattie called Poolie to eat with her and Abi. With heads bowed and eyes shut Hattie said the breakfast prayer. Abi said her own. Each face wore a smile as they ate every last morsel. They talked and told stories and laughed and sipped hot chocolate and basked in each other's presence like all good families do.

FOUR

Rebecca Sullivan Morgan is called the mother of Jonathan Morgan's children because it says so on their birth certificates. She is not fond of motherhood because it is quite bothersome. Tending to children is something she does when she has nothing better to do, Rebecca has been heard to say, after a few drinks.

Rebecca Morgan grew up the privileged only child in a rich banking family and evolved into an eccentric, overly-dramatic, self-absorbed lush. She took to heavy drinking just before she married Jonathan, when they attended the University of Alabama. Her best friends at that time were a couple of sorority sisters, who were major party girls. During her sophomore year, her last at the university, many noticed a gradual change in Rebecca. Her friends asked her about it, but she denied any problems. She entertained absolutely no discussion on the matter. It had been rumored she was jilted by a boy she deeply loved and hoped to marry. A boy no one knew. Gradually withdrawing herself from her friends, the classroom became the venue for her only social interaction. Not long after that, she and Jonathan were married.

Bumping into consciousness that smelled of downstair's bacon grease, the lush flung the drool-stained, gold and jade paisley comforter off her antique four-poster bed because she had to puke.

With all the grace God gives a new-born colt, she reached the commode just before the first rush of bourbon-tinged discharge.

Oblivious to the time of day or her husband's whereabouts, Rebecca knew full well that this Saturday morning would be spent like most Saturday mornings, convalescing beneath drawn blinds that cast creeping shadows on drooled paisley.

***

Poolie raked the last of the yellow maple leaves into a small, neat pile then traded the rake for the wood-splittin' gloves in the shed. Not that he was goin' to do any wood splittin' but the gloves would keep his hands free of cuts, splinters and blisters. He needed his good hands tonight. Tonight, young Mr. Cassius Clay Buford had some serious designs on gettin' himself all spiffed up for a Saturday night date with one fine specimen of young black womanhood by the name of Esther Bolay. Esther and her grandmother had moved down here from Detroit to take care of Esther's aunt, Romelia, who got the sugar and was near death; at least she was six months ago.

Poolie, by his own admission, had a real fondness for the ladies. The boys down at The Tan Man Pool Hall, where Poolie earned his nickname because he used to hang out there so much, had dubbed him Lincoln's baddest lady-killer. A title he wore proudly, didn't argue with and tried his best to live up to.

***

Hattie and Abi always enjoyed doing the Saturday morning dishes together. As bits of oatmeal and egg rose out of growing mounds of suds in the sink, Hattie drowned cups and plates with scalding water. Hattie could always put them in the dishwasher but then she and Abi would miss out on this special time of theirs.

As Hattie grabbed a frying pan, she caught Poolie out of the corner of her eye sitting in the Buick listening to that music again.

"Would 'ya just look at that boy o' mine," Hattie said. "Sittin' out there with his head a' bobbin' and a' weavin' like he be havin' some kinda' spell. Um, um, um. I declare I'm gonna have to lay into him, now. Out there, listenin' to that trash when he's supposed to be stackin' the judge's firewood. Sometime's I don't know if I raised that boy good or not. Just look at him!"

"Sure you have Hattie," Abi said, "you're the best mother I've ever seen."

Hattie told Abi about some of the difficult times with Poolie and how she often felt overwhelmed raisin' him by herself. "If Roosevelt hadn't died, I know we would've raised him proper," Hattie proclaimed. She turned her big brown eyes to Abi and said, "Abi, you're so lucky to have a good daddy. A good daddy means so much in bringin' up a chile today."

A good father? A good father? Abi screamed in her head. Nobody knows the father I have. Her hands trembled and her eyes blinked in an attempt to restrain her tears. She turned her head towards the table trying to avoid Hattie's eyes. Her fingers lost control of a plate that fell to black and white tile exploding egg-covered shards to all but one corner of the kitchen. Frightened and embarrassed, Abi turned and ran through the dining room, up the stairs and fell onto her bed gasping for air between sobs, face down in her pillow.

Stunned, Hattie's jaw dropped. She wrung her wet hands on the dish towel as she rushed up the stairs, trying to hurry, but not wanting to bother Miz Becca.

Hattie entered Abi's room and sat down on the side of the bed. "Abi, honey, don't you go worryin' yo' self 'bout that plate. It ain't nuthin' to get upset over. Lawd, we got so many plates I think I'll go back down and break a few more. You wanna' help me?" Hattie said, tryin' to make Abi feel better.

Abi could not speak. She shook uncontrollably clutching Teddy tightly to her chest.

Hattie thought it best not to push Abi to talk, but to let her get her cry out, even if it was just over a plate.

As she waited, Hattie stroked Abi's damp hair and gave thought to their talk in the kitchen, tryin' to study on what had been said.

Abi was taking steady, deep breaths, now, gaining composure with each passing minute. Then, she turned over and with a red-splotched, pillow-creased face and no emotion said words she thought she'd never hear herself say. "Hattie, daddy makes me do things." After these words left her mouth, she wasn't sure she had heard them. Maybe she only thought she had said them. Not sure if she could repeat them, she waited behind matted eyelashes to see if Hattie would respond. Then she would know if she had actually said what she thought she had said. She did not breathe.

"What do you mean he makes you do things?" Hattie asked.

Abi's cold, trembling hand searched for Hattie's warm hand, found it and squeezed, not ever wanting to let go. Dry-crying, Abi realized she was at the point of no return. She couldn't turn back now. Ever so slowly the words escaped her lips. "He makes me do sex things. You know... like what a husband and wife do."

Not believing words like these could ever come from this child's lips, Hattie was shaken down to her soul. Trying to regain some composure, Hattie pursued. "Are you tellin' me that he makes you do... the... wifely thing... the thing that a man and a woman do... in private?" Feeling inadequate in her manner of questioning, Hattie wished she could take the question back.

Abi buried her face in Teddy's arms and nodded, too ashamed to look at Hattie, now.

Stabbed, Hattie could not draw air. Instinctively, she continued to stroke Abi's hair, unaware of what she was doing.

Drained, Abi could talk no longer.

Sensing Abi's exhaustion, Hattie felt the need for a spiritual connection and began humming *'What A Friend We Have In Jesus'*. It brought swift, sweet sleep to the precious child's overwrought mind.

Gathering herself, Hattie tried to settle the whirlwind of thoughts of what to do next. As she searched her mind, a great, heavy fear consumed her. A fear of what could happen to not only Abi and the entire family, but to her. The realization of serious implications flooded, then froze her mind. Numbness and confusion bred the beginnings of panic. Questions sped, blurring her mind, one after another, with no pause. Should I tell? Who? Miz Rebecca? The law? Confront the judge?

Hattie needed time to think. She stood, then tip-toed out of the bedroom, careful not to wake Abi and returned to the kitchen to be alone with her thoughts. As she entered the kitchen she glanced outside at Poolie listening to his music in the car. No longer was that the problem it once was.

Needing to feel the safeness of familiarity, Hattie grabbed the broom and began sweeping. Wide-eyed and numb, she swept, feeling the ill wind of danger growing with every pass of the broom. She prayed for guidance and the courage to do what needed to be done.

Reality had never been so cruel. She felt sick. Her cold, sweaty palms grabbed the corner of the counter as she wrenched and then exploded the vile sputum of the rottenness she had just heard.

FIVE

In the fourth floor conference room of the First Southern Savings and Trust Bank, high-backed mahogany and leather executive chairs separated from the claw-footed mahogany conference table, as the nineteen member board of the Rutherford County United Way stood adjourned from their meeting. The eleven-man, eight-woman board glad-handed and back-slapped one another in celebration of the largest single financial commitment in the history of the county.

The majority of the board's membership is comprised of representatives from area agencies including the Department of Children's Services, the Department of Youth Services, the Community Action Agency, the Department of Mental Health, as well as the police department, the Sheriff's Office and the city and county school systems. Two bankers and Mayor Emerson Fitzpatrick round out the board and give it the punch it needs.

Thanks to Judge Jonathan Morgan's tireless efforts and the persistence and commitment of the entire board, three-hundred- thousand dollars had been pledged to the construction of the Rutherford County Children's Advocacy Center in Lincoln. With federal matching funds the center could be well on its way to completion by next fiscal year.

As a haven for abused and neglected children, the center will offer children a less threatening environment in which to be interviewed by law enforcement and social workers. With its informal atmosphere, the center will offer children the familiarities and warmth of home. In exceptional circumstances, requiring a court order, overnight stays will be permitted.

The members stepped from the boardroom into an adjacent conference room with a floor-to-ceiling mural depicting the working poor of Dublin, Ireland. The bank's owning family, the Sullivans, had migrated from Dublin to the United States in the late 1800's to make the family fortune loaning money. Not coincidentally, the largest single benefactor of the center was the Sullivan family, in-laws of Judge Morgan. Joseph Sullivan, the family patriarch, had guaranteed Jonathan whatever amount he needed in order to ensure the success of the development of the Advocacy Center. Joseph Sullivan couldn't care less about the center or the children who needed it. But he does care about the public's perception of his son-in-law.

Jonathan's public image, meticulously groomed by his father and grandfather, has always been of paramount importance. After he graduated from law school, in the top five per cent of his class, Jonathan went directly to work with the American Civil Liberties Union in Montgomery, cutting his teeth on class action law suits representing the poor, the homeless, the environment and anyone claiming to be a minority. He returned to Lincoln a year later joining the family firm, making himself known from one end of the county to the other; searching for cases that drew media attention. High profile cases, bolstering name recognition.

Last year's election signaled a bright future for Rutherford County's rising political star and both families, the Sullivans and the Morgans, committed themselves to doing whatever is necessary to ensure that Jonathan's meteoric rise will continue. They will blackmail. They will bribe. They will extort. They will step on anyone in the way. Judge Jeremiah Morgan, the family octo-generian, told the men of the family that before he dies, he wants to see his grandson in the governor's mansion. And Judge Jeremiah Morgan is not taken lightly.

Wafts of ceremonial cigars layered between crystal chandeliers as preparation for television coverage was underway. With the working poor of Dublin in the background, Judge Morgan buttoned his charcoal gray double-breasted, ready to put his signature on this page of Rutherford County history. As reporters closed in and lights beamed, the crowd focused on the handsome gentleman in front of the potted palms. As the clock struck noon, "Three, two, one... you're on," the technician pointed.

"Good afternoon ladies and gentlemen. I am Judge Jonathan Morgan, this year's chairman of the United Way. To my left and to my right are my fellow board members with whom I have proudly and diligently worked. Today we have made history. Today we have taken a stand and we are proclaiming to all who live within the boundaries of Rutherford County that we, today's leaders, place our children, tomorrow's leaders, at the top of what's important in our county. Today, we have committed three- hundred-thousand dollars to begin construction of the Rutherford County Children's Advocacy Center in downtown Lincoln. This center will provide our county's children with a non-threatening atmosphere in which they can talk with counselors, social workers, nurses and police. Thousands of children in this state are fortunate because they have good, decent, loving parents who can take care of them. But many are not so lucky. To those children and their families we say Rutherford County stands committed to breaking the cycle of abuse and neglect."

Knowing the scene called for sensitivity, Judge Morgan paused, took a deep breath and biting his lower lip, said, "I have met with social workers, nurses and police who have shared their horror stories of hurt and frightened children who live in situations you and I can't even imagine." He paused for emphasis. "I have seen, in my own courtroom, mothers and fathers who don't give a whit about their children, who are obsessed with their own selfishness to the extent that their own children are mere afterthoughts. And I have looked into the eyes of these children and seen the depths of their despair, silently screaming for someone, anyone to help them. Well we are saying, today that help is on the way."

The judge let his words hang in the air while he looked into the eyes of the crowd to gauge his effect. He was pleased with what he saw. He, then, thanked all of the appropriate people, organizations and businesses, who contributed, then opened the floor to questions from the media.

There were the predictable, obligatory questions regarding the capacity of the center, qualifications of the staff and budgetary issues. Then the white, pockmarked face standing next to the American flag asked, "Is the center gonna take in children from other races?" Collectively, eyes cut and jaws gaped as the man with the pockmarked face steeled himself for a follow-up, "Cause if ya' are, y'all know what'll happen if our young'uns take up with niggers, spics and…" Cut off in mid-sentence, the man surrendered to the judge's imposing baritone.

"Sir," Judge Morgan admonished, "children in Rutherford County are not judged by the color of their skin and we will not abide the likes of you or your kind, with your blatant bigotry. I suggest you seize this opportunity for the gift that it is intended and kindly remove yourself from the premises." Taking a breath and flexing his jaw muscle for emphasis, the judge added, "Before it is done for you."

The cameras were still rolling. Spontaneous applause for the judge reached a crescendo amidst several loud 'yeahs' from the men in attendance. With that, the man with the pockmarked face gave the judge the finger and exited the room then the building. "Atta boy, Judge. Tell him what for," someone yelled.

The judge was encircled by grateful, adoring citizens, black and white, who wanted to get close to the new hero. The media lapped it up. The speech and the spontaneous confrontation with the racist whack-job were rushed to their stations for the night's six and ten o'clock newscasts. The judge with a backbone. The judge who looked evil in the eye and spat in its face. The judge who shielded citizens of all colors. The judge who protected our children. Great stuff!

***

An hour from Rutherford County, the man with the pockmarked face's standard white van with heavily tinted windows and Mississippi plates turned onto I-65 South towards Birmingham. After entering Jefferson County, he entered the men's restroom at a Cracker Barrel restaurant and lifted the lid off of the second commode tank from the door. Taped securely to the underside of the lid in a ziplocked bag wrapped in aluminum foil were five crisp one-hundred dollar bills and a note. Smiling into the note, pockmarked face read, 'Job well done. Until later.'

***

Knowing that television coverage can be like manna from heaven, a sitting judge should always be mindful of the hungry masses. With orchestration it can be a moment of historical proportion etching itself into the minds of voters for years to come. Saving kids and bringing the multi-colored masses together. Not a bad day's work.

SIX

Abi trembled as she lay curled around Teddy, her mind racing. She knew change was fast approaching. Now that she had told, her life would never be the same. She did not know what to do next, but she knew what she didn't want to do. She didn't want to live here another day.

She was afraid that what her father had told her might come true; that if she ever told anyone, she and her brother and sister would be taken from home. She could not stomach the thought of her brother and sister being pulled out of their home, screaming and begging to stay.

She had reached the point where she believed that there had to be something that could be done; something that wouldn't devastate the entire family. She didn't know how to go about finding out what this something was, but she trusted her instincts. And her instincts told her that today was the day she would have to do something. Especially since she had told someone.

Shallow, nervous breathing warmed the top of Teddy's head. As she lay on her side with her eyes half-closed, she gazed at her wall covered with photographs and memorabilia. Photos of her running with a kite on a windy beach in Fort Walton Beach, Florida. Of her and her sister at the school book fair, winning a cake walk. Of her handing out medals to handicapped children at last summer's Special Olympics. That was one of her favorites. There was something that drew her to those kids who had so much to overcome. She had always been impressed that they never complained. They tried as hard as they could to run fast and throw far, but they never could. And it didn't matter to them. They loved the running and the throwing for the joy of it. She admired their persistence and determination and noticed that they were always happy. She wanted to be like them.

She couldn't take her eyes off that photo. Then a lightning bolt of a thought struck her. Running! That's it! Run away and never be found! That way her brother and sister would never have to leave home. She could get what she wanted and the family would not be ripped apart. It could work!

Her mind was trying, unsuccessfully, to keep pace with her hands which were grabbing and stuffing shirts, pants, underwear, shoes into her army surplus duffel bag. Then, it hit her. Hattie! Hattie was still in the house. Her excitement rocketed. She could leave with Hattie. No! That wouldn't work. There would be the problem of Hattie's complicity. Abi knew full well her father was smart enough to file charges against Hattie, probably kidnapping, and make it stick. She couldn't do that to Hattie.

Hattie's trunk! It's never locked. It's rusted out and tied shut with an electrical cord. She could get away without putting Hattie in any legal trouble because Hattie wouldn't even be aware of what was happening.

Abi grabbed Teddy, kissed his nose, gave him the last vacancy in her duffel bag and scurried down the stairs without making a sound.

Untying the electrical cord from the rusted-out trunk latch, Abi tossed her duffel bag in and quickly followed. Now, the wait. Taking deep breaths, she relaxed and allowed the soothing blackness to comfort her.

The sound of an approaching car triggered Abi's adrenaline. It pulled along side the Buick. The sounds of the door, opening and closing, and the high-pitched beep of the remote door-lock were familiar. Size ten, black wingtips crunched loose gravel as the left, then the right shoe met concrete.

She heard her father's voice, "Good morning, Poolie." Poolie was giving extra attention to the freshly stacked firewood so that the judge could see what a conscientious worker he was. She could hear only Poolie's humming after her father entered the backdoor.

Judge Morgan hung his keys on the backdoor key holder and hollered for Hattie to get him some coffee. His baritone startled her, as she sat like a punch-drunk fighter at the kitchen table.

Coming to herself, Hattie muttered, "Yessir, Judge, comin' right up." Pouring the coffee, she didn't know if she could look him in the eyes.

"Where's Rebecca?" the judge asked, reaching for the newspaper.

"She be restin'," Hattie replied. "I hadn' seen or heard from her this mawnin'," thankful that the newspaper hid the eyes of the newly-strange man. "Must not be feelin' well."

"No doubt," he retorted, with a grin, "no doubt."

Hattie untied the knot in her apron. "The twins are in the den watchin' cartoons and Poolie, he's done with yo' firewood, so's we be getting' ready to head on home, directly." She hated leaving Abi, but she had to remove herself from all of this and allow herself some thinkin' time. "I guess I'll go on up and say good-by to Abi," Hattie said, already headed toward the stairs.

The judge sipped his coffee, never looking up. "Okay, Hattie, we'll see you Monday."

Hattie heard his comment, but couldn't respond.

Tapping a forefinger lightly on Abi's door, Hattie stuck her head inside expecting to see Abi asleep. She wasn't there. She noticed the teddy bear missing from his usual post between the pillows.

"What's the matter, Hattie?" Rebecca asked, freshly showered, wrapped in her terry cloth robe and showing signs of recovery.

"Uh, I, we was just fixin' to leave and I was goin' to say good-by to Abi, but… she's not here, so's I guess I'll be on my way," Hattie said.

"Oh, she's probably in the den or the game room," Rebecca said, turning away, toweling her tangled auburn hair. "You can catch her on your way out. We'll see you Monday."

"All rightee, Miz Rebecca," Hattie said, without looking back. She could feel sweat forming on her upper lip.

Bouncing down the stairs, Hattie heard Poolie washing his hands in the kitchen sink and yelled, "Come on, Poolie. You ready to go?"

"Yeah, mamma. Let me dry my hands."

Leaving the backdoor, Hattie had a feeling like she'd never had before. She couldn't define it but she thought it must be akin to what an inmate feels when he breaks out of prison.

Hattie opened the heavy car door, tossed in her purse and jumped behind the steering wheel. Poolie, in one fluid move, flung his coat in the back, hit the radio button, closed the door and kicked off his boots. Hattie turned the key with the silver cross key chain and engaged the Buick. She stopped a moment to gaze at the house, longing for the warmth of the past. She wanted to feel like she used to, but couldn't. The cold reality of the present obscured her memory of good days gone by. Like a giant ship just minutes from sinking, the grand old home seemed gutted beyond repair, her future inevitable.

"C'mon momma, turn this horse a' loose," Poolie directed, impatiently. "I got things to do."

Hattie could barely muster the strength to depress the accelerator. As she backed out of the driveway, the crepe myrtles passing her windows waved permanent good-byes. Through watering eyes that blurred her view of the yard, Hattie realized that her future was as unclear as her vision. She was now a stranger in her own world. Nothing was the same.

SEVEN

Even from across the street, passers-by could read the chalk lettering on the Victory Café's hanging blackboard. It hung next to the neon Budweiser Clydesdales in the window, giving it that extra bit of light. According to the blackboard, today's lunch special was a fieldhand's helping of turnip greens, black-eyed peas, corn on the cob, cole slaw and pork chops with hot apple pie for dessert chased by a hot cup of coffee.

This Saturday, just like the past two years of Saturdays, Police Chief Joe Lee Bush will sit down, alone, at the third booth on the right about 1:10 P.M. for his blue-plate special. And as usual, Myra, the Victory's most popular waitress, will make sure his lunch will be waiting on him. No need for the man who'd sworn to serve and protect to have to wait for his meal.

"Goat, I'm headin' out to lunch. Can I bring you anything?" the chief yelled to the office of Jerome 'Goat' Witherspoon, dispatcher.

"Naw, Chief. I'm good. Darlene packed me a couple of her taco gut-bombers and if I come home with anything but tacos on my breath, I'll catch hell. Thanks anyway."

The chief laughed, "All right, Goat, I'll check ya' later." As he closed the office door, slid on his Ray Bans and opened the car door, he heard the courthouse clock strike one. Just like one of Pavlov's dogs, his mouth watered.

Just as he crossed the intersection of Fourth and Adams, he heard the screeching of tires and the sound of metal crunching metal. It sounded bad. He turned on the siren and hit the gas. Approaching the corner of Hickory and Second, he could see smoke rising from the wreckage. The smell of burnt rubber and gasoline permeated the air. A crowd had gathered, pointing and gasping. Mothers pulled their little ones back from the street and hid their little faces in skirts.

Radioing for back-up and an ambulance, Chief Bush pulled his car into the center of the intersection to stop traffic. As he stepped out of his car, he saw that nobody was moving in either vehicle.

"The Buick ran a red light!" a voice from the crowd hollered.

The Buick got the worst end of the deal with its driver's side crushed by the station wagon.

"I s-saw the whole th-thing," the little man stammered, not wanting to get involved, but knowing it was the right thing to do.

As back-up arrived, Chief Bush directed Officer Perez, the department's first and only female officer, to take the statement from the little man, while he checked the injured.

The little man, stuttered as he told what he had seen, to the officer, who repeatedly directed him to take a deep breath and calm down. She could tell he had panicked. The wet spot in the crotch of his trousers told everyone else.

"I was st-standing right here on th-this s-sidewalk, officer, waitin' for the light t-to change, so's I c-could c-cross the s-street. I was g-goin' to get some washers f-for my kitchen f-faucet and I was headin' to C-Cramer's Hardware. Th-That red and white B-Buick never stopped, n-never hesitated or nuthin'. It j-just barreled right th-through that red light." He pointed with a crooked and trembling forefinger. "See, there ain't a sk-skid mark out th-there from th-that Buick. Th-They never hit th-their br-brakes." With that, the little man took in air and asked Officer Perez if she could tell him the location of the nearest restroom. She did and he was excused.

One other witness was willing to come forward. He gave the same account as the little man. He was a sixteen-year-old veteran of the county detention center and was the more articulate of the two witnesses. Officer Perez was not surprised at the young punk's ability to speak well. Budding young criminals learn at an early age that words are tools to be honed and fine-tuned. If someone chose to believe those words, that was their problem. The art of articulation was a necessary weapon in the on-going battle against authority in general and cops and women, in particular. As he combed his long, black, oily hair with his right hand that had 'L-O-V-E' tattooed on his fingers, he gave his name as Romero B. Goode. He proudly told Officer Perez, "And that's the truth, baby, Romero B. 'very' Goode," as his eyes ran vertically over the officer.

The officer ignored the punk's comment but questioned him about being in school. He cocked his head to the earring side, struck a match off of his boot-heel, lit a rolled cigarette and told the officer he hadn't been to school since the very minute he turned sixteen. Needless to say, his pants were dry. Just a wreck, man. Just a wreck.

The chief strode across the hot asphalt towards the Ford, its hissing radiator out-dueling the cries of children and the yelling of onlookers. Leaning in the driver's side open window he saw a middle-aged female who, it seemed, had just come from the grocery store. She was the only occupant. Although she was unconscious, there were no signs of injury. Seat-belt still on. The smell from a busted can of tuna permeated the interior. Flintstone vitamins floated in a cool pool of milk under the accelerator. He checked her pulse. It was strong.

As he stood back from the Ford, he could hear the ambulance approaching. He directed the crowd to disperse except for anyone else who may have witnessed the accident. Children begged their mamas to leave as the ambulance's wail became deafening.

The chief walked around the front of the Buick to the passenger side. Although the window was up, he could see there were two occupants, an older female and a younger male. Both were unconscious. Neither wore seat belts. Blood dripped from a gash from the protruding tibia of the left leg of the driver. She looked familiar. Her door, the point of impact, was crushed inward about one-third of the way across the front seat.

The passenger was half-way down in the floor facing his door. He seemed twisted too much to the right. Both had pronounced head injuries. The driver was lying down in the front seat with her head resting against the boy's back, squarely between the shoulder blades. Her legs were pinned by the warped door. Both were breathing. He let the paramedics take over from here. He could hear the slapping of their hustling footsteps in sync with the rap music moaning from Buick's radio.

As the chief headed back to his car, Officer Perez met him to tell him that Witherspoon ran a check on the tags. The Ford was registered to Houston Freeman and the Buick to Hattie Mae Buford.

As the ambulances sped off to Lincoln Memorial Hospital, Tony's Wrecker Service prepared both vehicles for removal.

EIGHT

Rebecca Morgan turned the bottom of the clear bottle with the black and white label to the ceiling, splashing its amber contents over three cubes in a coffee cup. Too early in the day for highball glasses. The cup afforded her the illusion that she wasn't really drinking. The amber liquid was the one thing, each day, she could depend on because it always delivered what it promised.

Tilting the cup to her lips, she swallowed hard. It burned wonderfully on the way down.

Rebecca was not a happy woman. Although it hadn't always been this way, the pleasure she gets from life, now, comes from a bottle. She has few friends.

She knows that most folks think that she thinks she is better than most. They are right. They also think she has a past. They are right. Rumors of different varieties have circulated ever since she married Jonathan, but no one has ever been able to validate any of them.

One rumor alleged that Rebecca had been married to two men at the same time while in college, a result of her heavy drinking. Another was that Rebecca married a black man just before she married Jonathan and that her family paid him to leave the country. And yet another implicated the entire Sullivan family in a murder-for-hire plot to dispose of an old lover of Rebecca's. Most thinking people don't put much stock in these rumors. They just chalk it up to small town gossip about a family most don't like.

As Rebecca sees it, her past is just that. Hers and past. That is where it belongs and that is where it will remain.

NINE

Dispatcher 'Goat' Witherspoon pulled up his standard-issue khakis as he shuffled from the bathroom to the ringing telephone, cursing Alexander Graham Bell for inventing the damned nuisance. Cinching his britches with his right hand, he snatched the phone with his left. Not hiding his irritation, he answered, "Police department, Witherspoon here, what 'cha want?"

"Goat?" the shaky voice on the other end asked.

"Yeah. Who is this?" Witherspoon asked, reaching for his chair.

"Goat? This is Tony, you know, from the wrecker service."

"Yeah, Tony. What's up?"

"Goat, we got ourselves a little problem out here at the junkyard."

"What kinda' problem you got out there?" Witherspoon asked, beginning to toy with Tony, as he detected a little panic in Tony's voice.

"Well, I worked that accident in town a little while ago. You know, the one where those three people… uh, all had to go to the hospital?"

"Yeah, I heard about it. Sounded bad," Witherspoon said.

"Well, Goat, you ain't gonna believe this, but," Tony could hardly spit it out, "but there's another body in the trunk of one of them cars."

"Aw hell, Tony. You messin' with me?"

"Goat, I ain't lyin'. I swear!" Tony began to hyperventilate. "You gotta send the chief out here, now… it's a girl. She's unconscious, but alive. Listen, I'm the only one here today, since it's Saturday, so I better get back and keep an eye on her. You get the chief out here, pronto. Okay, Goat?"

"Okay, Tony, I'll get right on it. Hey, do ya' know who she is?"

"Naw, I ain't never seen her before. Listen, Goat, I better go. Hurry up and get somebody out here," he said, as he threw the phone down and headed back to the junkyard to watch the girl.

TEN

The telephone woke Rebecca from her afternoon nap. She hoped Jonathan would answer the screaming thing, but with each passing second, realized he wouldn't. Grabbing the receiver as if to choke it, she blurted, "Hello!"

"May I speak to Mr. or Mrs. Morgan, please?" a female voice asked.

"This IS Mrs. Morgan," Rebecca retorted, "Who is this?"

"Mrs. Morgan, this is Florence Joiner, R.N. at Lincoln Memorial Hospital. I am the on-duty nurse in the emergency room and I'm calling to let you know that Virginia Abigail Morgan was admitted to the hospital this afternoon and I'd like to know if…"

"What do you mean Virginia Abigail Morgan was admitted to the hospital?" Rebecca demanded.

"Well, Mrs. Morgan, a Virginia Abigail Morgan, age thirteen, who was involved in an automobile accident, was transported by paramedics to the hospital earlier this afternoon and I am trying to contact her parents to let them know. She had this telephone number among her possessions. Would you be her mother?" the nurse politely, but firmly, asked regaining control of the conversation.

"Well… I do have a daughter named Virginia Abigail," Rebecca muttered. "But, I thought she was here in the house. Are you telling me that she is at the hospital?"

"Well, she had this telephone number, as I said, so I'm assuming she could be your daughter."

"What in the world has happened to my daughter?" her mind reeling. "How can this be possible?" she pleaded, as her left hand reached for a Kleenex.

"Mrs. Morgan, I know this is very hard on you. Please bear with me and I will tell you all we know, which is not very much."

As gently and as completely as she dared, the nurse informed Rebecca about the accident, omitting the part about Abi's being discovered at the junkyard. She felt that that was the police department's job. She concluded by informing that preliminary tests indicate that Abi is in stable condition and her prognosis is favorable. She urged the Morgans to come to the hospital at once.

A hand that didn't seem to be Rebecca's hung up the phone as shock spread. Her first conscious effort toward the liquor cabinet fell short when she dropped to her knees. "Jonathan!" she screamed. "Jonathan!"

Jonathan raced from the den, up the stairs into the bedroom to see his wife kneeling on the floor screaming into her hands.

"Rebecca, what's the matter?" he asked, kneeling and reaching for her hands. She kept shaking her head as he helped her to the side of the bed. He, then, headed to the bathroom for aspirin.

"Jonathan, a nurse from the hospital just called … and said that Abi … has been in a wreck and has been admitted to the hospital."

"What did you say?"

"I said the hospital called to inform us that Abi has been in a wreck and has been admitted to the hospital. But, they think she will be okay," she said, striving for a little composure.

"How in God's name could Abi have been involved in a wreck? I thought she was in her room!"

Grabbing the aspirin from his hand, she replied, "That's one of the reasons they want us to come to the hospital. So we can find out how all this happened." She threw the aspirin to the back of her throat, chased it with the afternoon coffee and said, "So, you'd better get ready." She rose from the bed and headed to her closet.

"Did you ask who she was with?" he continued.

"No, Jonathan."

"Did you ask about Abi's injuries?"

"No, Jonathan. I did not. I was too upset to think. And when I heard her say that Abi would be all right, I didn't need to know anything else. Let's get ready to go. I don't want Abi to be alone another minute. God, she must be terrified," Rebecca fretted, as long-dormant maternal instincts began to surface.

ELEVEN

Eddie Mack Monroe, Hattie Mae Buford's younger brother had assembled a sizeable gathering of family and friends at the hospital to coordinate plans to take care of Hattie's affairs. The time had come for him to be there for her, for all the times she had been there for him. He strutted with pride from relative to friend coordinating schedules. He mapped out plans for volunteers to oversee her daily mail, pay her bills and with the help of the good Reverend Whitlow, scheduled round-the-clock house-sitting shifts.

Thieves and con-men comb newspapers for the unfortunate who are away from their homes for any length of time and Eddie Mack would see to it that Hattie would not fall victim to these vultures. He would make arrangements with his employer for his work schedule to allow him to handle this crisis. He was mighty pleased with himself for being able to help his big sister.

Eddie Mack stepped from the noisy gathering into Hattie's darkened room to check on her. The shades were lowered and the television was off and he could barely make out the silhouette of Miss Fannie Cutshall, Hattie's life-long friend, as she sat in the recliner near the bathroom door. Miss Fannie had agreed to spend the first night with Hattie and was settling in, arranging her snacks, magazines and crossword puzzles. She was known all over the county as a crossword puzzle wizard. She once won a hundred- dollar savings bond in a contest in the Lincoln Gazette. Eddie Mack whispered to Miss Fannie asking if she had everything she needed. She patted his hand and told him she would be fine, for him to go on home and she'd see him tomorrow.

Hattie had been in and out of consciousness but, now, was fast asleep. He held her hand and longed to tell her she didn't have anything to worry about because he had everything under control. He wanted to give her that secure feeling of being cared for that she had given him all of his life. Looking into her almost smiling face, he remembered when he was fifteen and almost sent to a lock-up facility near Birmingham, for stealing some rich kid's custom-made bicycle. Hattie had convinced the judge, over the assistant district attorney's objection, that if he would allow Eddie Mack to live with her, she'd make sure the court would have no future problems from him. Eddie Mack remembers that day like it was yesterday and he remembers thinking that it might be worse living with Hattie than going to lock-up.

He learned a great deal living with Hattie. If he was pressed to name the most important thing he learned from her it would be to live each day as though you were being graded by the good Lord himself. She used to tell him that all the time.

"Well," she would ask him at the end of every day, "how'd you grade out today, Eddie Mack? You on the A-B Honor Roll yet? If'n you ain't, you better be on it tomorrow or you and me's gonna have us a 'come-to-Jesus meetin' out back? You hear me?" He didn't like those meetin's out back by the woodshed. No sir. Eddie Mack would always tell her at the end of each day that he knew he hadn't done as well as he could've, but he'd try harder the next day. And after a while, he realized that that's what she wanted him to get in the habit of doing. Trying harder every day to do the right thing. It didn't take too long before Eddie Mack was a well-behaved kid; one folks were beginning to compliment. After a few months, Hattie saw to it that he sent the judge a thank you letter telling him how much he appreciated his second chance. He even began cutting yards, for free, for some of Hattie's widow friends. Hattie told him it would help him get in the pearly gates and he figured he needed all the help he could get.

When Eddie Mack stepped out of Hattie's room, he was told Chief Bush had dropped by to ask about Hattie, on his way to the Morgan girl's room. He had told the chief, earlier, that he didn't have any idea why that girl had been in Hattie's trunk. He hoped he was believable, because it was the truth. Eddie Mack did not like answering questions from lawmen and even though he liked Bush, it didn't come easy for him to trust cops, seeing as how he'd had some run-in's with the law in his past. Eddie Mack knew this had the makings of a serious matter and he wanted no part of it.

Dr. Nadillya, the on-call emergency room physician, entered the waiting room, accompanied by the second floor charge nurse. He asked to speak to the next of kin. The doctor was from Calcutta, India with a heavy accent.

"I'm in charge, here, doc. Eddie Mack Monroe, Mrs. Buford's brother," he said, extending his hand.

"Glad to meet you, Ed Mack," the little brown doctor said, shaking Eddie Mack's hand. "I want to tell you that Mrs. Buford's prognosis is good." Flipping through his chart, he added, "Her lapses of consciousness are 'spected to decrease rapidly. Soon, she will be able to talk to you very well. Other than surgery on her leg scheduled for Monday, Mrs. Buford has no serious medical concerns. But she will be very sore for a while." Twisting his little, thin moustache, Dr. Nadillya asked if Eddie Mack had questions.

Eddie Mack wanted to know only two things: how long Hattie could expect to be in the hospital and would she have any long-lasting effects from her injuries. Dr. Nadillya assured him that Hattie should not be in the hospital over a week and that there should be no long-lasting debilitating effects.

A broad smile showed Eddie Mack's relief. "Thank you, Jesus," he proclaimed.

Poolie's condition was more serious. Preliminary x-rays indicated damage to the spinal cord. "Mrs. Buford's son is going to be airlifted to UAB Hospital in Birmingham tonight, where he could remain for up to three weeks. We are hopeful that after a reduction in swelling of his spinal cord, neurosurgeons there will be able to alleviate any potential long-term problems. We were able to determine that he has no life-threatening injuries, but when it comes to spinal cord surgery, we defer to Birmingham." Nadillya peered over his glasses, "Any further questions?"

"Can I see Poolie before he leaves?" Eddie Mack asked. "I want to tell him everything's gonna be fine and that his mother is okay."

"Poolie?" Dr. Nadillya asked.

"Uh, yeah, Cassius Clay Buford. Mrs. Buford's son," Eddie Mack explained.

"Oh. You call him Poolie. Ah, I see. He is in the trauma unit being prepared for flight. If you will come to the unit in fifteen minutes, I will see that you can speak to him, before he leaves. Okay?"

"Thank you doc. I'll be there in fifteen." They shook hands. Eddie Mack then shared what he had learned with the crowd.

Dr. Nadillya was heard to say to his nurse as they turned to walk down the hall, "See, I didn't need you. They understand everything I say. My southern accent is coming along, isn't it?" Her laughter echoed the length of the entire floor.

***

The hum of the fluorescent ceiling light was the only sound in Room 220 as its patient slept. Blue-gray light jumped about the room from the elevated, muted television. In a corner of the room Chief Bush, rested his foot on a tall waste basket as he lip-read an old Humphrey Bogart movie. He had been told by the doctor that Abi was the luckiest of all of the accident victims. Her being in the trunk of the Buick surrounded by her duffel bag and a half a bale of hay kept her from serious injury.

Other than some minor bruising, Abi suffered only from a slight concussion. The nurse expected her to rest peacefully for most of the evening. He was relieved when the nurse told him there would be no medical reason preventing him from asking her some questions. He had heard the nurses' rumors about why the girl was in the trunk. Speculation was rampant. The duffel bag indicated that the girl was planning to leave home, but what he needed to know was why she was in the trunk. He thought he'd hole up in her room a while and if he got lucky, she'd wake up while he was there.

Joe Lee Bush was no stranger to hospital rooms. Watching Abi sleep in the antiseptic-white room reminded him of the days and nights he had watched over his six-year-old daughter during the final weeks of her struggle. Leukemia. He remembered how hard his only child had fought for her life. He'd never seen another human being struggle for survival like his Jennifer. Thinking of it now, five years later, still made his heart hurt. After she died, her mother never got over it. She took her own life a month to the day after they buried Jennifer. He visits them every Sunday, on their birthdays, Christmas and any time he feels a need to talk to them, which has been a lot lately.

Abi rolled onto her back and moaned, her eyes still closed. She seemed a little uncomfortable, writhing as though her back hurt. The chief leaned over to see if a tube or something was up against her back. He gently rolled her to her right and saw that the safety pin holding her gown together had rubbed a sore in the center of her backbone. He fiddled with it and freed it from the gown. As he sat back down, Abi opened her eyes.

"Hey, how're you doin'," he asked, returning to the side of the bed. It took her a moment to focus, but she soon recognized him. She smiled.

"How're you feeling?" he whispered, stroking her hair back from her forehead.

"Not bad," she said. "Am I… still… in the… hospital?" She remembered being told where she was by one of the emergency room nurses when she was admitted.

"Yep, you're still here," Bush smiled. "Can I get you anything?"

"I'm thirsty… can I have a coke?" she whispered, her voice cracking from dryness.

The nurses had left cokes and ice in case she awoke and wanted something other than water.

After she had a sip or two and some small talk the chief pressed for some answers. "Abigail, if you don't mind, I need to ask you some questions. Is that okay with you?"

Abi hesitated, but consented, "Yes sir."

The chief settled into his chair, crossed his legs and opened a coke of his own. "The nurses told me that it's okay for us to talk but if you start feeling bad, let me know and we'll stop, alright?"

She nodded.

He thought it would be best if he led off with what he knew about the wreck, such as how the witnesses said it happened and the condition of the victims. As he talked, he could tell Abi was upset about the injuries to the Bufords, but relieved that their prognoses were good. He poured her some more coke and fluffed her pillow before getting to the question that he felt she would like to avoid.

"Abigail," he said, trying to read her eyes. "Can you tell me why you were in the trunk of Mrs. Buford's car?"

Wanting to tell but not really wanting to tell, Abi could not find the words. Her eyes never left his. She hoped they would speak for her. He reached for her hand when the silence did not break. It was cold.

Diverting her eyes, she brought herself to say, "I was running away from home." She couldn't bring herself to look at him so she fixed her eyes on her duffel bag in the corner.

The chief watched her for a minute. Seeing what she was looking at, he asked, "May I get you something from your bag?"

She nodded, jostling a tear from her eye. "My teddy bear."

He found the teddy bear and gave it to her, along with a tissue. She put her coke down to hold Teddy with both hands, clutching him to her breast.

Sitting back down, he waited a moment, and then asked, "Abigail, can you tell me why you wanted to leave home?"

This was the moment she knew would eventually come. Could she tell this thing that would destroy her family? Could she be that selfish? She didn't have to tell any outsiders if she didn't want to. She and her family could handle this. Why couldn't she just work it out with her dad? She remembered thinking this morning that once she took the first step, there would be no turning back. But maybe she could turn back. Maybe. She thought about not saying anything. Let the gossip mongers assign whatever reason they wanted to her running away.

But the more she thought about it, the more she began to feel something like anger. It wasn't real anger but it was close. Her confidence began to grow and she began to feel that she might be able to say what needed to be said. She was brought up hearing, 'Always tell the truth'. 'The truth shall set you free,' Hattie preached.

Summoning the strength that her thirteen years had given her, she forced the words, "I was running away from home... because my daddy has been"... There was a loud knock at the door.

Mrs. Morgan burst into the room. "Abi! Abi, honey! Are you okay?" She rushed to Abi, oblivious to the chief's presence and cupped her face with both hands.

Judge Morgan followed, heading to the other side of the bed. He saw Bush, attempted a half-smile and thanked him for his handling of the accident and the special attention he was giving Abi. He reached for Abi's hand with his left while he wiped newly formed sweat from his upper lip with his right.

"Well, Judge, you're welcome. But, I haven't been here very long. I just dropped by the hospital about a half-hour ago to see how all the victims were doing. Matter of fact, Abi just woke up a few minutes before y'all came in." Bush noted everyone's demeanor. He studied Abi's face. He continued, "The nurses and the doctor say she's gonna be fine. Just a slight concussion and some minor bruising."

The chief knew from experience that there were certain times that you didn't continue questioning, even though vital questions had been unanswered. Given the possibility that Abi was about to discuss a sensitive issue, he didn't want to put her in the position of talking in front of her parents. "Well I guess I better get back to the office and let you folks have some time to yourselves. Judge, when you get time, give me a holler and I'll go over the accident report with you."

The chief looked at Abi and saw 'thank you' in her eyes. He gave her a reassuring wink and said, "Little lady, if there's anything I can help clear up for you about the accident, you know where to find me." He knew that she knew what he meant. "Y'all take care now." The chief nodded to Mrs. Morgan and Abi as he left the room.

"It surely was nice of the chief to come by to check on you," Judge Morgan said, looking for any clues that trouble might be brewing.

"Yeah, he's a real nice man," Abi replied, showing no emotion.

"Abi, honey, tell us what in the world happened," Rebecca said. "I couldn't believe it when the hospital called. We had no idea you were gone!" Rebecca's lips trembled and her eyes filled. Clenching Abi's hands, Rebecca bowed her head, as though she had lost the strength to hold it up and said, "I can't believe we almost lost you."

Abi noticed that the chief had pushed her duffel bag out of sight behind the over-stuffed chair in the corner. And Teddy was well covered by sheets and blankets. If she was lucky, she wouldn't have to explain the duffel bag, tonight, anyway. "Mom, dad, I'm so sorry. I just can't believe this has happened."

Anxious for answers, Judge Morgan ignored her apology and asked, "Abi, your mother asked you how all this happened. Don't you think we deserve an answer?"

Abi knew she did not want a confrontation in the hospital, especially, with her mother present. She had no choice but to lie. She cleared her throat and said, "It was really a stupid thing, but I thought it would be fun, like when I was little."

"What, honey... what are you talking about?" Rebecca pleaded.

"You know, mom. Remember when I was six or seven and I used to hide in the backseat of Hattie's car and I would wait until she drove almost all the way home before I would jump up and scare her? I used to love her having to take me all the way back home because I could always talk her into stopping at the store for coke and peanuts. Remember how I used to put all my peanuts in my coke bottle and drink it that way?"

"Yes," Rebecca said, remembering, "I surely do."

"But... this time it didn't work out like I planned. I'm so sorry," Abi said, studying her parents' faces.

"Baby," Rebecca said, "This wasn't your fault. This was an accident." Patting Abi's hand, Rebecca looked at Jonathan for his reassurance to Abi.

Taking her cue, Jonathan said, "Your mother's right. You had nothing to do with Hattie having an accident. Don't go beating yourself up for something you didn't do. We are just thankful that you are okay."

Abi listened to their words knowing they were wrong. She knew she had everything to do with the accident. She knew Hattie had to have been upset after listening to her this morning. "Have y'all heard anything about Hattie and Poolie?"

Her father replied, "Yes. We talked to the charge nurse before we came to your room and she thinks they'll both be alright after their surgeries." He took the last sip of Abi's coke. "So you're telling us that all this was just your attempt at re-visiting the good old days?" She nodded. "Unbelievable," he said, tossing the can into the wastebasket.

It had crossed the judge's mind more than once that Abi could have been trying to run away. He was relieved to hear what she said and hoped it was the truth, but he couldn't shake his doubts.

"I'm so sorry, daddy. I can't believe this has happened," Abi cried.

He bent down to give her a kiss on her cheek. "It's okay, baby. It's okay." Wanting to project a compassionate, fatherly image, he asked everyone to bow their heads to pray for Hattie and Poolie and to give thanks for Abi's well-being. After the prayer he hugged Abi and Rebecca and said he was going down the hall to look in on Hattie and Poolie.

The drive to the hospital had been a blur of ignored stop signs and red lights. Jonathan hadn't had time to collect his thoughts about what had happened and the potential consequences. He needed a few minutes to sort things out. Dropping quarters in the vending machine, he punched coffee with creamer and strolled the halls.

He replayed Abi's explanation over and over. By the time he reached the bottom of the coffee cup, he decided she was telling the truth. That belief overrode his apprehension. She gave him no reason to doubt her. What he had heard her say was exactly what he needed to hear. His instincts were over-ruled by his rationalization that nothing was wrong. Nothing had changed. He could feel the burden lift.

He tossed his empty cup into a trashcan in the hall corner and headed to the nurses' station to learn the room numbers of Hattie and Poolie. He was told that Hattie was sedated and unable to have visitors but that relatives were receiving visitors in the second floor lounge. Poolie was being prepped for airlifting to Birmingham.

He found Eddie Mack making a pot of coffee in the lounge's kitchen, asked the questions to which he already knew the answers and offered to be of whatever assistance he could be in the days ahead. Eddie Mack was grateful and agreed to call the judge if they needed anything. He asked about Abi and stated he hoped she recovered quickly. Eddie Mack thought the judge must be upset about his daughter, because worry was hanging heavy on his face.

TWELVE

A thick layer of smoke blanketed the poolroom and the bar at Loretta's, a place where the locals could go when they wanted to avoid the eyes of the nosy. Located about two miles west of the city limits, it was just a five-minute drive from downtown. The Saturday afternoon crowd had dwindled after the end of the Alabama-Tennessee football game, which Tennessee had won for the fourth straight year. That didn't sit well with folks here, but it sold a lot of beer and whiskey.

"Hey, Spence, Ben's headin' for the jukebox again," Loretta yelled to the card table as she wiped down the bar. Spence looked up from his cards and watched his seventy-five-year-old father shuffling across the dance-floor towards the jukebox. From time to time old Ben, a salty character, was prone to feeding too many quarters to the juke.

"Be careful, Pop, there've been many a wild woman in here, tryin' to separate a man from his money. Don't want to let your guard down," Spence shouted. He wanted to send a message without admonishing his dad in front of his friends, to be a little more frugal. Last Saturday, Ben spent all of his allotted fifteen dollars on the juke and Spence didn't want a repeat performance.

"A dollar says he plays Hank Williams first," said Ray Pomeroy, the town barber. He threw a dollar in the center of the table. "Bet?"

"You're on, big boy," said Spence. "He doesn't play Hank unless he's had a little Jim Beam and wants to reminisce about the good old days. I know for a fact he ain't in that kind of mood. Let's make it two dollars."

That brought a hatful of bills from the remaining players who figured Spence knew his old man better than Pomeroy.

Heads turned and eyes squinted through the haze as old Ben fed the quarters to the juke. He turned, flashed his store-bought smile, rolled up his flannel sleeves and walked over peanut hulls to Loretta.

The static of the phonograph echoed, "*Your cheatin' heart will tell on you*," Ben lip-synced the just-paid-for voice of the one and only Hank Williams. He bowed to Loretta. She dried her hands, returned his bow and consented to one dance, like she has for most Saturdays the past couple of years. It was like therapy for Ben, since his wife died and he'd moved in with Spence. He was a sweet, harmless old man, one she didn't have to fight off, like some of the others. Gentle Ben, she liked to call him.

"Damn it, Spence. It cost me hard-earned money to learn you don't know enough about your own old man to win a two dollar bet," whined Butch, the town's Chevrolet salesman.

Spence shrugged, raking his fingers through his thinning blonde hair. "Sometimes I know him, sometimes I don't," he said. "He must have wrangled a shot of Beam out of Loretta behind my back." His smile belied his words. He liked seeing his dad enjoying himself. For too long, Ben had wallowed in the depression that followed Spence's mother's death.

"Are we gonna play poker or are we gonna watch some old fart drool all over Loretta," Butch asked, holding three Kings that were ready to change his luck.

"Well boys, with the hand I'm holding, it'd pay me to just sit back and watch old Ben and Loretta trot the fox. I fold," proclaimed Ralph, the county's Budweiser distributor. He scooted his chair away from the table, crossed his arms over his ample belly and let his eyes dance with the couple on the floor.

"Me, too. I'm out," said Spence. "I haven't drawn a good hand all afternoon." He ambled over to a barstool, ordered a cold one and watched his father. He and his father had become real close these past couple of years. Although, initially, Spence didn't like the idea of his father moving in with him, it had worked out better than both expected. Spence always knew the time would come when he would have to take care of his dad, but he didn't think it would come as soon as it did. They're the only Danes listed in the book. You call one Dane you get two. No extra charge.

After Hank finished, Ben pecked Loretta on the cheek and escorted her to the bar. "I got her warmed up for ya', Spence. Your move." Loretta and Spence laughed, as they always did after Ben always said that after every dance. Ben hoisted himself up on a stool, leaned over to his son and whispered, "She's a pretty damn good dancer, but, you know, she needs to lean a little bit closer to the razor. Know what I mean?"

Spence elbowed his dad, "Pop, you better hold your voice down!" He glanced at Loretta, hoping she hadn't heard. She was occupied drying a glass and returning it to the mirrored shelf behind the bar.

The vibration on his belt told Spence that he was being paged. "Pop, I've got to make a call," he said, sliding off his stool. "You just sit tight, okay? Loretta, can I make a call from the office? I just got a page."

"Leave your usual quarter," Loretta smirked. Spence motioned his head for Loretta to keep an eye on his dad. She winked and mouthed okay.

In Loretta's office, Spence learned from the service that Chief Bush wanted him to give him a call. He was told it wasn't an emergency, but Spence decided to respond immediately, since the chief didn't make trivial calls.

As he placed the call, Spence glanced at the pictures of Loretta's family. Johnny, now seven; Brittany, nine. Raymond, their father, still in prison for drug trafficking. For better or worse; in sickness and in health; till death do us part. Loretta says she meant it when she said those words eight years ago and every day she gets up to prove it. He was just trying to put food on the table and clothes on our backs, she always says. It's just a plant. If the good Lord didn't want those plants to grow on this earth, they wouldn't grow, she reasoned.

"Hello, this is Joe Lee," said the chief's baritone.

"Chief, this is Spence. I got a message you called. What's on your mind?"

"Hey, Spence. I've got a little situation I might need your help with. Is this a good time to run it past you?" The chief's wife could be heard in the background asking if he had lit the grill.

"Well, I'm still at Loretta's for dad's weekly R&R. Give me about half an hour and I'll drop by your house. That good for you?"

"That'd be fine. I appreciate it Spence. Tell Ben hello for me."

"Will do." Spence hung up. He slid a five-dollar bill under Loretta's phone. Kids gotta eat.

THIRTEEN

When the chief opened his front door, Spence was met with the smell of just-grilled-steaks. Rib-eyes or T-bones, he guessed.

"Dora just pulled some rib-eyes off the grill," Bush said, "and we threw one on for you. Hope that wasn't too presumptuous."

"No, not at all. I'm starving. I only had time to fix dad something and sit him down in front of the television. ESPN is my babysitter tonight. They're good and they're cheap," Spence said, unzipping his flight-jacket.

"Come on in, Spence," Bush said, closing the door behind him. "I appreciate you coming over on such short notice."

Following Bush through his house, Spence remembered how much more a house seemed to be a home when it had a woman in it.

For a moment he thought of Julia. He remembered smelling her cooking and seeing her personal, subtle touches in every room. He remembered her warmth on cold winter nights and her sleepy face over coffee on early mornings. Just knowing that she was on the other side of the door every night when he came home made him complete. He couldn't blame her for leaving. He was a real son-of-a-bitch in those days. In retrospect, he couldn't understand why she hadn't left sooner. Post-traumatic stress syndrome, the psychiatrists had called it. They had told him that Viet Nam had done that to too many young men and that he shouldn't be ashamed of it. They told him that he suffered emotional trauma so intense that he was psychologically scarred and would be for years until the magical powers of intensive therapy took hold. He thought that was psycho-bullshit. They said that was the reason he had been unpredictable, angry and violent and that his marriage could have easily been predicted to fail.

Walking into the aromas of Dora's kitchen, Spence's stomach growled.

"Spence! How's my favorite bureaucrat?" Dora leaned over from the oven for a kiss on the cheek. "My, don't you smell good," she exclaimed, arching an eyebrow. Dora was the chief's second wife. She was as soft-hearted a person as Spence had ever known. She volunteered three days a week at the cerebral palsy center working with two and three-year-olds.

"I get your drift, Dora. Sorry about the cigarette smoke. Pop and I have been at Loretta's and I haven't had time to change."

"Dora, honey, Spence and I need to talk a little business, so we'll be out back on the patio," said Bush, grabbing his sweet tea.

"Don't be too long. All I lack is the salad. Spence, is Chianti okay with you?" she asked.

"You better ask the chief, Dora. I don't know if he's getting ready to send me out on something or not," Spence replied.

"Aw naw. This ain't nothin' that can't wait until tomorrow," said Bush. "Pour him a glass now if he wants one."

Spence nodded and Dora poured. "Thank ya', ma'am," he winked.

Stepping outside Spence was met by Moe, one of the Bush's two Collies. Dora had named them after two of the 'Three Stooges', Moe and Curly. "What's on your mind, Joe Lee? You seem a little preoccupied."

As the head of the county's Child Sexual Abuse Unit, Spencer Dane was accustomed to area agency heads seeking his expertise regarding children in suspicious circumstances. It was the career he'd always wanted; one he had studied extremely hard for. He had received his Bachelor of Social Work from Troy State University and his master's from the University of Chicago. The Chicago opportunity was afforded him by his uncle, Thurman Dane, a stockbroker, who lived in the Waukegan area on Lake Michigan. He lived in his uncle's basement for the entire two years he worked on his master's. From there, he completed a research project in the field of sexual deviancy at Dartmouth, studying under the tutelage of J. Vernon Goforth, Ph.D., Professor of Clinical Psychiatry at Dartmouth Medical School. Spence has been with the Department of Children's Services in Rutherford County for nineteen years. His opinion was valued.

"I guess I am a little squirrelly, Spence," Bush said, as he paused for thought and a sip of tea. "Have you heard about the wreck in town earlier today?"

"No. I've not heard anything."

"Well, around noon there was a two-car accident at Second and Hickory. It was pretty bad. The driver of one of the vehicles is the housekeeper for Judge Morgan. You know him, don't you?"

"Yeah. We cross paths occasionally."

"Well, Mrs. Buford, the housekeeper, and her son were in one vehicle and the other vehicle was driven by a Mrs. Freeman. All three were banged up pretty bad, but they'll all be okay with a little patchwork. Now, here's the kicker. After all three occupants were removed and transported to the hospital, my office gets a call from the junkyard saying there's another person in the Buford car. In the trunk! Well, we beat a path out there and find a teenaged girl in the trunk. She's unconscious at that point but we find some ID in her belongings. Turns out, she's Judge Morgan's daughter. Without bogging you down with too many details, I'll skip to my conversation at the hospital. She was on the verge of telling me why she was in the trunk when her parents came in. She didn't look like she wanted to keep talking, so I didn't push her. But I do remember her saying she was running away from home because her father had been doing something. Now, she didn't actually say he was doing something to her but I think she was about to."

The chief took a long sip of tea, "What do you think, so far?"

"Well, I don't know. May be something; may not. You didn't hang around after the parents got there?"

"No. I got the feeling she didn't want me there after her parents showed up. I noticed when they entered the room she pulled the sheet over her teddy bear. She had just asked me to get it out of her duffel bag. Now, why would she try to hide something that she just asked for? I'm pretty sure she didn't want them to see it because if they had, they would've discovered she had packed some things to leave the house. By their behavior, I don't think they knew she had run away. Before I left, I re-positioned one of those over-stuffed hospital chairs in front of her duffel bag so they couldn't see it."

"Interesting. I gather you didn't exactly tell them that their daughter was found in the trunk of the car?"

"You gather right. If my gut feeling is right, I would have put that girl in a bad situation if I had brought it up. I thought it best to give her a little time."

Spence slowly shook his head. "I don't really have a feeling one way or the other on this. Any chance she was just mad at daddy for not letting her date some kid he didn't like? You and I see that every day. Maybe that 'something' she referred to that her father was doing to her was simply keeping her from some creep who was wanting to have some fun with his daughter."

"I thought about that. But talking with this girl, I got the feeling there was something more, something serious. I think she's got a real problem. I don't run in to these situations as much as you do, Spence, that's why I want you to go talk to her."

"I take it you haven't been able to talk to Mrs. Buford or anyone else about this?" Spence asked.

"Right. She's been in and out of consciousness and her son has been airlifted to Birmingham. I did mention it to Eddie Mack Monroe, Mrs. Buford's younger brother, while I was at the hospital. He didn't know anything about it."

The backdoor opened and Dora yelled, "Dinner's ready. If you're not in here in two minutes, Moe and Curly eat well."

"Spence, I know this has the makings of a real ticklish situation, especially with the judge and everything, but I really think this girl needs your help."

"Maybe," Spence said, sipping his Chianti. "But, man, I hope you're wrong. That'd be a tough situation to be in. What do you think she's telling her folks tonight?"

The chief stirred the remaining ice cube and looked at Spence, "I wish I knew."

The two men fell silent and stared into the night.

FOURTEEN

The digital clock flipped to 2:27 A.M. and found Rebecca Morgan awake on a portable bed parallel to Abi's. She gazed at the ceiling tiles and smiled as she remembered how she and Abi had laughed at old *I Love Lucy* episodes a few hours earlier.

One of the nurses had smuggled in some popcorn and they sat and munched and laughed at three episodes that CBS ran during their 'Lucy-thon'. She was glad that Jonathan had agreed to take care of the twins so she could stay with Abi. She wished Abi could have stayed up longer, but the nurses were adamant about the doctor's orders.

Abi slept well early, even when the nurses checked her vitals. Rebecca positioned her bed close to Abi so she could touch her throughout the night. It was a touch she realized she had missed for a long time.

The events of the past several hours had caused Rebecca to reflect on herself as a mother. She was not pleased with the picture she saw. For too long, she had distanced herself from her children and had not been a part of their lives. Hattie had been the mother they knew. Rebecca made a vow that starting tonight, she would change. She sealed her vow with a prayer asking for the strength, wisdom and guidance to live each and every day for her children. They would be proud to call her their mother.

Rebecca wanted a cold coke. There were only warm ones on the nightstand. She sat up and reached for her purse on the windowsill. When she opened her pocketbook, two quarters sprang out. She caught one; the other fell and rolled to the far corner. She tiptoed to the corner and looked under the over-stuffed chair.

In the dim light she couldn't make out the bulky figure. It was big and dark. Moving the chair, she bent down to touch it. It was a duffel bag. She opened it and reached in. She pulled out underwear, a pair of jeans and an Alabama sweatshirt. She smelled them. She smelled Abi.

She heard a whimper. Turning around, she saw a faint glimmer of light from Abi's tear-stained cheeks.

Abi couldn't speak. The inevitable was unfolding. And this time, there was nothing she could do to stop it.

"Abi, honey, is this your bag?"

"Oh, momma," Abi cried. She held out her arms for her mother. Rebecca took her hands, then hugged and patted her. "Honey, what's the matter?"

Clutching Teddy to her breast with her left hand and holding her mother's hand with her right, Abi said, "I hoped you wouldn't see the duffel bag, momma. I hoped I would never have to tell you any of this." She closed her eyes.

Rebecca watched her daughter wrestle with her thoughts. Whatever it was, she knew Abi would tell her in her own time. At 2:45 A.M., there was no reason to be impatient.

Opening her eyes, Abi pulled her mother to her. It felt good to feel her mother's cheek on hers.

"I love you, Abi," Rebecca said. "I love you so very much. I don't know what I would have done if something had happened to you. And whatever it is that's troubling you, we'll work it out together. I promise."

Abi could feel the warmth of those words on her face. Her mother raised her head up and looked into her eyes.

"Whatever your problem is, you and I will take care of it together. That is my solemn vow to you… now and forever."

"I love you. I've missed being close to you momma," Abi whispered.

"I promise things will get better, baby. I promise they will. I know I've grown apart from you. That's something I regret. But, I can't change the past. I can change the future and I promise you I will do everything in my power to be the mother you and your brother and sister deserve. Whatever the problem is with that duffel bag, we can take care of it."

Abi took a deep breath and said, "Momma, what I have to tell you is going to hurt. It hurts me to say it, but, now, I have to." Her hands tightened on her mother's. "Momma, I was trying to leave home. That's why I packed my duffel bag." She saw her mother start to speak. "Momma, please let me say this while I can," holding up her hand. "I was wanting to get out of a bad situation, one that you didn't even know about. I didn't want to leave because of you. It was daddy." Abi knew the next words would be the hardest, but bolstered by her mother's support and Hattie's words of wisdom, the truth shall set you free, Abi did not stop.

"I was trying to leave home because daddy... has been... having... sex... with me." Her mother gasped and yanked her hand from Abi's.

"What?"

"Momma. Please. I don't want to say it again. You know what I said. You heard me."

Rebecca stood and said, "Abi, tell me you didn't say what I thought you said."

"Momma. I'm sorry."

"Abi, tell me that's not true. Tell me," her voice louder. The blood rushed from her face.

"But mother, it is true. Please tell me you believe me," Abi begged. She felt her mother slipping away.

Rebecca turned her back to Abi and walked to the window, not able to breathe much less speak. She couldn't control the trembling hand that covered her mouth. She looked outside, dizzy from a blur of thoughts and emotions. This was too much. More than she could handle. She turned, walked past Abi, left the room and slammed the door behind her.

Abi stared at the place where her mother had stood and wondered if she would ever return.

Rebecca raced down the hall, unable to see through her tears. The nurses at their station heard the waiting-room's bathroom door bang open and saw her run in. She grabbed some tissue and stared at the scared face in the mirror. God, how could this be? Could Abi be saying this for another reason? If it had been happening, how could I have not known? Where could it have happened? Where was I? Her mind was numbed by sickening images that she couldn't stop.

She sat down on the edge of the commode seat, elbows on knees, and her face in her hands. The longer she thought about it, the closer she inched to believing Abi. She knew her drinking had distanced her from Abi and Jonathan. She also knew that her and Jonathan's sex life was non-existent. Thinking back, Abi had become distant over the past year. Coincidental?

The one constant overriding all of her doubts was the simple fact that Abi would not say something so devastating if there weren't some truth to it. Rebecca knew her daughter. Abi was a truthful, responsible child who loved her family. Jonathan, she knew from experience, couldn't be trusted. She knew of two affairs he'd had. She'd threatened to leave after the second one. If her father and his father hadn't stepped in, she and the children would have left years ago. But this! This should be beneath even Jonathan.

Rebecca paced the length of the bathroom. She patted her eyes dry and stepped out into the hall. As she walked back to Abi's room, forcing slow, deep breaths, she thought of the horrors her poor Abi must have gone through. Reaching the room, she slowly opened the door and saw Abi still in bed, her back to the door.

Abi heard the door and turned.

She was about to speak when Rebecca said, "Abi, don't say a word." She placed a forefinger on her lips then on Abi's and whispered, "Shhhhh." A long moment passed as they looked into the other's eyes. Neither spoke. Rebecca muffled her sobs with her hands and drew breath when she could. She picked up Abi's hands, kissed them, then pressed them to her heart, and said, "I am so disappointed in myself... for not being there for you. Will you forgive me?"

"Oh, momma. You do believe me," Abi cried. "Momma, I love you so much."

"Abi, I'm sorry I made you think I didn't believe you. When you hear something so devastating it takes a while to work through it. I needed some time. I am so disappointed in myself that I..." she couldn't finish. She laid down next to Abi and held her tightly as mother and daughter cried themselves to a peaceful sleep, whispering soft, 'I love you's' because they felt so good to say.

Abi's mother had returned.

FIFTEEN

The shower splashed as usual Sunday morning but it was not followed by his usual humming. Judge Morgan was not his usual self. He'd fixed the twins their cereal and was preparing to take a shower. Rebecca had thought it best if he stayed with the twins so that they could keep their regular Sunday morning schedule of Sunday school and church.

He missed his Abi this morning. Just walking past her bedroom on his way to the shower, had aroused him and he was consumed with thoughts of her baby-soft skin and her sweet smell and the way her hair fell around her face when they were together. He needed her this morning. Closing the shower door behind him, he positioned the shower-head on the back of his neck, stiff from a fitful night's sleep. He let the hot water relax him, as he breathed in the rising, caressing steam. As he lathered himself, he could feel Abi's delicate, slender fingers touching him where he directed, massaging him, gently at first, then faster and harder then slower and gently, repeated over and over, until finally she brought him to the point of no return.

***

Sunday mornings usually let Spencer Dane slide until at least 8:00. But today, 5:00 found him warming his hands around his second cup of hot coffee, staring out at the season's first frost.

Spence had had a restless night after being called late by his director, Jane Covington, who wanted to talk about the Morgan girl. She had heard on her scanner that the chief had called Spence about the girl and Ms. Covington wanted all the details. He hated these after-hour calls from her. They were pointless. She always wanted to know all the comings and goings in Lincoln, just so she could spread gossip to her bloody-mary, bridge club buddies. The director was an incompetent, melodramatic old maid who had been appointed the director twenty-one years ago by the out-going director and rubber-stamped by the county board. She was constantly a burr under his saddle, always intruding in his cases, doing more harm than good.

Sipping his coffee in the pre-dawn darkness, he mentally prepared himself for his meeting with Abigail Morgan.

After a bowl of cereal, he scanned the newspaper. Buried in the second section was the usual scant coverage of area accidents, the names of the victims and their conditions. There was no mention of the Morgan girl. This was good because Spence didn't want any reporters sniffing around before he concluded his investigation.

Before he left Chief Bush's last night, they discussed the possibility that one or both of Abi's parents may have stayed with her overnight and could be with her when he visited this morning. In that case, he would just have to make the best of it. Both he and Bush thought it was more important to see Abi as early as possible this morning, regardless of who is present. Time was becoming a factor. Since Abi's physician saw no medical reason for her to remain in the hospital, she would probably be ready for discharge by noon.

***

As he raised his hand to knock on room 220, Spence could hear voices from inside. They were female. That meant, in all likelihood, Abigail's mother was with her. That was probably a good thing.

"Come in," the deeper voice said. Spence opened the door and saw Abigail sitting up in her bed, smiling. It was obvious that this was a pleasant moment. He hated he had to interrupt it.

"Good morning, I'm Spencer Dane." he said, "I'm from the Rutherford County Department of Children's Services," smiling his best 'I mean you no harm smile.' It was at this point that people would recoil in abject horror, but these two did not.

SIXTEEN

After only a few minutes with Abi and her mother, Spence was struck by the composure and calmness of both. It was as though they were in complete control of everything and that they could handle anything, together. There was a bond between the two that gave them a sense of oneness.

"Mr. Dane, we realize that you are here to help Abi get out of a difficult situation," Rebecca said, speaking confidently. "And we very much appreciate your concern. My daughter, over the course of last night and this morning, has told me what she has had to endure, over the past year. It was hard for me to believe at first. But I know my daughter and I know she is not the kind of person who could say this if it weren't true." Rebecca saw a look of reassurance on Abi's face. "We welcome your advice but I'd like to assure you that we are very capable of taking care of this problem now that it is out in the open. There is no reason for your department to be involved."

Spence picked up on Mrs. Morgan's 'get the hell out of here' innuendo that was pleasantly couched in her comment. "Mrs. Morgan, having just met you and your daughter, it is obvious that both of you are capable individuals. I'm very glad to learn that Abi has confided in you and that you believe her." He didn't want to bulldoze his way into their lives but slowly and gently evolve into being a part of the remedy in this matter. In his investigations, he was always hopeful that the non-offending parent believed the victim and was supportive. He found that that was essential in protecting the victim and usually an early indicator of a successful resolution of the case.

As the sun filtered through the blinds, Spence reviewed agency protocol and procedure. He emphasized his main concern was Abi's protection. He explained that in many cases such as this, all family members could remain in the home while treatment is being provided, so long as the child is not at risk of abuse.

Rebecca resented Dane's intrusion but thought better of making an issue of it. She didn't want to risk upsetting Abi any further. She decided to let him have his little say so that he would soon be on his way.

Abi made a point of telling Spence that she didn't want her family split up or anything bad to happen to her father. She just wanted her father to stop what he was doing. She told him that she and her mother had talked and they feel they can handle this problem.

Spence admired Abi's boldness and smiled at her mother. "Abi, you and your mother may very well be able to handle this. But, I'm required by law to help you, also. Don't get me wrong, I don't want to split your family up, either. But, I do want to make sure that your problem is resolved and we may be able to do that without anyone having to leave home. Okay? How does that sound?"

Abi looked at her mother for a cue. Rebecca winked and nodded her approval.

"Mr. Dane, Abi made me promise, last night, that we wouldn't leave her father. I told her I couldn't see how I could live with him, knowing what I know. But, we talked long and hard about it. She convinced me that the most important thing is to keep our family together."

"I've got to tell you," Spence said, sitting back, "I don't believe I've ever seen such conviction and such a sense of purpose from a mother and daughter in this situation, in all my years. I admire your commitment to your family."

"Mr. Dane, it's like this. I love my father… as my father. Not as anything else. I don't like this other person he is. I want him to stop what he's doing so that I can get my old father back. Do you understand?" Abi said, her eyebrows raised.

Spence nodded, "Yes, I do. That's what I want, too. And that's what we are going to try to do. Get your old father back. Okay?"

Abi smiled and seemed pleased. "Okay."

Spence asked if Rebecca or Abi wanted something to drink before he continued. Neither did. "In order for me to know the extent of the abuse, I will need to talk with Abi in great detail. I can do that privately or I can continue as we are, whichever you all prefer." Spence glanced at Abi then Rebecca. Their faces told nothing.

"Well, she told me a great deal last night," Rebecca said, not really knowing what would be more comfortable for Abi.

"Mom, I don't mind if you're in here."

"Okay, I'll just scoot over here in the corner, sort of out of the way," Rebecca said, sliding a chair backwards, up against the duffel bag.

After everyone was situated, Spence proceeded. "Now, some of this may be redundant but please bear with me. Okay, Abi, let's start with the obvious question. Why did you leave home yesterday?" He prepared to take notes.

"Well, it's like I told my mother, I wanted to leave home because of what daddy was doing, you know, the sex stuff." Abi stroked Teddy's head.

"When you say 'sex stuff', what do you mean?" Spence asked.

"You know... sex. Like... you know... like husbands and wives do." Abi saw in his face that her answer was incomplete. "You know... intercourse." Her face reddened ever so slightly.

"Now, Abi, I'm going to have to ask you what you mean by intercourse. Many children think it means something that it isn't. So, if you would, please tell me what you mean."

Rebecca squirmed in her chair.

Abi cleared her throat. "You know... when the man puts his private part... in the woman's private part. That's intercourse." Abi looked at Spence with raised eyebrows, hoping she wasn't wrong.

"Okay. Now, when you say his 'private part', what do you mean?" Spence probed.

Now, come on, Rebecca thought, surely you know what she means. She started to speak but decided not to slow this process down. She wanted him gone as quickly as possible.

Abi tilted her head. "You know... his... penis," she said.

"And when you say your 'private part', what do you mean?"

Rebecca squirmed.

"You know... my... vagina," Abi said, staring at the top of Teddy's head.

Spence took this occasion to inquire of mom and daughter if both were okay and if they felt good enough to continue. Abi said she was fine but eager to get this over with. Rebecca looked Mr. Dane dead in the eye and said, "I would like for you to wrap this up. Do you think you can do that in the next minute or two?"

"I know this is not easy, Mrs. Morgan. If you will just bear with me a little longer. I just need to get her complete statement for the record." He looked over to Abi and smiled, "And I promise I won't stay one minute longer than I have to."

He looked back down to his notes and said, "Now, Abi, can you tell me about when your father first had intercourse with you?"

Abi, now, realized that it might have been best if her mother didn't have to hear everything. "Well," Abi said, thinking back, "I think it was about... last Halloween when... we had... intercourse for the first time." She stuck a finger to her lip. "Yeah, I think that's right."

Rebecca tried to act composed but was having a difficult time restraining her emotions.

Spence continued. "And can you tell me how that came about?"

"It happened late one night after momma and daddy had been to a Halloween party. I can remember being in my bedroom asleep when daddy came in. I could smell that he had been drinking." Abi paused to gather herself. She wasn't going to let herself cry, now. She'd done enough of that. "I remember he got in bed with me and started touching me all over. He kept telling me how much he loved me and that... because he loved me so much... he wanted to share a special love with me." Abi swallowed hard.

"Abi, do you remember where your mother was at that time?"

"I think she was in their bedroom asleep."

Rebecca felt a twinge of guilt.

"Do you remember if he threatened you, in any way?"

Taking a deep breath, Abi said, "No, not that night. That night he told me that it was 'our secret' and that if I loved him, I would never tell anyone, not even momma." Abi looked at her mother. "Momma, I really wanted to tell you, but ... I was scared." Rebecca sprang from her chair to hug Abi. "Baby, you did what you thought was best. It's okay." She squeezed Abi and stroked her hair. "You don't need to feel guilty about what your father did. The blame is his, not yours."

At this point, Spence suggested a break, took everyone's order and went down the hall for coffees and a coke. He had some more questions but they looked like they could use a break. He retrieved the drinks, made a quick call to check on Ben and headed back.

He knocked to let them know he had returned. The coke was Abi's, the black coffee, Rebecca's and the coffee with everything, his.

Everyone assumed their positions.

"Okay. I don't have much more to go over, but before I start, do either of you have any questions about anything we've gone over?"

Neither had any questions.

"Abi, when I asked you earlier if he threatened you, you said, 'No, not that night.' Does that mean that he did threaten you on another occasion?" Spence asked.

Swallowing a sip of coke, Abi thought. "Well, I don't think you could say that he's ever threatened me, but he would tell me that if anyone ever found out, my brother and sister and I would be made to leave the family and placed in a strange home, never to see him or my mother, again."

Rebecca sipped her coffee with a poker face, but her rage smoldered.

"Let me back up a bit, Abi. You have said that intercourse began around Halloween of last year and you have said that intercourse is why you left the home yesterday. What I have to ask next is, during this time span of a year how often or how many occasions did intercourse occur?"

Without hesitation, Abi blurted out, "There's no way I can tell you how many times. There are too many to count." Embarrassed, she bowed her head.

Rebecca gasped, but her hand held the sound in.

Spence turned to give her a 'get a hold of yourself or leave the room' look. Turning back to Abi, he proceeded. "Well then, about how often would you say he had intercourse with you? Would it be once a month, once a week or once every couple of months? Just give me your best estimate."

"I think, at first, it was about once a month. Lately, I think it's been more like about... once a week." Abi could hear her mother stirring in her chair and she forced herself not to look in her direction.

That son-of-a-bitch, Rebecca screamed inside her head, clenching her teeth.

"Abi, do you know where your mother was during these occasions?"

"She was in bed, I think. It was usually early in the morning, before he took his shower. I don't think anybody else was awake."

"Abi, I need to ask some questions even further back than last year. Okay? Can you remember, before your father had intercourse with you, if he ever had any other kind of sexual activity with you?"

This was not a difficult question to answer. "Yes, he has."

Rebecca clenched a fist.

"Could you tell me what kind of sexual activity this was?" Spence asked.

Abi forced the words, "He'd put... his mouth... on my private part and... he made me put... my mouth on his."

"Okay... let me ask you this. Do you know what ejaculation is?" Spence continued, taking careful notes.

Searching for the right words, Abi offered, "Isn't that when something comes out... of a man's penis?"

"That's right. That's when a man has an orgasm. Fluid comes out of his penis. Can you tell me if your father has ejaculated during any of the sexual activity that you have mentioned?"

"Yes, I'm certain he has," Abi said.

"And how is it that you are certain?"

"Well... most all of the time after... intercourse, I could feel something sticky... you know, down there between my legs. And I thought it had to be from him."

"What about during the occasions of oral sex, when he would make you put your mouth on him?"

Abi dropped her head. "He would always bring a towel with him... like he was going to the shower. And just before he would... you know, have his orgasm... he would do it into the towel."

With that, Rebecca stood up, hand over mouth and walked into the bathroom to vomit.

Spence lowered his voice and asked, "And where would this take place?"

"In my bedroom."

"Anywhere else?"

"No."

"Can you tell me about how long a period of time the oral sex went on, you know, like what month or year it began?"

"I believe it started when I was about... eleven... yeah... I think that's right, because that's the year I had Mrs. Worley as my fifth grade teacher," Abi said.

Rebecca cleaned herself up and checked herself in the mirror. She could really use a drink. She stepped from the bathroom quietly and returned to her seat in the corner. She opened a Coke and steadied herself for the remainder of the interview while Spence changed the course of the questioning.

At Spencer's request, Abi thought back even further and remembered instances of subtle touching, which at the time seemed harmless; but in retrospect, appears to have been some type of conditioning. Spence said her father could have been grooming her by getting her used to different forms of subtle sexual contact such as frequent touching of her vaginal area or gradually sensualizing his kisses when he'd kiss her goodnight.

After scribbling more notes, Spence asked a question neither Abi nor her mother had thought of. "Do either of you feel that Abi's father poses a danger to Abi's sister?"

Both thought a moment. Both said they didn't think so, but with everything that Abi had just said, how could they be sure.

SEVENTEEN

The oatmeal was all gone and so was the orange juice. All that remained of Hattie's little breakfast was a sip of black coffee and half a piece of toast. She ain't had nothin' that tasted this bad since the last time she was in the hospital three years ago with the gout.

"Fannie, I'm tellin' you the truth, if a body ain't sick when they get here, eatin' this food will sho' 'nuff do the trick," Hattie mumbled chewing the last of the tasteless dry toast. "And this oatmeal? Good lawd! I believe they use this stuff to hang wallpaper. But, I guess I ought to quit whinin' 'bout it 'cause I'm so empty, I got to eat it."

"Well, Hattie, you know you got to go by the doctor's orders. Ain't no sense in carryin' on 'bout it," said Miss Fannie, without looking up from the Lincoln Gazette's crossword puzzle.

Hattie reached over to the bedside table where Miss Fannie's tray lay, strewn with the remnants of her scrambled eggs, grits and sausage.

"I don't think so!" blurted Miss Fannie, grabbing her plate. She looked Hattie dead in the eye, ate every last morsel right in front of her and said, "I ain't gonna let you go against doctor's orders, Hattie. Not on my watch. 'Sides, I promised Eddie Mack I'd see to it you was well cared for. So you see, I can't let you go puttin' food inside you that might hurt you."

"I see you don't have no trouble puttin' food inside you that might hurt you," complained Hattie.

"Well, I ain't fixin' to have surgery in the morning, either," rebutted Miss Fannie.

A knock at the door put a hold on the bickering.

"Come in," Hattie yelled. "We'll finish this little talk later," she whispered to Miss Fannie.

"Good morning, Mrs. Buford. I'm Spencer Dane and I'm from the Rutherford County Department of Children's Services. How are you feeling today?"

"Oh, I'm not feelin' too bad. I think I'd feel better if I could have something to eat," she said, cutting her eyes at Miss Fannie.

"Mrs. Buford, I was hoping that this might be a good time to spend a few minutes with you to talk about your accident. Do you think that would be okay?"

Hattie scrunched her eyebrows together in a puzzled look. "Yessir, we can talk a few minutes. But I'm a little confused 'bout what my accident has to do with Children's Services."

"Well, that's part of what I need to talk to you about," Spence said, pulling up a chair. "Would it be possible for us to talk privately?"

"That won't be no problem, will it Fannie," Hattie smiled to Fannie. "Oh! Where are my manners? Mr. Dane, this is my best friend, Miss Fannie Cutshall."

"I'm pleased to meet you, Miss Cutshall. Looks like you've been taking real good care of Mrs. Buford."

"Oh, Hattie Mae's real easy to care for… long as you do what she wants… when she wants it… and you don't never cross her," Miss Fannie said, with a smart-aleck grin. "I'll let myself out. Pleasure to meet you, Mr. Dane."

"Alright, Mr. Dane, what can I help you with?" Hattie asked, adjusting her injured leg and patting her hair as though that helped her appearance.

"Mrs. Buford, I need to talk to you about Abigail Morgan."

"Lord, I woke up this mornin' wonderin' how that precious girl was doin'. I was plannin' to call her after a while to see how she was getting along." Then it hit Hattie. Did this stranger know what she knew? Her eyes widened. "Is Abi alright?"

"Yes, ma'am, she's fine. Did you know that she is right here in this hospital?"

"What? She's in the hospital? What has happened to her?"

Spence raised an eyebrow, "Am I correct in assuming that you didn't know she was in your car at the time of your accident?"

"She was what? She couldn't have been! Just Poolie and me was in that car," Hattie exclaimed.

"You didn't know that Abi had gotten into the trunk of your car before you left the Morgan house?"

"No, sir. I sure did not." Hattie reached for the damp washrag on the table at the side of her bed and patted her forehead. "What did she do that for?"

"She told me a few minutes ago that she had gotten in the trunk before her father had gotten home, about fifteen minutes before you left for the day. She said she was running away from home."

"Oh, my Lord." Hattie took a moment to catch her breath. "Was she hurt in the wreck?"

"Not seriously. The doctor said she came out luckier than anyone because of her duffel bag and some hay that was left in the trunk. She had a slight concussion. She was held overnight, primarily for observation. She has been cleared for discharge around noon today."

"Well, I'll be." Hattie shook her head, "I heard it, but I can hardly believe it." She thought of her conversation with Abi. "So, you've talked to Abi about why she wanted to leave?" Hattie asked, testing the waters.

"Yes ma'am, I have. She explained that she confided in you that morning and that's the part I would like to ask you about. Is it okay to do that right now, Mrs. Buford?"

"Yessir, that'll be just fine."

"Can you tell me what you remember about what Abi told you yesterday morning?"

"Yessir. Abi had gotten upset while she was downstairs in the kitchen with me. I had said somethin' 'bout what a good daddy she had. After I said that, she dropped the plate she was holding and ran upstairs, cryin'. When I got up to her room, she told me about what Judge Morgan had been makin' her do."

"Do you remember the words she used in telling you what that was?"

"Yessir. I believe she said he made her do 'ugly things… sex things… like what a husband and a wife do.' Yeah, I think those are the words she used." Hattie grabbed a kleenex to wipe her upper lip. "She fell off to sleep after that and I went downstairs to get ready to go home."

"Mrs. Buford, have you ever suspected anything like this with Judge Morgan and any of the children?"

"Absolutely not. Far as I could tell, this was one of the best families I'd ever known. 'Course they had their problems like all families."

"What kind of problems are you referring to, ma'am?"

"Well, over the years, like in many families, husbands and wives kinda' grow apart. You know what I mean?"

"Yes, ma'am. Do you mean they weren't close in any way?"

"That's right. Not close at all. She had her friends and he had his. And they seemed especially distant to each other these past few years. Mrs. Morgan, she kinda drinks a little too much, but I guess it's 'cause she ain't got much else to do and nobody to do it with. And the judge, he stays gone most of the time, usually to the country club or with some of his lawyer friends. I guess 'cause he feels there ain't no reason to stay home with somebody who don't really care if he's there or not. 'Bout the only time you'd see them two together would be at some important social happnin' that the judge had to be at and he'd have to make her go. You know, it'd look better if'n they's both there, rather than one without the other'n, to be respectable 'n all."

"Mrs. Buford, did Abi ever give you any reason to suspect that anything like this was going on?"

"No sir, Mr. Dane. None whatsoever."

"Mrs. Buford, before I wrap up here, is there anything else you can think of that might be helpful to me in this matter?"

"No, Mr. Dane, not really. I can't think of a thing. You got any idea what's gonna happen next?"

"Well, I told Mrs. Morgan and Abi that I want to talk to Judge Morgan before Abi's discharge, so I'll be going to his home to talk with him, probably right after I leave you."

"Before you go, can you tell me what usually happens in these matters?" Hattie asked.

"Well, in situations where there is a protective adult in the home, it would be possible for the child to remain in the home if the child is not subjected to continued abuse. In this matter, it seems that Mrs. Morgan, who has just learned about this, is going to be very protective of her daughter. Additionally, Abi, who is thirteen, seems to be an assertive, determined young lady, who, now that everything is out in the open, is very capable of protecting herself. She is, now, very willing to report any mistreatment by her father, now that she has the support of her mother and my department. So, together, Abi and her mother comprise a very impressive protection mechanism as far as I'm concerned. This will give Abi the opportunity to remain at home while treatment services can be put in place to effect the necessary changes regarding this family's relationships."

"Mr. Dane, I sho' am glad to hear Abi can stay home. That child sho' 'nuff loves her family." Hattie thought a moment. "I don't know no other way to say this… but do you think that Judge Morgan would be… stupid enough… to try something with Abi, now that everything's out in the open, with everybody watchin' 'n all?"

"That's the big question, isn't it? But, based on my experience, it is highly unlikely. Doing something that idiotic would most likely reserve him a suite at the state penitentiary, wouldn't it, Mrs. Buford."

"Lawdy mercy, Mr. Dane, I sho' reckon it would," Hattie chuckled.

EIGHTEEN

Jonathan's BMW turned off Hickory on to Third Street headed to the Lincoln United Methodist Church just as Spencer Dane pulled into Morgan's driveway. Finding no one home, Spence left his card in the door and headed home to check on Ben.

He punched up the Sheriff's number on his cell.

Dora answered the phone with her hair dryer on full-blast and hollered for Joe Lee.

"Joe Lee, here," said the chief, with a mouthful of toothpaste.

"Morning, Joe Lee. This is Spence. Just wanted to check in with you on the Morgan girl. Yeah, I just came from the hospital and swung by the Morgan home to try to see the judge, but no one was there."

"How'd it go with the girl?" the chief asked.

"It went well. And you were right, Joe Lee. She's had some serious problems with her father for quite a while. I don't want to go into any detail over this cell phone, but I'm talking real serious."

"So, you're to the point where you need to confront him?"

"Yep. Everything up to this point has been good. I think we may see a successful resolution of this thing in the very near future. I'm real impressed with the mother and the girl. Strong people. No doubt about it."

"That's good to hear, Spence. I really appreciate your help in this matter and I appreciate you calling me to bring me up to date."

"Joe Lee, I'm going to let you go, now. I'm on my way home to get a quick breakfast. Then I'll swing back by the Morgan home to interview the judge. Talk to you, later."

"Thanks, Spence. I owe you one. Hey, if you need any assistance, you know, an officer to accompany you, let me know."

"Don't think this will be one of those situations, but thanks anyway."

***

As Abi showered, Rebecca packed Abi's clothes in her duffel bag to prepare for her noon discharge. She thought about Mr. Dane's question regarding Sara Beth and knew, without a doubt, that Jonathan would never abuse her. Jonathan knew Sara Beth was his child. He knew Abi was not.

When Rebecca attended the University of Alabama, she dated another young man at the same time she dated Jonathan. A handsome young man named Landon Moreau from Baton Rouge, Louisiana. Jonathan knew of Landon and didn't like him. In fact, had an intense hatred of him. Landon was Creole. His people came to Louisiana from Martinique in the West Indies where they had made a small fortune distilling rum. He lived with relatives in Baton Rouge in order to obtain his education in America while his parents remained in Martinique.

Jonathan didn't like Rebecca dating anyone else but him, but especially hated Landon because he was of French and Latin descent. Although Landon was quite light-colored, Jonathan racially slurred him at every opportunity.

Rebecca dated both Landon and Jonathan for several months and became intimate with Landon during the last half of her sophomore year. Just before his graduation, Landon left without saying good-by and she never heard another word from him. Before he left, Rebecca had begun to believe there was a future for her and Landon that included marriage. She was devastated at his cruel, abrupt departure. However, Jonathan was there to pick up the pieces and within a month, they were married. Seven and a half months later, Abi was born, a constant reminder to Jonathan of Rebecca's love for another man.

***

Spence pulled into his driveway and dashed into the kitchen for a late breakfast. Throwing his jacket on the table and some of Ben's leftovers in the micro-wave, he yelled, "Hey, Pop, where are you?" He could hear ESPN blaring from all three televisions in the house. "Hey, Pop!" Spence yelled. No answer.

Spence poured a cup of room temperature coffee and headed through the house to look for Ben. Not in the living room. Not in the den. He heard the toilet flush. Turning around, he saw Ben walking from the bathroom towards the kitchen with the sports page under his arm, talking on the phone, unaware of Spence's presence. "That's right, one o'clock, here at my house. I've got the chips, dip and pretzels and one six pack. How about you and Rusty knocking the dust off your wallets and bring over some more beer. Naw, you don't need to bring food. We can make sandwiches here," he said, opening the refrigerator door and taking inventory. "Yep, looks like we're in good shape. Yeah? Hell no. No way. No women! This is an estrogen-free zone. Okay, see you then."

Spence stood with his hands on his hips and an 'I can't turn my back for a minute' look on his face, waiting for Ben to speak.

"What? What'd I do?" Ben asked, tossing the paper down next to Spence's just-warmed, hard scrambled egg leftovers.

"Are you getting ready to have a party?" Spence asked.

Ben rinsed out his coffee cup. "Naw, I'm not having a party. But some of the guys are coming over to watch the ballgames this afternoon. That okay?"

"Well, I guess it is, since you've already invited everybody and his brother," Spence whined, sticking his fork into his rubbery egg, not really sure why he was giving Ben a hard time.

Ben fired back. "Now, dammit, Spence, I hope you ain't gonna start badgerin' me like some naggin', PMS-afflicted female. We've got some dad-gum good games on today and some of the guys want to come over and watch 'em. And there ain't one good reason they can't. Besides, out of your own mouth, you told me yesterday you were going to park your butt here, today, and watch the games with me."

It dawned on Spence that he was jumping on his dad for no good reason. Moving bits of egg around, he said, "Pop, you're right. I'm just bitching to be bitching. There's no reason you can't have the guys over. I'm just a little crabby because I'm having to spend my whole weekend on this case and now, after I force down this sorry excuse for a breakfast I've got to go out, again. I apologize, Pop."

"Apology accepted," Ben said, slapping Spence on the back. "Why don't you hurry up and take care of your case and high-tail it back here for the games. It'd do you a world of good." Ben paused and gave his face time to mount a serious expression. "You know, I ain't said nothing but you've been looking a little stressed lately, a little frazzled. You know?"

"It's the nature of the job, dad. That's just the way it is and the way it'll always be."

"Well, here's some free fatherly advice. If you're gonna work that hard, you're gonna have to play just as hard, just to balance it out. Otherwise, you'll end up on top of some building, downtown, like some deranged postal worker, shooting at folks like fish in a barrel."

Spence laughed, knowing there was a lot of truth to what his father said.

Speaking of the deranged, your director called while you were gone. Said she wanted you to call her as soon as you got in."

"How long ago did she call?" Spence asked, losing his appetite and scraping his plate in the trash.

"I think it was about forty-five minutes ago. She said it was urgent and that I better not forget to give you the message. You know, I don't think that woman's got both oars in the water. What she gonna do... fire me?" Ben retorted.

"That woman," Spence said, shaking his head. "Don't worry about her, Pop, she's harmless, for the most part. She just has to make everything so melodramatic. You know, life is just a damn stage to her." He grabbed the phone, stepped out the backdoor and punched each number as hard as the phone could take. "Anyway, thanks for the message, dad."

NINETEEN

Miss Jane Covington, blew a gray funnel of smoke from the side of her mouth as she grabbed her phone. "Spencer, thank you for calling me right back," and in her nasal twang asked, "what are we going to do in the Morgan case?" The lack of a 'Good Morning' or 'How are you doing, Spence?' really jacked Spence up.

"Miss Covington, I haven't completed my investigation. So, it would be a tad premature to know exactly what we are going to do, yet."

"Well, I've talked to a friend of mine at the hospital and the word is that the Morgan girl has been sexually abused and should be placed in a foster home," she said, spewing a second funnel. "Isn't that what you plan to do?"

He could feel his blood pressure rising. A friend at the hospital. Great. Another case of sticking her nose where it didn't need to be. "Miss Covington, yes, the girl has been sexually abused. And at this stage of my investigation and with my findings, I am not of the opinion that she will have to leave home."

"Why not?" Covington asked, not getting the answer she wanted.

"Look, I have talked to the girl, her mother and the family housekeeper. I am very impressed with the girl and mother. They seem to be very committed and determined individuals capable of weathering this storm. The mother just learned of the abuse last night. Had the girl ever gone to her mother, she would have been strong enough to stop it, but the girl didn't. Mother and daughter seem to have an impenetrable bond. The girl is thirteen and very capable of reporting any future threatening behavior by the father. I don't believe it will ever happen again because of all the attention being focused on the family and the ability of the mother to protect the girl. All indications are that this will be a case where the child can remain with her family while treatment repairs the inter-family relationships. This is what the girl says she wants to do and she has convinced her mother they can save their family."

"Spencer, from all that I'm hearing, people are beginning to wonder why we haven't already put that girl in a foster home. They are saying that if this was some other family, we would have already done it." Being in a semi-political position, Miss Covington had been known to collapse under public pressure.

"Have you heard ANYTHING I've said?" Spence yelled.

"Spencer, don't take that tone with me!"

"I don't give a good damn what people are saying. And you shouldn't either. People don't know what this mother and daughter have said, what they have done or what they are capable of doing. I think the family can work through this. Let's give them the chance, without ripping their children out of their home."

"I'm not so sure," she twanged at machine gun pace, "that it's best to leave that girl in her home. Look, Spencer, whether you like it or not there are some things we have to do to ensure our good public image. It's important that the citizens of our county have confidence in us to do our job. Look at it this way. If we remove the girl, the public sees us doing the job they're paying us to do. If we don't, the public sees us shirking our responsibility. Additionally, if we remove her, it guarantees that the girl will be one-hundred per cent safe."

"You can't be serious! Don't do this. The girl doesn't want this. She has convinced her mother that they can save their family. If you split them up, that could be the first step in the total destruction of this family. Let me finish my investigation and after I've talked to the rest of the family, you and I will sit down and go over every detail. This family is in a fragile state right now. If you compound that by tearing them apart, I'm afraid they'll be beyond repair."

It was dawning on Spence that gossip, not reason, had convinced the director that this child needed to be taken from her home. In all likelihood, the gossip had come from one of the county's blue-haired daughters of the Confederacy. One who was well-connected. Covington always lent them an ear.

In a conciliatory tone, Spence presented his argument again, only to be cut off in mid-sentence.

"Spence," more smoke, "as of now, you're off the case. It's being transferred to the Foster Care Unit. Finish up your paperwork and have it on my desk by tomorrow morning." With that the director hung up.

He stood with the phone still to his ear, not believing what had just happened. "Jesus H. Christ. What an incompetent idiot!" he yelled. He dialed her number back, a knee-jerk reaction, to satisfy his need to chew Jane Covington's brainless ass off. The line was busy.

He slammed the backdoor as he entered the kitchen and yelled for his dad, "Pop, I've got to run back to the hospital. I'll check in as soon as I can."

TWENTY

The sound of more than a few heavy boot-heels, in lockstep, echoed off the tile floor from the north hallway of Lincoln Memorial's second floor. Their destination-Room 220. Nurse Nunelly looked up from her charts at the nurses' station to see the four deputies, led by Deputy Ike Dundee, who carried, what looked to be some important papers in his right hand. No one in the bunch smiled.

Deputy Dundee, all two hundred and eighty pounds of him, strode up to Nurse Nunelly and with no pleasantries said, "I got a court order from Juvenile Court Judge Vincent that says I'm to pick up a juvenile by the name of Virginia Abigail Morgan, place her in the custody of the Department of Children's Services and remove her from these premises with no interference from anyone, including her family. It is my information that she's in Room 220. Is that correct?" With that, his toothpick returned to its usual place.

Nurse Nunelly replied in a heartbeat, "Yes, she is." She eyed the papers. "Would you like for me to run a copy of the court order for our records?"

"I got a copy for you," Dundee said, tossing the copy, as he turned and headed to the room. His minions followed as on-lookers gawked, anticipating some kind of showdown.

Dundee's knock on Room 220's door was loud enough to elicit a shout from the room across the hall to "hold it down out there."

Rebecca Morgan opened the door. The sight of the big man startled her but thinking he must be at the wrong room, she wasn't concerned. The other three deputies stood out of sight. "Yes?" she said. "May I help you?"

Deputy Dundee recognized Mrs. Morgan. He handed her a copy of the order and said, "Mrs. Morgan you have been served with a pick-up order from the Juvenile Court of Rutherford County ordering me to place your daughter, Virginia Abigail Morgan, in the temporary custody of the Rutherford County Department of Children's Services. The why's and the wherefore's are in the body of the petition and the order."

Stunned, Rebecca stood motionless and dumbfounded. What she was seeing and hearing had no connection, whatsoever, to her reality.

"Momma, who's at the door," Abi asked, curious as to why her mother was not speaking or moving.

Deputy Dundee's two hundred and eighty-pound frame filled the doorway. He took one step towards Rebecca to see if she would step aside. She didn't.

"You can't be serious!" Rebecca yelled, holding up a hand. It was sinking in that the deputy was acting on behalf of some court to take custody of Abi and place her somewhere. "Who originated this petition and what judge signed this order?" she demanded, hoping to clear up this matter and send Deputy Dundee on his way. She knew that there must be a mistake. Spencer Dane had promised this was not going to happen.

"Ma'am, this petition originated from the Department of Children's Services. Who signed it from that department, I don't know and I don't care. Juvenile Court Judge Gwendolyn Vincent signed this court order. That, I do know and that, I do care about. If I don't enforce this order, I'll be looking for another job by the time I get back to the office. So, all you and me've got to agree on is that both of us will obey this order. And that means that I take Virginia Abigail Morgan with me and that you don't interfere. Got it?"

The anger Rebecca had suppressed all morning listening to Dane's interview erupted. She was backed into a corner and was left with no alternative other than to stand her ground. "Nobody is taking my daughter anywhere. Got it?" Rebecca blurted, mocking Dundee and daring the big man to lay a hand on her.

This was not how Dundee expected this to go but it was his job to do and he was going to do it.

Turning around to his men he said, "Okay, boys, we gotta go in and get her. We don't want to hurt nobody so take it easy." With that, Dundee took another step toward Rebecca, ready to move her aside if necessary.

Because it was nearly checkout time, Abi was already dressed and packed. She had gotten close enough to the door to hear her mother's remarks and like her mother, she couldn't believe that Mr. Dane had lied to them.

"Deputy, I'm warning you. If you enter this room, you do so at your own risk." Rebecca drilled her eyes into the eyes of the six-foot four-inch Dundee. She could tell that he knew she meant it. She could also tell that he intended to do his job.

Nurses left their stations and patients came out of their rooms to watch. They'd never seen anything like this. Deputy Dundee made the first move. He reached both of his powerful arms to Rebecca's shoulders. True to her word, Rebecca proved to the deputy that he was entering at his own risk. With all of her might and a strong right arm, she slapped Dundee's sagging jowls hard enough for him to bite his toothpick in half. The sound echoed down all four of the second floor halls. While his head was still turned to his right, she quickly followed with a knee to his groin that caught him off balance and dropped him to one knee.

"Get that damn bitch," a gasping Dundee ordered his men. "Cuff her and place her under arrest!" he demanded, grimacing in pain.

Rebecca tried to close the door but was too late. Two deputies forced the door open, grabbed her flailing arms and forced her to the floor, where one put a knee to her back while the other cuffed her. The third headed to Abi. Out of fear and rising anger, Abi followed her mother's lead, resisting as much as she dared, swinging her arms wildly and kicking at the deputy's legs.

Dundee walked gingerly across the room. "Mrs. Morgan, it didn't have to be like this. This could have been a lot less painful."

Rebecca raised her tear-streaked face, as the two deputies stood her up and held her cuffed arms. "Less painful? You're taking my daughter and you're telling me it could have been less painful? Pain is not the word for this! Look at my daughter! Look at what you've done, you son-of-a-bitch!"

Dundee smarted off, "Looks to me, like this here petition and court order says you're the bad guy, not me." He stuck his fat, sweaty face so close that she could count the blackheads on his nose. He whispered, "Lady, I'm takin' your little girl with me and I'm takin' your sweet little ass to jail. So, if you know a good lawyer, other than the one who's been screwing your little girl, I'd suggest you get busy remembering his number, so you can give him a call when we get to the station. Got it?"

"You fat bastard!" Rebecca screamed.

By this time, the hallway was filled with gawkers. They watched as the deputies escorted Mrs. Morgan and her daughter from Room 220 down the hall to the elevator.

Rebecca yelled to the crowd as she resisted every step, yanking her arms from the deputies. "Look at how the law works in this town. They are taking my daughter from me… and I'm going to jail. We are not guilty of anything! You could be next!"

A deputy tightened his grip on Rebecca's arm. "Shut up, lady." He picked up the pace to the elevator.

One patient holding his IV pole with one hand hurled a wad of chewing gum at a deputy, hitting him in the face. Another yelled, "Let 'em go. They ain't done nothin'."

That spurred the crowd on. Half-eaten rolls, pens and one juicy wad of chewing tobacco were thrown at the deputies with surprising accuracy, before they could hustle their prisoners away.

The unbelieving crowd watched as mother and daughter cried and begged the officers not to do this.

The two deputies with Mrs. Morgan escorted her into the elevator on the right, as the two deputies with Abi stepped to the one on the left.

Rebecca and Abi stared from their elevators at the faces of the crowd down the hall. The faces that looked back were wide-eyed with horror. Some were crying. Others were frozen in disbelief. One made a sick joke. Most wished they'd never witnessed the spectacle.

Then, the elevator doors began to close.

"Baby, I love you. I promise this won't last. Be strong," Rebecca yelled, hoping her words found their way to Abi.

"Momma, I love you. I'll be waiting. I…" The doors slapped shut, leaving Rebecca and Abi with their own reflections in the cold steel doors. They descended. Rebecca to the basement and Abi to the ground floor.

TWENTY-ONE

With no make-up and short, oily, mousy-brown hair, the pleasingly-plump Trudy Waddle was no threat to ever be featured on a pin-up calendar. The deputies had joked in the elevator that there must be an un-written code that all female social workers in the state of Alabama were forbidden to look attractive. Least ways, all the ones they knew.

The deputies took Abi by the arms as they exited the elevator and walked towards Ms. Waddle, the county's foster care worker. Her forced smile looked worse than her brown sack dress.

"Hi! You must be Abi," she said. "I'm Trudy Waddle and I'm your social worker," she said, extending her hand to Abi.

Abi was not going to force a smile or any other pleasantry and she did not extend her hand. Her tears had dried and she was becoming angry and resentful, no longer the pitiful, sniveling kid people pushed around. She and her mother had been lied to and treated like criminals and she wasn't going to take it lying down.

The deputies left Abi and her duffel bag with Ms. Waddle but stayed nearby just in case.

Wanting to set the tone for their future relationship, Abi cocked her head and said, "Ms. Waddle, why are you doing this to me?"

"Now, Abi, don't you go worrying yourself about all this legal mumbo-jumbo. Everything's going to be all right. We're going to put you in a real good home where you will be very safe. Okay?" Waddle said, flashing the fake smile.

Abi meant to get an answer from this woman, who either didn't have one or was being evasive. "Ma'am, do you even know what's going on with my family and your department. We've been talking to Mr. Dane and we all had agreed that this would not happen. Did you know that?"

Taken aback, Waddle stammered, "Well, no... uh, I didn't know all of the details about what you and Mr. Dane had..."

"Well, ma'am, are you in the habit of taking kids from their homes without knowing what's going on?" Abi wanted to help this woman look like the fool she was.

"No! Of course not." Waddle shrieked, her upper lip twitching. "Now, listen here young lady, I've got a court order here that says I've got to take custody of you and I don't have to know all the details of what's happened before the case became mine."

"So, it's your case, now? Does that mean it's not Mr. Dane's any more?"

"That's right. You are my responsibility now, not Mr. Dane's. So, you might as well make the best of it, dear. Do you understand?"

"Well, if Mr. Dane and my family had an agreement, wouldn't it be binding?" Abi pressed, knowing that all this was bigger than she was and that she couldn't change anything.

"Little lady, I don't have time to be standing around here all afternoon just because you've got a few questions," Waddle retorted in a pious, nasal tone. "I know this is not easy for you and that..."

"You KNOW! You don't KNOW anything! How can you stand there and tell me that you know. You, clearly, don't know what's been going. And you can't stand there and tell me that you know what it feels like to be in my shoes. So, don't even try." A crystal-clear understanding linked their eyes and Trudy Waddle already wanted off this case.

"Abigail, grab your duffel bag and follow me to my car," Waddle ordered, as she turned and walked. She had had enough.

Abi grabbed her bag and followed. As bad as her life was at this moment, there was a curious promise of hope in the air, fueled by her newly-found, spitfire spirit. She took a deep breath of October air as she stepped outside and remembered her mother's last words. 'Be strong.' Until now, Abi didn't know she could.

TWENTY-TWO

Jonathan pulled the BMW into the shaded 'For Patients Only' area and hurried into the ground floor entrance. He hoped all the paperwork had been completed and that there would be no delays. He wanted away from this place and fast.

He exited the elevator and turned left to Abi's room. He noticed more people than usual around the nurses' station and in the hallway. They all seemed to be talking excitedly, pointing and gesturing. He wasn't sure if it was his imagination, but some seemed to stop talking when they noticed him.

He tapped once on the door as he opened it. "Okay, girls. All aboard! This train's ready to pull out." He stopped dead in his tracks. The room was empty. He saw no signs of Abi's clothes or her bag. Wrong room, he thought. He checked the room number. He walked around the room looking for anything familiar. Nothing in the bathroom. The television was on but barely audible. He stepped on a toothpick in the doorway on his way out of the room to question the nurses.

The small crowd dispersed as he headed to the nurses' station. Nurse Nunelly began shuffling some papers when she saw him coming. The closer he got the faster she shuffled.

"Excuse me, Nurse uh... Nunelly," seeing her identification tag. "I'm Jonathan Morgan and I'm here to pick up my daughter, Abigail, who was in Room 220. She was to be discharged at noon, but I don't know where she and her mother are. Do you know where I might find them?"

Nurse Nunelly took a measured breath and said, "Judge Morgan, you... will need... to see Ms. Murdock in our Social Services department in Room 110. That's in the west wing of the first floor." She looked back down to her papers.

"Social Services? Is that part of the discharge procedure, now?"

"Um… yes sir, in certain matters."

Jonathan didn't understand the reasons for many of the hospital's policies, so he figured this was just another in a long list.

"Alright. Did you say Room 110?"

"Yes sir. And ask for Ms. Murdock," Nunelly said, loosening her stomach muscles.

***

Spence had telephoned the second floor nurses' station en route to the hospital, while waiting on a train. He was told that Abi had been placed in the custody of the Department of Children's Services and had been taken from her mother during a nasty altercation with deputies and that Mrs. Morgan was taken to jail.

He could not believe how badly this was turning out. Damn Covington. She had to have called Judge Vincent at home to get the pick-up order this quickly; then paged someone in the foster care unit. Probably Turnbow or Waddle, her two favorite lackeys.

Since there was nothing he could do at the hospital, he made a U-turn to head to the county jail. He wished the city police were involved with this little matter rather than the sheriff's office; he'd much rather be dealing with Chief Bush's officers than the sheriff's deputies. But, by law, Alabama's sheriffs' offices carry out the orders of the county juvenile court. By the time he arrived at the sheriff's office Mrs. Morgan had been finger-printed and booked.

Spence asked the big-haired, bottled-blonde receptionist if he could speak to the arresting officer in the Morgan case. Her black false eyelashes batted in synchronization with her ruby-red, bubble-gum-smacking lips, as she said that the arresting deputy was Ike Dundee. She seemed to get a thrill just saying his name. Spence was escorted to a door that had Chief Deputy Dundee in big black, gold-trimmed letters on it. The receptionist pecked once on the door, leaned in and mumbled something soft and incoherent.

"Deputy Dundee will see you, now," she smacked.

Spence stepped into the overly-heated, ill-lighted cubicle barely big enough for two grown men. Dundee's desk was piled with unfinished paperwork, wadded up Three Musketeers wrappers and empty Dr.Pepper cans.

"What can I do you for?" Dundee said, holding out his massive hand.

Spence shook the hand and handed it his card. "I need to see someone that I was told you just brought in. It's regarding a case the department is working on. The Morgan case. Are you familiar with it?" Spence chose to remain standing, hoping he wouldn't have to spend much time in the tiny room with the big man.

Dundee leaned back in his swivel chair and grunted, "Yeah, I'm familiar with the case. See this little love tap she planted on me?" he said turning his head, revealing a reddened, five-finger badge of the morning's battle.

Spence winced. "Is Mrs. Morgan okay?" he asked, wondering if the deputy retaliated.

"Aw hell. Ain't nothing wrong with her; we didn't lay a hand on her. And she's lucky we didn't because we sure had every right to. Charged her with assault and battery, though. Had to. Couldn't let that slide after what she did to me in that hospital." Dundee snickered, "Damn strongest woman for her size I believe I've ever come across. And I've come across plenty."

"Well, all I want is to be allowed a few minutes with her. Can that be arranged?"

Dundee looked up from Spence's card. "I don't see no problem with that. But, you can't stay long. Husbands don't take kindly to us letting other men visit their wives, back there out of sight, if you know what I mean."

"I won't be staying long. Just long enough to explain a couple of things."

The deputy leaned over to grab his phone. "Darlene, would you show this gentleman to the penthouse suite, please ma'am. He needs to see Mrs. Morgan. And when you're done with that, how 'bout bringing me one of them Three Musketeers and a Dr. Pepper."

TWENTY-THREE

Judge Morgan closed the door behind him that had Lincoln Memorial Hospital Social Services written on it and asked the receptionist if Ms. Murdock was in. The receptionist phoned Ms. Murdock in another room and was told to have the judge to come on back.

Jonathan stepped through another doorway and proceeded down the hall to the very last office. He knocked and was told to come in.

"Judge Morgan, I'm Hilda Murdock; how are you?"

The judge was struck by the color and the height of Ms. Murdock's hair and the amount of hairspray it must have taken to keep it there. "Glad to meet you, Ms. Murdock. And to answer your question regarding how I am, I must confess I'm a bit confused. I was scheduled to pick up my wife and daughter around noon today, but I can't seem to find them. You all haven't gone and lost them, have you?" Jonathan smiled.

"Judge, please sit down," said Murdock.

They sat simultaneously. She tugged at the lapels of her gray blazer, as if she was now safer that way, all covered up underneath a lifetime of plaques, awards and degrees that the world needed to see. She opened a folder and sorted the papers inside, so that she could easily read from them if the need arose.

"Judge Morgan, earlier this morning, the hospital received a copy of a court order served by the sheriff's office stating that they were to remove your daughter, Abigail Morgan, from the hospital and place her in the custody of the Department of Children's Services." Before he could respond she said, "Therefore, we had no choice but to comply. I hope you understand."

He pushed his head forward, squinted his eyes and tried to buy some time to think. He said, "Could you, please repeat that?" As she did, he could feel the adrenaline coursing through his veins. The thing he feared the most had happened. His mind hazed with a whirlwind of emotion and he feared he might not be able to compose himself for the best possible response.

After Murdock repeated herself, she added, "Judge Morgan, I know this is terrible for you. I'm so sorry this has happened but the hospital's hands were tied. We had no choice but to comply with the order." Hoping to prevent any forthcoming retribution from the judge, Murdock said, "I'm sure this can be cleared up just as soon as you can talk to the judge in this matter. Probably just some mistake somewhere down the line." Her words belied her thoughts.

The judge had not heard a single word. He was calculating his response, waiting for her to stop talking. When her lips stopped moving, he spoke.

He decided his first reaction should be one of shock and dismay, followed by the proper dose of righteous indignation. "What in the world is going on here?" he said, slamming his hand on her desk. "I come to pick up my daughter and you tell me someone else has taken custody of her? Is that what you're telling me?"

Ms. Murdock started to speak, but he wouldn't let her. "Where was Abi's mother when this happened? Did she not try to prevent this?" He stood to portray an uncontrollable reaction. "Does anyone know where she is?" he said, his voice thinning.

Knowing that answer, but not daring to divulge it, Ms. Murdock said, "I believe someone at the sheriff's office might be able to help you with that since they served Mrs. Morgan with a copy of the order, too."

"Ms. Murdock," he said, keeping her on her heels, "do you have a copy of the court order with you?"

"Yes, Judge and I've made a copy for you." She shot the copy into his hand.

The judge scanned the one-page order. "Well, by God, somebody's going to have some explaining to do! I can't believe any judge would issue an order such as this without at least a hearing of all parties. Does that make any sense to you, Ms. Murdock?"

"No sir. I can honestly say it doesn't," Murdock rubber-stamped the judge's assertion.

To display the appropriate amount of anger and disgust, he pushed over his chair and slammed the door as he left a relieved Murdock.

***

The Rutherford County jail was built in 1949. It is a brick and sandstone structure that the sheriff has been trying to replace for the past ten years. But, the townsfolk have no compassion for its inhabitants. Until it falls over and kills someone, the good citizens of the county will continue to exercise their apathy.

Rebecca's cellmate is eighteen-year-old Libby Durand, who was brought in last night, charged with drug trafficking and prostitution for the second time in three months. As Spence walked down the cold, damp, malodorous cellblock, he could hear Libby's explanation to Rebecca of how she was set up; that she was really innocent and that her boyfriend, the father of her four-month-old, was contacting a bail bondsman as they spoke.

Rebecca heard the crunching of footsteps off the sandstone walls.

Even in the dimly lit cellblock, Spence could see Rebecca's eyes locked on his. Every fiber of his being wanted to be somewhere else. "Mrs. Morgan, I can't tell you how sorry I am about what has happened. I came down here because I wanted to tell you that all of this was someone else's doing. I was taken off the case. My director and I had a difference of opinion about this and she gave the case to another staff member. Someone who would do her bidding. The director wanted Abi to be placed in a foster home and, as you know, I didn't believe it was necessary."

Her poker face never changed, "Mr. Dane, I'm not at all concerned about the in-house politics of your office, but I do appreciate you coming down here to tell me that you didn't lie to me. What I want to know now is… where did they take my daughter and when I can get her back."

"She's in a foster home. Which one, I don't know. As far as when you might get her back home, it depends. Usually, a hearing is held about a week or two after a child is placed in the department's custody, depending on how busy the court's docket is. However, depending on the wording of the petition and the existing order, there is a chance it could be within seventy-two hours from when they took her."

"A week or two! You can't be serious! We've got to have the seventy-two hour hearing. I can't stand the thought of Abi being forced to live with strangers for weeks. That child has been through enough."

"I've not seen the petition so I don't know which one you'll get. It very well could be the earlier one, but you never know. It'll be the judge's call." After a brief pause, Spence asked, "Have you talked to your husband yet?"

"No. And to tell you the truth, I, honestly, don't think I can." Rebecca's head lowered as she stared at the concrete floor. "I know I promised Abi that I'd try to keep the family together, but, you know," she paused and said, "I honestly think I can kill the bastard the moment I get out of here and not even lose a minute's sleep."

"Mrs. Morgan, I think I understand how you feel," Spence offered, with the predictable social worker response, "and that feeling is quite a normal reaction to what you've gone through, but..."

Rebecca raised her head and looked past Spencer. "Mr. Dane, please don't waste my time with any of your social work bullshit about how you understand what I feel and how you and your bureaucratic hand-wringers know what I need. What I should have done when Abi told me what her father had been doing, was get a lawyer, get my children and get the hell out. And the more I think about it that's exactly what I'm going to do when I leave this stinking jail. So, Mr. Dane, my suggestion to you is to finish your report this afternoon because my attorney will be contacting the Department of Children's Services tomorrow to discuss your interview with my daughter. Unless you have any further questions of me, I suggest you get busy."

"You know, Mrs. Morgan," Spence conceded, "I think you're right. Do it your way." He spoke as a man and not a social worker when he said, "It has a much better feel to it." Before he turned to leave, he smiled and asked, "You need for me to post your bail?"

Rebecca flashed a smile that had thought behind it. "No. I want Judge Jonathan Morgan to have to come down here to this God-forsaken place and cast his eyes on his wife behind bars, charged with assault and battery for attempting to prevent the county government he works for, from taking custody of his daughter because he's been fucking her. That's what I want."

TWENTY-FOUR

Trudy Waddle's salary afforded her a five year old, beige Ford station wagon that rode as rough as a cowboy's buckboard. The 98,000 miles hadn't been easy ones.

There had been no words spoken since Waddle had told Abi to get in. The only sounds made during the whole trip, other than the Ford's rattles and groans were Waddle's cigarette sucking noises. Abi thought, at the rate she smoked she would be dead in a year.

She watched the landscape grow dense with pin oaks, pines and birch saplings as they traveled the two-lane blacktop westward toward Pinto Lake. They had left the Lincoln city-limits fifteen or twenty minutes ago and Abi estimated that if they didn't arrive at their destination shortly, they'd soon run out of Rutherford County.

Waddle turned right off of the two-lane onto a winding gravel road at a sign that read, Kilroy's Landing, 1 mile. Twenty-five yards or so due east of the sign was an old dilapidated plank store with broken windows that looked to be the home of the four blue-tick hounds lounging on the front stoop. The ancient structure pitched severely to the left and was not far from being gravity's next victim.

The entire length of the gravel road was swallowed by tall, thin pines on either side but every quarter mile or so, Abi could catch a glimpse of patches of blue sky crisscrossed with thin wisps of windswept clouds and vapor trails of the Memphis to Atlanta 747s.

Down deep, Abi was worried about where she was going, but on the surface she was cool; there was no way she was going to ask Waddle about it. She was not going to give her the satisfaction of knowing that she was even giving it a thought.

She already missed her family and even Boomer. The heavy reality that she was not going home tonight struck her hard. She wanted to cry, to scream at the top of her lungs at the injustice of it all. But that would do no good. She realized there was no sense in whining about it. 'Be strong,' she remembered her mother saying.

It scared her to think that strange people in a strange house somewhere were waiting for her. And that these strangers would be responsible for caring for her, feeding her and who knows what other stuff. Too eerie to think about, she thought. But she couldn't stop. What would they look like? Would they be ugly? Would they be harsh? Cruel? Kind and sweet? She wondered what her bed would feel like. Would the unfamiliar sounds at night be scary? Different smells? She hoped the house wouldn't stink.

***

Jonathan Morgan was deep in thought as he pointed his BMW away from the hospital and toward the county jail. Although the court order that removed Abi from his custody was a serious problem, he had shaken off his initial worry and had come to the realization that it could be overcome with strong legal representation executing timely maneuvers. This might be easily achieved in the juvenile court system, which is flexible in its procedural rules, particularly relating to sworn testimony. What was beginning to weigh heavily on his mind was the potential for criminal charges, should he lose his case in juvenile court.

If he was thinking clearly, and he thought he was, his first move should be to convince Rebecca that everything was going to be all right and that things were not what they appeared to be. By doing this, he would be achieving two goals, simultaneously, learning the specific allegations of the petition and repairing whatever damage the allegations had done to their relationship. He would need Rebecca by his side throughout all of what was to come and the sooner he could convince her that this is all about nothing, the sooner he could get his life back. He knew that if he could bring Rebecca over to his side, Abi would follow.

A block from the jail, his cell phone rang.

His father, W. Henry Morgan, spoke low and serious. "Jonathan, where are you?"

"Father, I'm downtown." Jonathan had no time for idle conversation. "And I'm in the middle of something. Can I get back to you?"

"Jonathan. Listen to me. I know you've been to the hospital and that you're probably on your way to see your wife and it is my opinion that you're on the verge of making a serious mistake. Your grandfather and I would like for you to come to the office for a family meeting, now."

Jonathan was stunned. How could his father know?

"Do you understand, Jonathan?"

Recovering, Jonathan said, "I'll be there in five minutes." He rarely questioned his father or grandfather because they always had his interest at heart. And it seemed that whatever was good for Jonathan was good for the family. This, it seemed, was one of those occasions.

***

Jonathan entered the small conference room adjacent to the law library. The shades were drawn with only one table lamp spreading thin orange light over the room. Smoking his pipe and leaning forward over a cup of coffee at the head of the table was eighty-one year old Jeremiah Morgan, Jonathan's grandfather, the undisputed head of the family. To his right sat Jonathan's father, wearing a tired, strained face and to his right sat a man unknown to Jonathan, whose face hinted cunning and coolness. The stranger's brown, oil-slicked hair reflected the orange light from the lamp and shot it to the ceiling. His tan trench coat gave him the look of an under-cover agent. His gaunt and pale face and hands told Jonathan that this little man shunned the sun.

In the center of the table was a speaker-phone. At first glance, one of the lines appeared to be on.

"Jonathan," spoke his father, "please sit down."

He did so without comment. His father rose and strode across the burgundy and gold Oriental rug to the armoire for brandy. "We have very important things to discuss."

Jonathan knew he would be doing the listening. The elders were in charge.

Brandy was served and the meeting began. The elder Morgan put down his pipe, cleared his throat and said, "Jonathan, we are here today to keep this family's good name from being irreparably harmed. If we fail in our endeavor, you, your father and I know that your political future will be over. And as we all know, there are people all over this state counting on this family to be in the governor's mansion in two years. The purpose of this meeting is damage control. It has come to our attention that you are having some, shall we say, difficulty with your family." The old man's voice wasn't as smooth and strong as it was during his years as the county's circuit judge, when the ears of the convicted heard pointed opinions and dreaded sentencing, but it still served him well. "The discussion today will be strictly of a legal nature."

The grandfather noticed that the puzzled expression on his grandson's face had not dissipated since he entered the room. "Jonathan, do you have a question?"

"Grandfather, may I inquire as to what you know and how you learned it?" Jonathan raised his voice ever so slightly, but not enough to offend. "And may I ask the identity of the gentleman here at the table with us?" Jonathan nodded to the stranger, who reciprocated.

"You may," the grandfather said, sipping his coffee. "And we shall answer the former question, first." He proceeded, "Just a bit earlier this afternoon, this family's good friend, Sheriff Rayburn, shared with your father that his office had received a court order from Juvenile Court Judge Vincent. With his hands legally tied in this matter, our good friend wanted to let us know, as soon as possible, what was coming."

Jonathan's father set down his brandy to interject, "Jonathan, do you know where you wife is?"

Jonathan saw that look on his father's face that he'd seen so many times as a child. That look that bestowed disgust and disappointment and told Jonathan that he just didn't quite measure up. "No, sir. I only know that hospital personnel suggested that I talk with the sheriff's office since the deputies served the order on Rebecca at the hospital. That's where I was headed when you called."

"Well, you were heading to the right place; she is in jail," his father said, shaking his head as though Rebecca was the scourge of the family. "Sheriff Rayburn told us his deputies had no choice but to arrest her for assaulting an officer at the hospital."

Jonathan's open mouth and widening eyes prompted the grandfather to caution, "Jonathan, this is the time to respond with your brain not your emotions. We suspected you were on your way to the

Sheriff's office and from what we've learned, that would not have been the optimum course of action. We have been told by our good friend that your wife has made a comment that could be construed as a threat against your life. Don't get me wrong. We did not think you were in any kind of danger from her; we just felt that her statement reflected a hostile frame of mind and we did not want you confronting her with no more than you knew, while she was in that mindset. It could have led to complications, legally. "Let's see, how did she say it?" He looked to the stranger and nodded.

The stranger's cadaverous hand pulled a tape recorder from his coat pocket and hit 'play'. Filling the room was Rebecca's emotionless, flat-lined voice. "I honestly think I can kill the bastard the moment I get out of here and not even lose a minute's sleep." The stranger returned the tape to his pocket.

Jonathan slugged down his brandy. "Where was she when that was recorded... and how was it recorded?"

"Jonathan, would you, please get me another cup of coffee?" grandfather asked. Jonathan complied and as he did, his grandfather responded. "She was recorded in her jail cell. Our good friend has bugs in all of his jail cells that the exterminators have never been able to get rid of. Let's just leave it at that."

After pouring his grandfather's coffee, Jonathan helped himself to a second brandy.

Jonathan's father took over in order to head the meeting toward its conclusion. "Jonathan, earlier in the tape you just heard, Rebecca made a comment about how Abi had told her that she wanted the family to stay together and that Rebecca had promised Abi that she would agree to that. The legal significance of that statement is rooted in the fact that your daughter has no desire to seek any legal remedy for the petition's allegations. And as you can ascertain, if she is not seeking any legal remedy, that increases the likelihood that this matter can be disposed of discretely. Jonathan, if this gets into the newspapers, you can kiss running for governor goodbye. Hell, you can kiss running for anything goodbye, forever. Of course, there exists a big 'if' in winning this case. And the big 'if' is whether or not Rebecca is still willing to go along with Abi's desire to keep the family together. If she is not, then we've got our work cut out for us. If that statement of Rebecca's that we just heard represents her intentions then this will not be easy. Because Rebecca is now one of the keys to winning this case, we wanted to sit down with you before you went to see her. Do you see the importance of this meeting, now?"

His grandfather spoke as Jonathan nodded. "Jonathan, we have taken the liberty of retaining counsel. Because of everything that's at stake here, for you, our family and those across this state who are counting on you, we have hired the best legal representation money can buy in this state; J. Wendell Nixon of Birmingham." Turning his gaze to the speaker phone, he said, "Mr. Nixon, please say hello to my grandson, Judge Jonathan Morgan, Circuit Court Judge of the Thirty-First Judicial Circuit of the great state of Alabama and the odds-on favorite in the next gubernatorial election."

Jonathan straightened up in his chair and stared at the conference speaker as if he was going to shake its hand.

"Judge Morgan," the polished baritone of J. Wendell Nixon said, "it is quite an honor to meet you, even though it is by long distance. I apologize for this telephonic meeting but it was the best I could do on short notice. Judge, let me say that it is a privilege and an honor to work for you and your family, who have a well- deserved reputation all across the state of Alabama. It is with humility and gratitude that I accept your offer of employment and I can assure you that I will do everything in my power to ensure that we win this case."

Every lawyer in the state knew well the reputation of J. Wendell Nixon. He was a high-priced, high-profile, cut-throat attorney, who would sell his mother into slavery to win a case. Mr. Nixon never met a reporter he didn't like and had a tendency to try almost all of his cases in the newspaper, which made Jonathan uneasy. "Mr. Nixon, it is quite an honor to meet you, sir. I wish it were under more favorable circumstances but unfortunately that is not the case."

"Judge, let me assure you that I have no doubt of your innocence in this matter and before I am through, everyone involved, from the Department of Children's Services to your juvenile court judge will be thoroughly convinced you are the victim in this unfortunate and sad affair." It was said that Nixon had more confidence than any ten men, and while that might get most men in over their heads, Nixon had always come through when the chips were down.

The stone faces of Jonathan's grandfather and father were shattered with broad smiles that told everyone, 'We picked the right guy. No doubt about it.'

"Gentlemen, as you know I have a prior engagement this afternoon, but I wanted take the time to speak to each of you in order to answer any preliminary questions you may have before I leave you in the capable hands of my associate, Mr. Ward. So that you will have no concerns about Mr. Ward's abilities, I would like to inform you that since he has been an employee of mine, this firm has not lost a case on which he as worked in two and one-half years and if memory serves, Ward, doesn't that constitute twenty-one cases?"

"Twenty-two, Mr. Nixon," Ward replied.

"That's right; twenty-two. I just pulled it up on the screen here. I'd forgotten the McMurtry case. So as you can see, gentlemen, Mr. Ward does not like to lose. Of all the associates that we use around the state, Mr. Ward, is the most efficient and aggressive. And the fact that he lives in Dalton County just across the river from you all means he knows your area and the people in it. He will be quite an asset in this matter."

"Mr. Nixon," Jonathan said, "Is Mr. Ward an attorney?"

"No, no Judge, he's not. I apologize if I gave you that impression. Mr. Ward is not an attorney. He performs some of the, how can I say this… some of the 'behind the scenes work' for the firm. He acts as my 'eyes and ears' and believe me when I tell you, he makes significant contributions in all of the cases in which he works. In time, I'm sure you'll understand."

"Mr. Nixon, when can you and I sit down to discuss the case?" Jonathan pressed.

"Hopefully, tomorrow, Judge. I'm hoping to come up to see you by noon, but I'll call before I leave Birmingham to give you my estimated time of arrival."

Wanting to pick Nixon's brain before he hung up, Jonathan asked, "Mr. Nixon, before you go, I'd like to ask your early opinion of what it will take to win this thing. Can you share your thoughts on that at this time, given what little you know about this matter?"

There was hardly any hesitation before Nixon answered, "The girl. The girl is the key." He launched into a mini-seminar regarding admissible evidence. "Listen, there are no witnesses. The only people who could possibly know one iota about the allegation have to be people whom the girl has told. That's all hearsay and carries no legal weight. It doesn't matter what the Department of Children's

Services alleges or what Aunt Sally or Uncle Bill say the girl said. I firmly expect that we can convince the girl to recant her story. And when she does, it's over. Game, set and match. Judge, I must bid you farewell; we will talk in much greater detail tomorrow about short and long range strategies. I look forward to seeing you then. It's all yours, Ward."

Jonathan now realized the extent to which Nixon and Ward would go to win this case.

Nixon hung up and every face at the table, except Ward's, beamed with visions of victory. His presented its viewers with the pale mask of determination and single-mindedness of purpose. His face doesn't smile until the job is done. Ward pulled out his notepad to review the immediate strategy that he and Mr. Nixon had formulated prior to the conference call. As far as he was concerned the meeting had just begun.

TWENTY-FIVE

"Home, sweet home," Ms. Waddle said, as the Ford wagon topped a steep hill that unveiled Abi's first glimpse of her new home. About a quarter of a mile away down a slight grade, stood a small, white, wood-framed home surrounded by huge cedars and a white wooden fence that bordered both sides and the back of the house, keeping four horses in a half-acre corral. As they drove down the hill, they passed acres of fading green pasture with fat, white cattle grazing near a pond shaded by weeping willows.

Abi could feel a heavy beat in her chest as she took it all in. A red barn outside the corral caught her eye. Something was written across its tin roof, in large white letters, but she couldn't make it out. There were bluebird houses on practically every other fence post and on most of the trees. A horse was tied to a long steel rod that walked the horse in a circle like a slow-motion merry-go-round. She figured it was some type of training device to get unruly horses used to doing something that they, by nature, didn't really want to do.

She could see the writing on the barn's roof now, as they were almost to the house. It read, 'Seven days without Jesus makes one weak.' It brought a smile to her face; she thought it was clever.

"Abi," Ms. Waddle said, "Welcome to the home of Reverend and Mrs. Malachi Peace. Look. There's Mrs. Peace rocking on the front porch; you'll really like her."

As the car came to a stop in the gravel drive, Abi saw a lady, probably in her fifties, with graying hair, arise from her rocker and with a smile stretching from ear to ear, say, "Welcome, Miss Trudy, it sure is good to see you. I see you've brought us another blessing."

Waddle got out and walked to the front of the car and gave Mrs. Peace a hug. They'd done this many times before. Abi hesitated to get out of the car, letting Ms. Waddle dispense with the preliminaries. In a minute both ladies turned and headed for Abi's door.

Ms. Waddle opened the door, leaned over and asked Abi to step out and meet her foster mother. Abi stepped out, right into a bear hug by the surprisingly strong Mrs. Peace. Mrs. Peace was no taller than Abi, about five-three and was rather plump but surprisingly light on her feet, seemingly weightless.

"Abigail," Mrs. Peace's mellow voice said, "I can't tell you how glad we are to have you with us. I want you to know right up front, that me and the good reverend consider it a true blessing that the Lord has sent you to us."

Abi, at first, wanted to offer a similar response, something with the word 'blessing' in it, but couldn't think of how to phrase it without it sounding awkward, so she just relied on what she had been taught; 'always be polite and properly pronounce your words when you meet strangers.' So, she told Mrs. Peace that she was glad to meet her.

"The reverend and me, we want to make you as comfortable as we can for however long you're here. We know that the girls who visit us sometimes don't really want to be here, but we hope that before long you'll come to think of our home as your home, even if it's in some real small way. Do you like the country, Abigail?" Mrs. Peace asked, sweeping her hand across the view of their property.

There seemed to be a very real goodness about Mrs. Peace. It was comforting to Abi and helped her forget for a moment about the incident at the hospital. "Yes, ma'am. I do like the country." Abi was so nervous she could barely respond much less make conversation.

Mrs. Peace sensed Abi's anxiety. "Abi, how about you and me getting your bag out of Miss Trudy's car and going inside. I'll show you around the house then we'll go to your room and let you settle in." She put her arm around Abi's shoulders and gave her a quick hug. "And if you feel like it, then we'll sit down and have us a piece of apple pie I just pulled out of the oven. Is that okay with you?" Mrs. Peace had kind, caring eyes lined with deep creases she'd earned from years of laughing and crying with children. Her ruddy complexion hinted that she'd spent many an hour working the twenty-acre farm, tending to the cows, horses, garden and general yard upkeep.

What with all that had gone on today, Abi had had very little to eat. Hot apple pie would be great; maybe even with some ice cream on it. While Abi wondered if Mrs. Peace's pie would be as good as Hattie's, she could tell her mouth was watering.

Ms. Waddle motioned for Mrs. Peace to come over to her side of the car. They spoke in hushed tones. She nodded a couple of times, as did Mrs. Peace. The only difference being, Mrs. Peace smiled when she nodded.

With their conversation complete, Ms. Waddle, turned and told Abi that she would be checking on her tomorrow. Abi felt like being polite to Ms. Waddle, since she felt she had won their first battle back at the hospital and because she wanted to make a good impression on Mrs. Peace. Abi smiled and said, "Thank you, Ms. Waddle. I look forward to it."

As Ms. Waddle drove away, Abi grabbed one end of her duffel bag and steadied herself to heave it up the steps to the porch. Mrs. Peace quickly grabbed the other end of the bag and said, "You know, hun, totin' this big duffel bag is a lot like the heavy burdens life throws your way. If you can share the load with someone, it can be a whole lot easier."

Abi smiled and said, "Yes, ma'am." Negotiating the steps, she thought how much Mrs. Peace sounded like Hattie with her common sense approach to life. And she was beginning to think that she could probably cook like Hattie, too.

As they entered the front door of the two-bedroom home, the smell of the just-baked apple pie blended with another familiar aroma. It stirred Abi's hunger pangs. She couldn't quite place it, but thought it smelled like baked chicken in some kind of sauce, maybe cream of mushroom soup.

Walking through the front of the house, she saw several yellowed black and white photographs, of hard, straight-faced men and women. They were all confined to the wall above the small television that sat on a plastic plant stand. Abi thought they could be photographs of parents or ancestors since it was her experience that people back then didn't smile as much as people today. Below them were color photos of smiling young folks who Abi guessed to be the Peace's children.

The hardwood floor shined like a new penny and Abi wondered if special pains had been taken by Mrs. Peace to wax the floor for her arrival or if Mrs. Peace was such a good housekeeper that the floors looked this good all of the time. Braided throw rugs every five or six feet muffled the sounds of their steps as they walked to the last room on the right. Abi's room.

The ten by twelve-foot room had a six by six, dark green carpet bought on sale at a remnant store to match the curtains on the lone window of the room. A pine bunk bed let Abi know that she might not be the only occupant. There was an old, worn desk in the corner with a stack of books on algebra, English composition, European history and biology that was pushed to the side to make room for a Seventeen magazine that was folded open to an article entitled 'Can You Catch Him Without Bait?'

Mrs. Peace walked over to the magazine, read the title of the article, shook her head and let out a half sigh, half laugh. Her eyes watered as she raised her head and stared out the window. After a moment, she turned to Abi and said, "Well, sweetie, I guess by the looks of this room you probably think you have a roommate." Her eyes were full of sadness as she continued. "Up until last night you did. As sweet a girl as you'd ever want to meet. Her name was Sonya. Sonya Jett. She was with us for, I guess, goin' on six months."

Abi felt as though she should console Mrs. Peace in some way but then she thought, well, she really didn't know her that well, so she just listened.

"Sonya ran away, last night," Mrs. Peace said, reaching for the wadded up tissue in her apron. "We're pretty sure she left with the Elrod boy. His father is Doyle Elrod who works at the tire and rubber plant in town. I don't suppose you know the family." She dabbed her eyes.

"No ma'am," Abi said, shaking her head.

"Reverend Peace and I, we'd been worried for some time that Sonya would leave with the first boy that showed her any kind of attention. I sure do hate it," she said. "You know, with the mother that she had, Sonya never really had a chance. Her mother was only concerned about herself; always trying to catch herself a man. And boy, could she pick 'em. The last boyfriend she had was, I believe, a twenty-three-year-old Mexican, who talked her into going to California. He'd convinced her she could be in the movies there. Well, after she heard that, she couldn't leave fast enough. The only things found in Sonya's refrigerator when the Department of Children's Services found her were two blocks of cheddar cheese, five wine coolers and eight frozen Salisbury steak dinners." Shaking her head, she said, "Have you ever heard a' such?"

Again, Abi shook her head.

"Oh, I shouldn't carry on so… I got no call to burden you with any of this." But Mrs. Peace couldn't let go of it. "It just devastates me and the reverend… to see how some kids are raised with hardly a chance in the world of growing up right. It just rips our hearts out. Most of these kids are good kids; they just got sorry parents. Parents who couldn't care less about 'em. No-good folks who only care about themselves and what they can steal from the day. Parents whose only intention when they wake up each morning is to figure out how they're gonna get high or who they're gonna steal from or how they're gonna get by at work with doin' as little as they possibly can. I really get sick and tired of it. They got no value system to speak of. No direction. It's no wonder these kids turn out like they do. And it's no wonder sweet little sixteen-year-olds like Sonya cling to the first warm body that shows them the slightest bit of affection and what they think is love. If I was in her shoes, I'd probably end up doin' the same thing." She pondered what she'd just said, then validated it. "Yep, probably would." Staring at the pine floor, Mrs. Peace returned to herself. "Honey, I'm sorry to vent like this in front of you." Before she could finish her thought, Abi hugged her and told her how lucky Sonya was to have been able to spend the time here that she did and even though it was brief, it was a time that she will always be able to look back on and say that she was truly loved and wanted. Mrs. Peace returned the hug. It felt good to have another child in her home. Another girl whom she had the opportunity to help. For how long she didn't know. But she was finally learning not to care how long they stayed. Just how much she could help them and love them while they were there. That must be how it really was to have children, she thought.

Before Mrs. Peace left Abi's room they reviewed some of the ground rules of the home such as the times of the daily meals, bathroom schedules, telephone and mail privileges and bedtime, all of which were acceptable to Abi, because she didn't expect to be here long anyway. She knew her mother would be coming to get her soon. Mrs. Peace allowed Abi some private time in her new room, while she went to prepare two pieces of apple pie, one topped with vanilla ice cream.

Abi removed her belongings from her bag, folded them neatly in the bottom two empty drawers as Mrs. Peace had instructed and placed Teddy on top of the pillow on the bottom bunk. She patted Teddy on his head to console him and told him everything was going to be all right; that they'd be home soon and for him not to worry.

***

As she and Mrs. Peace ate apple pie and chatted at the kitchen table, Mrs. Peace with coffee and Abi with milk, Abi listened to Mrs. Peace reminisce about how she and Reverend Peace have lived here since the day they were married some thirty years ago. She also learned that they had never had children. Abi, now, realized that most of those photographs on the wall were other people's children.

Mrs. Peace talked about herself and her husband and how, about thirteen or fourteen years ago, Mr. Peace, who had been a brick mason for some twenty years, came to her one day out of the blue and told her that he had a calling to give his life to the Lord. Mrs. Peace said in a hushed voice, that her husband came from a family that was not 'with the Lord', but that something had happened involving one of his three brothers that really changed Mr. Peace. He never told her or anyone else, as far as she knows exactly what it was that had happened. And she never pried, figuring he would tell her if he wanted her to know. Anyway, she had thought she'd like being the wife of a preacher. It had a nice ring to it.

She said that after he got his own church, an air of contentment and a sense of purpose enveloped Mr. Peace that he'd never before had. He wore the mantle of 'reverend' well.

Mrs. Peace always spent a lot of time talking about herself and her family when a new child came in to their home. She was good at helping her foster children lose some of their initial awkwardness and embarrassment. When a new foster child would arrive, she would talk for hours, to take the focus off the child and his or her problem. It seemed to help them blend in.

The second helping of pie and ice cream was eaten while Mrs. Peace began preparing supper. That aroma that Abi smelled when she entered the house was, indeed, baked chicken in mushroom soup. Joining the chicken on the table tonight would be sweet potatoes, fried corn, green beans and cornbread.

Mrs. Peace explained that after supper, Abi would be joining the Peaces at Reverend Peace's Sunday evening service at the New Life Freewill Baptist Church. The reverend was at the church, now, distributing fliers on every pew, to inform the flock about next weekend's Halloween hayride for the teenagers.

After they set the table and covered the dishes, Abi and Mrs. Peace, spent a good half hour strolling up past the barn to the pasture and around the pond. Rabbits and squirrels cast in the fading glow of the sunset were tending to their rituals in preparation of their night's sleep.

Blackbirds, in huge flocks, were gathering in the oaks and poplars for their night's rest, while on their seasonal migratory journey. There was a realization at that moment for Abi as she watched bird after bird landing on frail, little limbs, trusting something bigger than themselves to help them complete their journey. By the hundreds they landed, not knowing what tomorrow would bring but knowing tonight they had to be where they were simply because it had to be. Abi could see that she was like them. She could see that all of God's creatures were on their way somewhere and just like the oaks and the poplars were to the blackbirds, the Peaces were to her.

TWENTY-SIX

An hour after Nixon hung up, everyone had their marching orders from Mr. Ward as he concluded the meeting with the Morgans. He meticulously reviewed everyone's responsibilities until he was convinced they knew their roles. There could be no screw-ups, he warned them. The first order of business was Rebecca. The plan called for Jonathan and Mr. Ward to go to the jail. While Jonathan and Mr. Ward were with Rebecca, Jonathan's father was to go to Rebecca's parents. Jonathan's grandfather would man the phones at the office.

The sheriff met Jonathan and Ward at the county jail to process the paperwork for Rebecca to be released. Afterward, they instructed the sheriff to bring her to an adjoining office to talk privately. They had no desire to confront her in the presence of the jail population where she could put on a show. They wanted her on their turf where they could be in control.

When Rebecca opened the door to the little office Jonathan stood to hug her. "Rebecca, are you okay? I couldn't believe it when the hospital told me what had happened. I am so sorry you had to go through what you did."

Rebecca allowed herself to be hugged but didn't reciprocate. She measured her actions because of the stranger with Jonathan who watched her every move. As Jonathan offered her his chair, he introduced Mr. Ward as an associate of J. Wendell Nixon's, their attorney. Mr. Ward nodded to Rebecca.

"We have an attorney?" Rebecca asked, emphasizing the 'we'.

"Well, honey, don't you think we need one?" replied Jonathan with his ready answer. "Our daughter has been stolen from us without a modicum of due process and you were arrested and thrown in jail for simply trying to prevent what was obviously a miscarriage of justice. So, yes, we have an attorney. Some heads are going to roll over what has happened to us. I can guarantee that. Mr. Nixon plans to be here tomorrow to go over the case, which has been set for Tuesday at three o'clock. He expects that Abi will be back home in no time and that all this will be behind us very soon." Jonathan felt as though his speech had come out right and he wanted to look at Ward for confirmation but dared not.

Rebecca asked if she and Jonathan could be alone.

Ward nodded and stepped out. Rebecca turned to her husband. "Jonathan, I know what's been going on… with you and Abi. I know everything." She gritted her teeth and paused to let the rising anger subside. She knew she had to gauge her words and her actions, now that Jonathan had acquired an attorney. But she did allow herself one indulgence. She leaned over and with a 'go to hell' smile on her face, whispered, "I'm coming after you and everything you've got, you low-life, son-of-a-bitch." It gave her great pleasure to see the whites of his eyes grow.

"Honey," he said, "please don't tell me that you believe that stuff that was alleged in that petition. The sheriff showed me his copy while we processed your paperwork. I couldn't believe the garbage that's in that thing. I was shocked. Rebecca, I beg you, do not believe those scurrilous charges."

"You bet I believe those charges," she said, pointing a finger in his face. "I don't have one doubt in this world about those charges. The moment I heard Abi say those words, down deep, I knew they were true. At first, I wouldn't let myself believe her; I was holding out hope that what she was saying was not true but knowing you like I do, my hope was simply wasted."

With as much conviction as he could muster, Jonathan prepared to speak. He knew he had to pace his speech to project the illusion of being in control and being concerned about her, even though his heart pounded mercilessly. "Rebecca, please sit down. There is something that you need to hear, something that I've kept from you that maybe I shouldn't have. I may have made an error in judgement in not telling you, but I was trying to spare you and protect you from what was happening. Obviously, now, I wish I hadn't kept it from you." He got her a chair, placed his hands on her shoulders and gently pressed her into the chair.

Jonathan had Rebecca's attention although she didn't really want to give it to him; she wanted to remain angry and threatening. But before she could come to herself, he struck.

"Rebecca, some six or seven months ago, it was brought to my attention that Abi was hanging around a bad kid from Blocton, you know, in Dalton County. I was never clear on where they met, but my guess is, at the skating rink here in Lincoln." Jonathan could see a growing fire in Rebecca's eyes prompting him to plead, "Please, let me say this; you have to know what I know." She relented.

"This kid, who's on probation for assaulting a teacher, has a history of picking up young girls at skating rinks and bowling alleys in our three-county area and shall we say, sweeping them off their feet. Well, on more than one occasion, the owner of the skating rink called me to let me know that the kid was hanging around Abi. To protect you, I specifically instructed the owner not to talk to you if you answered. A time or two, I drove out there to watch from across the parking lot to see if I could catch him with Abi. The owner said that a lot of the kids would often hang out in their cars in the parking lot. We figured that's where he and Abi spent a lot of time. Anyway, to make a long story short, I didn't ever catch them, so I hired a private investigator. You just met him; Mr. Ward. A month or so after that, Mr. Ward saw them together in the kid's car. By the way, this kid is seventeen." Jonathan could see that what he was saying was making an impact on Rebecca.

He sat down, scooted up to where his knees touched hers and reached for her hands. "I hate to have to tell you this, but... Mr. Ward has photographs of this kid and Abi... involved in... sexual activity. They were in the kid's car in the parking lot." Jonathan awaited Rebecca's response. There was none. Her hands were limp. Jonathan continued the assault. "I subsequently confronted Abi with this and of course, she denied it. I really thought I could scare her into not seeing this kid and I thought, being a judge, I could scare the kid away. It didn't work. She lied to me and convinced me she wouldn't see him anymore but the rink owner told me, later, that she did. In hindsight, I should have brought you in on this but I thought I could handle it without getting you all upset. I was afraid of what you might do, you know, the way you were drinking. Anyway, she's become infatuated with this little creep and thinks she's in love. I intercepted a letter at the house from him in which he told her he was going to come get her late one night and that they could live with his aunt in Dalton County. I confronted her with it and she blew up and threatened to leave. And it wasn't but just a few days after that when she hopped in the back of Hattie's car and well, you know the rest." With those final words, Jonathan felt two things: relief that his speech was over and creeping confidence that his performance was good. He was optimistic that he had planted the necessary seed of doubt in Rebecca's mind.

Rebecca was numb; her mind was about to burst with the scrambled contradictions of Jonathan's and Abi's words. Her mind's picture of Abi and Jonathan was blurred with the new picture of Abi and this seventeen-year-old kid. Did he say there were pictures? Pictures don't lie. Coming to herself, she muttered, "Did you say there were pictures?"

Thinking that he was turning this thing around, he consoled her. "Honey, I'd rather you not see them; they'll only upset you. But, if you insist, I'll get Mr. Ward to bring them to my office next week and you can see them then." Ward had told Jonathan earlier that he could produce photographs when necessary. In the shadows of the skating rink, at night, across a parking lot, the girl would resemble Abi, in the kid's lap in the front seat of his car.

"Rebecca, this kid has control of Abi. He has convinced her that if she did as he said she could leave us and live with him and his aunt in their little den of iniquity. Many a teenager's dream, I'm sure. Earlier this week, Mr. Ward and I had a meeting with this kid and told him in no uncertain terms that we were playing hardball. We were able to get a signed statement from him acknowledging that he and Abi had sex on a regular basis and that he supplied her with alcohol and pot. He also stated in writing that he would never see her again. We threatened the kid's aunt with criminal charges against both of them and since she was on probation already, she was most receptive. She got his attention quickly; slapped him in our presence and threatened him worse than we did. We told her we would be keeping the signed statement for future use, in case the kid tried to renege on our agreement. When I told Abi about the signed statement she went ballistic and threatened to leave, anyway and said nobody could stop her. My guess is that when her attempt at leaving home was foiled, she resorted to allegations against me that were sure to get her out of our home. I have no doubt that the little punk is behind all of this."

The blank look on Rebecca's face wasn't telling. Jonathan did not have a clue what she was thinking. Then, her eyes widened and watered and her lower lip trembled. Her pupils shrank to pin holes and her face flushed. Instinctively, he felt a need to step back but he was too slow.

Rebecca sprang out of her seat and caught Jonathan by surprise before he could stand. She let out a blood-curdling scream as she pounded his chest with rapid, forceful blows from both fists sending him reeling over his chair, sprawling on the floor. She shoved his chair across the room and as he flailed his arms and legs trying to regain his balance, she landed horrible, crunching kicks to his ribs and face, the last of which snapped his head back against the cinder block wall knocking him unconscious.

Mr. Ward and the sheriff, listening in another room, immediately scurried to help Jonathan. On his way down the hall, the sheriff hollered for Deputy Dundee. Ward got to the room first. As he opened the door he could see that Jonathan was on the floor unconscious and Rebecca was still kicking his bloody face, snapping his head back like a rag doll.

"Mrs. Morgan, stop!" Ward yelled. After one more kick to his ribs, she stopped and looked at Ward as though she did not know what had happened. She was breathing so fast she could not speak. A tangle of hair that had fallen over her face had been sucked in her mouth by the force of her inhalation. Ward moved quickly to Jonathan's side and dropped to a knee to check for signs of serious injury. Rebecca fell into her chair. Deputies rushed in, but there was nothing for them to do. Rebecca was sitting, elbows on knees, sobbing into her hands.

The sheriff started to call 911, but heard Jonathan coughing and saw that he was coming to. Ward convinced the sheriff that this little matter needed to be kept confidential and that it wouldn't be a good idea if 911 were involved. The sheriff was relieved when Ward told him that he did not believe Jonathan had sustained serious injury.

"Help me sit him up," Ward requested of Deputy Dundee. They propped Jonathan up against the cinder block wall. He opened and closed his eyes trying to focus, as he turned his head from side to side. Ward handed him a handkerchief and told him that he had a bloody nose and should apply pressure with the handkerchief. Rebecca continued to cry uncontrollably.

"Judge Morgan, do you know where you are?" Ward asked.

Wiping his nose, Jonathan, slowly replied, "Yeah, I'm sitting on a cold floor... somewhere in the sheriff's office." He didn't want to actually say the words that would describe what had just happened. He was too embarrassed to say that he had been beaten up by his wife. So he rubbed the back of his head, looked at Ward, then Rebecca and back to Ward. "Looks like everybody's okay." This brought a half smile, half smirk from Ward as he patted Jonathan on the shoulder and told him that everything was, indeed, going to be okay.

Darlene was called in to help Mrs. Morgan to the ladies room to straighten up. After helping Jonathan climb into his chair, Mr. Ward confided that he and Mr. Nixon had considered an alternative plan should Mrs. Morgan not be receptive to the story about the seventeen-year-old. He laid it out for Jonathan, who thought it would be the best option, given what had just occurred. And the phone call was made.

TWENTY-SEVEN

W. Henry Morgan and Joseph Sullivan had been more than mere in-laws since the marriage of their children, some fourteen years ago. They were essentially business partners. They were two of the most influential men in the northern half of the state and the merging of their families only made them more so. The influence peddling of the Morgans and Sullivans reached into the realms of the banking industry and the judicial arena, not just in Alabama but throughout the southeast. But, more impressively, their influence was revered in the Alabama state legislature and the governor's mansion, where it affected state legislation, state-held contracts and political appointments.

So it was not an altogether difficult assignment for Mr. Morgan to be the one to inform Mr. Sullivan about Jonathan's and Rebecca's difficulties with Abi. He requested the meeting to be with Mr. Sullivan, only. No need for irrational female reactions, Mr. Morgan thought. He would let Mr. Sullivan explain it to his wife later. Anyway, she was babysitting the twins and couldn't part from them at the moment.

The Sullivans knew about Abi's automobile accident but had no knowledge of her running away. They had talked with Abi yesterday afternoon but not in person, since her doctor limited her visitors. She sounded fine over the phone. They had no idea of the serious underlying problems.

They met for only a few minutes in the study, a spacious room of mahogany and leather, with the obligatory stuffed animal heads mounted on the walls, denoting true Southern manhood. Businessmen can say quite a lot in a few minutes since their primary interest is the net result.

Mr. Morgan informed Mr. Sullivan that there were indeed, some very serious problems with Abi. He kept to the script that had been authored by Mr. Ward, the focal point being Jonathan's trouble with the seventeen-year-old kid from Dalton County. He spoke slowly and with emphasis, especially when detailing the photos and the signed statement by the kid. He concluded his summarization with the Department of Children's Services' knee-jerk reaction that placed Abi in foster care without finding out all of the facts and without due process. "Heads are gonna roll," Mr. Morgan promised. He told that this afternoon Jonathan hired J. Wendell Nixon of Birmingham who assured the family that they will win this case and that everything will return to normal in a day or so. And Mr. Morgan emphasized that those people responsible for this egregious mistake will lose their jobs over this. All those responsible would pay. Last, Mr. Morgan told Mr. Sullivan that all of this was taking a terrible toll on Rebecca and that Jonathan is worried about her being able to cope with all of this.

Joseph Sullivan, like many businessmen married to their careers, is quite detached from his family, and in his particular case, especially from his daughter, Rebecca, who has been another man's responsibility for over fourteen years. He has a 'bottom-line' mentality. He hated hearing the problems that Rebecca and Jonathan were having with Abi but he knew he could count on Jonathan to take care of them. Bottom line. He expressed his dismay and added that he and Mrs. Sullivan would do whatever necessary to help the family. All the Morgans have to do is to give him a call.

***

It was different and not altogether unreasonable, Abi thought, as she watched the trees darting past her from the back window of the Peaces' church van. Two blessings at supper. The first, before supper, to ask for forgiveness and to bless the food they were about to eat and the second, after supper, to give thanks for being able to have a meal and to ask for guidance for tomorrow. The more Abi thought about it, the more she liked it. She liked the holding hands around the table during the blessing, too.

She sat in the right backseat as Reverend Peace hummed a familiar hymn during the ten-minute drive to the New Life Free Will

Baptist Church. The church was only about three miles from the Peaces but the winding gravel road made the going slow. The crunching of the gravel underneath the car had a soothing effect, almost lulling her eyes shut. She looked up at the stars peeking through gaps in the rows of tall pines lining the road and wondered about her mother. She wasn't really worried about her because her mother was tough but she wondered what her mother was doing now and how long it would be before she could get her back home. She was beginning to feel that heavy sadness deep in her chest, again. But she caught herself. She refused to be sad; she forced those thoughts out of her mind. 'Be strong! Be strong!' Abi told herself, trying to follow her mother's orders. Think positive thoughts.

The reverend's humming stopped when the van did, in a clearing about fifty yards from the church. The reverend said, "Abi, there's our little gift from God."

Bathed in the pale moonlight, Abi could see the little white, wood-framed church, sitting about a hundred yards from the rocky shoreline of Pinto Lake. It was as beautiful a sight as she'd ever seen. Like a painting. Pinto Lake, about a half-mile wide and three-quarters of a mile long, was fed by the mighty Tennessee River from the north. The only man-made structure on the entire shoreline was the New Life Free Will Baptist Church, with the remaining shoreline covered in mostly cypress, pine and oak trees that grew right up to the shore.

Across the lake, a creeping orange half-moon peeked over the pines of the eastern shore, spilling its beams onto the lake's glass-topped, black water. In the southern quarter of the sky, Abi identified the two most prominent constellations during early fall in Alabama, Orion and the Big Dipper.

"Baptized many a new believer in that lake," the reverend proudly exclaimed, "yes, sir, saved many a sinner." The reverend had a way of turning down the corners of his mouth most every time he spoke about his church. Abi thought it was his attempt at suppressing the grin of pride he projected every time he spoke of his church.

As members of the church arrived, Abi saw, first hand, just how special this little church really was and how special a person Malachi Peace must be. There were just as many black members as there were white members and when they all sat, they didn't group themselves.

They all sat amongst one another and shook hands and laughed and were polite to each other just like the good book says they should be. The name of this church is most appropriate, Abi thought; this really is the 'New Life' church. Abi sat down front, in the far right corner, where the Peaces' foster children have sat for almost a dozen years. Mrs. Peace sat at the piano behind the podium. Beaming face after beaming face hurried down front to speak to the new foster child and to welcome her to their church family.

When there appeared to be no more stragglers arriving for the service, Reverend Peace took hold of the podium with his leathered hands and looked out over the faces, which brought an immediate, respectful hush. He cleared his throat and began his service with his usual greeting and a short prayer. He then updated the listeners on the church's financial condition and followed that with the announcement of three births, a son born Monday to Frank and Judith Simms and twin sons born yesterday to Jake and Ola May Whitson. After the obligatory oohing and ahhing from the audience, the reverend announced the Halloween hayride next weekend, which prompted unbridled chattering by the youth. He asked those parents who were interested in signing up their children to complete the application flyers that he had placed in the pews and return them when the collection plate is passed.

The reverend paused, jutted out his prominent chin and looked into the eyes of the front row milking everyone's attention. When he had it, he slowly cast his dark brown eyes from left to right and began. "Is Jesus really in your heart?" He paused for silent emphasis. "Or just on your car tag?" An enthusiastic 'Amen' reverberated off the sheet-rocked walls from a little black man in the back pew. The reverend was proud of his sermon's title; he hoped it would be an attention-getter. And it was. It was a stirring sermon that lasted thirty minutes, not counting the two interruptions of applause and the dozen or so 'Amens' from the salt and pepper audience.

The Reverend Peace was a charismatic man endowed with the gift of being able to evoke immediate trust from those who met him. With his longish, straight-back, white hair the six-foot tall preacher reminded Abi of Charlton Heston, performing great and wonderful miracles, as Moses, in "The Ten Commandments." In her eyes, he was already performing a miracle of sorts, right here in his own church, with his blended congregation. As the reverend boomed his message to the attentive flock, Abi stole a moment to bow her head to pray for her own miracle. Maybe, just maybe, she thought, Reverend Peace could be her Moses.

TWENTY- EIGHT

The anaconda-like strength in her attacker's arms crushed Rebecca's ribcage. She could not breathe and she was losing consciousness.

All at once, she swallowed a blast of freezing air and flashed her eyes to the soft, calming female voice coming from above. "Good morning," the monotone voice said. "It is 8 A.M. Please prepare for your morning medication to be dispensed in fifteen minutes. Thank you and have a good morning."

Rebecca gasped for air, her chest rising and falling in time with her heart, pushing tiny beads of sweat onto her flat pillow, as she lay strapped in her bed.

Her hands were icy from lack of circulation. Tight leather straps cocooned her arms against her sides and cut off the blood flow. The pain in her hands was giving way to numbness. She tried to move her fingers, but they were lifeless. Her brain received no signal that her fingers had moved.

Rebecca had no memory of where she was or why she was restrained. As much as she concentrated, she remembered nothing. Her breathing slowed to a normal rhythm as she tried to shake the cobwebs in her mind. She shook her throbbing head hoping the fog would lift.

She raised her head to peer over her sheet-covered feet and saw only a solid white wall free of any hangings. To her right a pea-green Naugahyde chair that could fold down made her think she was in a hospital. That would explain the intercom announcement. To her left, another solid white, blank wall. No window; no wall hangings, no clues.

Her head, heavy as an anvil, returned to the pillow with a thud. She was weak. It had taken all of her strength to raise her head.

Taking a deep breath, in an effort to supply her brain with as much oxygen as possible, Rebecca closed her eyes to concentrate, searching for any shred of a clue as to how she got here. Slowly some memory bubbled to the surface. She recalled sitting in the jail with Jonathan and his lawyer's associate, a Mr. ... a Mr. ... Ward. That's it. Ward. It was coming back to her. She remembered crying herself to exhaustion after she attacked Jonathan. She remembered Abi and the seventeen-year-old kid. The fog was beginning to lift. At some point, she had been helped to the bathroom where she remembered being sick. She could not remember anything after that.

The door cracked open and a ray of the hallway's fluorescent lighting knifed across Rebecca's face. A silhouette stood in the doorway. It was about four-and-a-half feet tall with a head full of tangled hair. Rebecca couldn't discern the silhouette's hair color.

"Hi, sweetie," spoke a coarse female voice, as the silhouette gave a quick peek down both sides of the hallway and skulked into the room. "I just had to shimmy on down here to welcome the newest piece of flotsam to our sea of human debris," she cackled, as a wide, eerie smile cracked her angular, forty-year-old face, now visible in the room's pale light. She slithered in quietly and closed the door without a sound as though she had done it a hundred times.

"I happened to be up late last night when they brought you in, darlin', " she said as she leaned against the door facing and took a sip from a plastic Listerine bottle that she pulled from the pocket of the open housecoat. Her left eye maintained a perpetual Popeye squint but was almost hidden by a tangle of red hair that seemed strategically positioned. She was a funny-looking little munchkin with her explosion of red hair rocketing in every direction, contrasting starkly with her pale, almost translucent skin. The big hair effect was an obvious over-compensation for her lack of height.

She screwed the cap back on the Listerine bottle and returned it to her housecoat before she said, "I would have welcomed you to our little family when you arrived last night but it was too late for me to put on my welcome wagon face. 'Sides, I was having a party of my own, if you get my drift," which Rebecca didn't. "But," she giggled, "mine paled in comparison to the one you obviously had had, dearie." Another cackle. "You were truly whacked out." She shook her head, restraining a giggle but her hair-sprayed rocketry didn't budge. "I really miss that. You know, that's the biggest problem with being in this place. You can't get really wasted when you want to." She reached for the Listerine.

Rebecca wanted to ask questions about where she was and how she got here but more than that she needed to be free of the pain in her hands. "Listen," Rebecca whispered, "I really appreciate you coming to see me and everything, but I need to ask a favor of you." Rebecca was wary of the strange little woman but she knew she couldn't pass up the chance to ease the pain in her hands. "My hands are killing me. Could you, please, loosen these straps?" Rebecca raised her head and nodded toward her hands.

"I told Gaylord last night when they strapped you down that they didn't need to do that," the little woman said, moving towards the bed. "But you know Gaylord. Since he was promoted to evening shift manager he does it his way or no way. Always by the book. He's one of those people that you come across every so often that can't take a crap if some book don't tell him how to do it. I can just see him sittin' on the commode, flippin' through some oversized bathroom etiquette manual lookin' for the chapter on how many times he should wipe." With that, she let out a ghoulish shriek of a laugh that unnerved Rebecca. "If it's written in black and white in some book, then Gaylord thinks it's gospel. Hell, he'd rather eat a bucket of worms than disobey manual policy. I think it probably has to do with the kind of upbringing he had, don't you?" She paused and cocked her head, listening for someone in the hallway.

"Tell you what I'm gonna do. I'll loosen the straps one notch, but no more. I can't take a chance on getting caught. 'Sides, I don't want to piss Gaylord off. Me'n him are kinda' together, if you know what I mean."

"Oh, thank you, so much. You can't believe how much these things hurt." Rebecca rolled to her right then her left as the straps were loosened and blood began to circulate.

"Where are my manners?" the little woman exclaimed, pulling Rebecca's sheet back in place. "I've gone on and on about nothing and haven't even introduced myself. I'm Maybelline. Maybelline VanDyke. You can call me May or you can call me Mable, but you can't call me Maybelline." She reached for the Listerine again. "Do you remember that old song, I believe it was back in the fifties, called

Maybelline? I think Chuck Berry sang it, I'm not sure. You remember Chuck Berry don't you?" she asked, not waiting for Rebecca's reply. "He was one of those real good Negro singers in the early rock 'n roll days. I got nothin' against blacks, you understand. Hell, Gaylord's black and me'n him's together. You know... we get together when we can," she said with a wink. "I guess you could say that's my little contribution to racial harmony," she said.

Without taking a breath, Mable sped on. She always talked as though she was running out of time. "Anyway, back to that song. When I was in school, boys would pick on me all the time. On the school bus, during classes, in the lunchroom, in the hallways... because I was ugly. I didn't used to be as pretty as I am now," Mable proclaimed, proud of her metamorphosis. "And they used to sing that song when they were making fun of me. I got so fed up with boys making fun of me with that song, I started spittin' at 'em, anywhere, any time." She raised her eyebrow at Rebecca and squinted her Popeye face even more and said, "That's right, I said spittin'. And I got damn good at it, too."

"Once there was this ole boy, the biggest dough-bellied bully in school, who rode the same school bus I did. I remember it like it was yesterday. It was the day John Kennedy got shot. You know they say everyone remembers where they were when Kennedy got shot. Well, it's true. I was sittin' in the left aisle seat of the third row on a big, ole rusted-out yellow school bus ridin' down Clark County road sixteen. Bobby Neal Eastep, the dough-bellied bully, had been razzin' me ever since we'd gotten on the bus and had pretty much raised my temperature to the boiling point. I knew I had to do something before I started bawlin'. Well, when he took to singin' *Maybelline* that did it. He and all of his little suck-buddies were having a big laugh at my expense. By the time he'd reached the third verse, you know, the one that goes, *'You done started back doin' the things you used to do'*, I nailed him. It was biggest glob of spit I believe I ever hurled. Best shot I ever made. Across the aisle and two rows back. Landed right in his mouth. Probably couldn't make that shot in another hundred years. He got so sick, he hung his big ole buffalo-head out of that bus and puked his fat-ass guts up in front of all his little buddies. It was a thing of beauty. Right then and there... I became a legend." Mable cocked her head back and gave it the starlet shake, as though she was waiting for the flashbulbs from fawning photographers to explode.

Mable's self-aggrandizing pause for emphasis allowed Rebecca to speak. "Mable... I need to know some things... and you're the only person I can ask," she asked hesitantly, for fear of how this weird little woman might react.

Mable's eyes refocused to the present in anticipation. "What's on your mind, doll?"

"Mable, my name is Rebecca... Rebecca Morgan." Staring at the ceiling, because it was easier than looking at Mable, she continued. "Mable, I need your help. I don't know where I am ... and I don't know how I got here." Cutting her eyes over to Mable, she asked, "Where am I, Mable? What is this place?"

"You really don't know where you are, lamb-chop?" Mable asked.

"No, I don't."

"Hell, Rebecca Morgan, you're in the damn loony bin, hun. You can't tell that by lookin' at me? I'm a dead give-away. You disappoint me sweetheart." Mable laughed that eerie laugh that shook the tangle over the Popeye squint. "This here's Graceview. The sanitarium. Trust me, darling, we ain't at the Holiday Inn."

Rebecca shut her eyes at the sound of the word. Sanitarium.

"Yeah, we got a little bit of everything here at Graceview," she said, off on another spiel. "But we only got a couple of what you'd call real grade-A whack-jobs... but they're ours and we're real proud of 'em. One guy can't shake the notion that he's a sixth-generation werewolf and the other'n thinks he's Jesus Christ. He's our real big trouble-maker. The first one, you see, only gives us a problem during full moons but the second one, it don't make no difference to him what kinda' moon there is. He's pretty much an around-the-clock pain in the ass trying to save us from being human and all. And he's always harping about how we're all going to hell if we don't shut up about his virgin mother. I'll have to give you the details on these two later; I don't have time just now. Mostly, we got your garden-variety snap-jobs... you know the typical baby-boomer who snapped under the pressure of making the mortgage payment, the car payments, the blackmail threats from the trophy girlfriends, the screaming, ungrateful delinquents and the nine to five hustle while trying to keep up with the Joneses." Another draw on the Listerine. "And then," she said, rounding out the menu, "we got your usual smattering of drug addicts and alcoholics thrown in for good measure. For the most part, everybody's harmless here. Just don't cross nobody." She let out a deep, prolonged breath. "Yep, no doubt about it, we're a well-rounded bunch."

Rebecca's eyes never left the ceiling as Mable raved on. Mable's voice receded into the background as Rebecca's thoughts reclaimed her full attention. The weight of the realization that she had been committed to a sanitarium sunk deep into her. Her mind was reeling. How could this happen? She knew that involuntary commitments were possible if a judge was petitioned. But that took time. Who was able to do this to her so quickly and why? Her mind, mired in the muck of confusion and chemicals, slowly revealed the probability that Jonathan was behind this. He had the connections and the authority. What purpose was served by her being committed? How long could she be kept against her will? What was Jonathan planning to do about Abi? Rebecca realized she needed someone to help her. She could do nothing while committed.

Mable's voice pitched and rolled reclaiming Rebecca's attention. There was an edge to her tone, now. "Sweetie, tell me you weren't ignoring me," Mable said slowly, emphasizing each word, as if she was talking to a four-year-old. "I don't like it when I'm ignored." She pulled a toothpick from her pocket and clenched it with her teeth. "Do you like it when you're ignored, Mrs. Rebecca Morgan? I'll bet you don't like it one bit and I'll bet you don't put up with it. Do you Mrs. Rebecca 'I'm Somebody' Morgan? Am I right?" Mable's eyes narrowed flexing a crease in her forehead as she bent over Rebecca until she was inches from her face. A vein stood out on her neck. "Well, Missy, I got news for you. Mable really, really doesn't like it! Not at all!" Mable scowled, her breath smelling of vodka and lemon. "Here I am opening myself up to you and what do you do? You ignore me. And when you ignore me you tell me that I'm nothing, I'm worthless, that I'm not even worth your attention, which don't cost you one damn dime! I tell you, Rebecca Morgan, you got a lot of nerve. That's what you got. A lot of damn nerve."

Rebecca cringed at this threatening behavior. For all she knew, the little woman was crazy enough to hurt her. She quickly replied, "Mable, I am so sorry. I wouldn't do anything to hurt your feelings. I've just got so many things on my mind. Please forgive me." She forced a half-smile as her eyes pleaded for mercy.

Mable raised her angry, red face from Rebecca's, turned and walked towards the door.

"Please don't leave me," Rebecca begged. "I need you. I'm sorry."

Mable grabbed the door handle to leave. She let it go and turned around. Her angular face broke into a wide toothy grin as the toothpick fell from its perch. "I knew you wouldn't let me leave. You like me too much. Ain't that right? Hell, I'm irresistible." Again, the starlet head-shake. "At least that's what Gaylord tells me every Monday, Wednesday and Friday night. Must be true."

Rebecca knew that Mable was her only hope at this point and she wasn't about to destroy whatever connection she had established. "Mable, I want us to be friends. Good friends. As long as I am in this place, I want you to know I'll be here for you and that you can come in here anytime you want to. Okay? Buddies?"

"Yes, by God, ma'am. Buddies it is! We gonna be good buddies, too, Rebecca Morgan. You wait and see," Mable exclaimed extending her hand for a good ole buddy handshake. Remembering that Rebecca couldn't shake hands, Mable said, "Sorry. I forgot. But how's about a peck on the jaw to seal the deal?" She leaned over, grabbed Rebecca's face with both hands and planted a big lemon-scented kiss on her cheek. Bobby Neal Eastep flashed into Rebecca's thoughts.

"Thank you for being my friend, Mable. I'll always be yours. You can count it," Rebecca said.

"Well, sweetie, you're as welcome as can be. And thank you for being mine. Listen, I better get back to my penthouse suite before the nurse comes by to give me my dope."

"Oh. I remember, now. The announcement said that would be in fifteen minutes. How long has it been?"

"Don't worry. In here, fifteen minutes really means thirty. Thirty means an hour and so on. You'll get the hang of it."

"Since I'm new, will they be coming to see me?"

"Naw. You won't be receiving your meds until tomorrow at the earliest. Today, they'll send a doctor by here to give you a quick once-over which'll take about or fifteen minutes, unless he takes a liking to you, if you get my drift. Then they'll take you down to the basement where you'll be issued some lovely in-house scrubs to wear. Victoria's Secret they ain't. And then, you'll be assigned your own room. Once you get your room, you pretty much got it made. Soon as you get it, take yourself a shower and relax a little. It'll be after lunch before I can get back to you. I got some group sessions I got to attend today."

"Before you go, Mable, tell me. Where are we? I mean what city?"

"Honey, we're in the wonderful port city of Mobile, Alabama. Gotta go." The muffled sound of the Listerine bottle in Mable's housecoat hitting the door facing was the last sound Rebecca heard as her new friend exited as quickly as she had entered.

TWENTY-NINE

The late morning meeting between Jonathan and J. Wendell Nixon at the Morgan home lasted just thirty minutes. Nixon ordered Jonathan to cease his comings and goings in public. No sense in giving the townsfolk more grist for the rumor mill. He was to confine himself to his house until the hearing that was going to be held tomorrow at 3 P.M.

Everything was falling into place. Rebecca had been neatly tucked away in Mobile thanks to Dr. Emanuel Sosa, a psychiatrist friend of Nixon's. Nixon had filed his response to the Department of Children's Services' petition in Judge Vincent's court and would return tomorrow for the hearing.

Potential witnesses for the hearing included Jonathan's father and grandfather who promised to testify of their knowledge of the troubles Jonathan has had with Abi's delinquent behavior. Likewise Rebecca's father, who will testify that his daughter has been under such monumental stress from all of this, that he, along with Jonathan, committed her to Graceview Sanitarium in Mobile, to get the professional help that she needs.

By tomorrow, Mr. Ward will have produced the necessary photographs of Abi and her seventeen-year-old boyfriend engaged in sexual behavior in the parking lot of the skating rink. This will be accompanied by the boy's signed confession of such behavior and that he was responsible for coercing Abi to make sexual allegations against her father so that she could move in with him. Mr. Ward will be with the boy, on 'stand-by' at the boy's home, in case the judge requests the boy's oral testimony.

The only testimony that the Department of Children's Services will offer is Abi's statement. As Nixon said, it should be a slam-dunk.

Even if Abi had told someone else, Nixon is convinced he will be able to prove that what Abi was telling was an out and out lie. Abi has no corroborating testimony. The preponderance of corroborating testimony lies squarely in Jonathan's corner. Nixon was right. Tomorrow would be no contest.

That new feeling of supreme confidence made it all the more difficult for Jonathan to accept his in-house confinement. As the afternoon wore on he grew restless. He hated the thought of being a prisoner in his own home. He felt like a dog on a chain, his every thought on breaking free. He tried watching television but he couldn't tolerate the inanity. There were no books in the house that he hadn't read. He paced from room to room. He poured himself a drink. Bourbon, neat.

Two hours and five drinks later, the alcohol and the evening shadows gave Jonathan the courage and the cover he needed for an excursion into the country. Between drinks three and four, he had made a telephone call to Mrs. Celine Moore, a diminutive twenty-five-year-old ex-topless dancer from Huntsville who lived in one of his seven rental houses on Castleberry Lane in the west end of the county. He had met Celine, then Celine Miller, when he was at a three-day tort reform conference two summers ago in Huntsville. She was dancing at Alice's Wonderland, a topless club in west Huntsville. With a little pillow talk, he subsequently convinced her that with his political and business connections in Rutherford County he could get her a much better job. She was hesitant, initially, but when he told her that he had a rental house for her she jumped at the chance to move out of her dilapidated, cramped mobile home.

Mrs. Moore's husband of six months, Roy, worked for a construction company that kept him, more often than not, out of the county. During these occasions, Jonathan visits the Moore home to see if Mrs. Moore needs any financial assistance. She always does and is always affectionately grateful for a reduction in the month's rent. Because she handles all of their finances, Mr. Moore knows nothing about any reductions in rent. But it has caught his attention that Mrs. Moore buys new clothes much more often than he thought they could afford.

Jonathan donned a Florida Marlin's baseball cap, faded jeans and a worn flannel shirt, climbed in his 1980 Ford pickup that he keeps in the old wooden garage at the south end of his property and headed west. The tan and white truck was used for hauling material for landscaping— wood chips, manure and grass squares; so it had plenty of dents, scrapes and early signs of rust and was quite inconspicuous. With a bag of Redman chewing tobacco on the dash and a couple of empty beer cans bouncing around in the truck bed Jonathan passed for just another good ole country boy.

He skidded to a dusty stop in Celine's driveway and took a quick swallow of bourbon. When he saw her peeking out from behind the pulled curtains in the living room he knew the coast was clear. If Mr. Moore had come home she would have opened the curtains completely and turned on all of the lights in the living room. That was the routine.

She met him at the front door with a worried look. "Jonathan, you can't come in. Roy just called. He's on his way. They've had rain where he is so the crew is coming home."

Jonathan smiled, as though he had heard nothing. He was not bothered in the least about this unexpected revelation. He knew what he wanted. Pushing on the door, he grinned. "Now, now, Celine, let's not be stingy. You know it won't take long."

Celine smelled the bourbon on his breath and began to worry that Jonathan wouldn't take no for an answer. "Jonathan, Roy is only ten minutes away. He called from his truck. We cannot do this. Not tonight. Please." She was dressed only in her housecoat having just showered in anticipation of Jonathan's arrival.

"A lot can happen in ten minutes. Know what I mean, Celine?" He pushed harder with his left hand while he reached for her with his right. She was no match for his strength.

"Jonathan, my husband will be here any minute. You can't…"

Jonathan grabbed her by the throat with his right hand, almost lifting her off the floor and closed the door behind him with his left. Her housecoat fell open arousing him even more. "I am not leaving until I get what I came for. So if your damn husband is ten minutes away or one minute away I don't care. You just get busy taking care of me. You understand?" He pushed her onto the sofa where she began sobbing. She'd only seen Jonathan like this once before. It was about a year ago and it was the biggest fight they'd ever had. He'd slapped her a couple of times, which required two stitches in her lower lip. He'd been drinking then, too and she had provoked him by demanding that either he divorce Rebecca and marry her or she would return to Huntsville.

Jonathan strode up to Celine sitting on the sofa, with her elbows on her knees, crying into her hands. "By my count, we got nine minutes left. What are you waiting on?"

Celine opened her eyes and raised her head to plead. He was standing so close her hair brushed his jeans. "Please don't do this. Don't…"

Jonathan grabbed her hair with his left hand and yanked it backward until her neck popped like cracking knuckles. She yelled. "Celine, it won't bother me in the least to let ole Roy know about that abortion you had about three months ago. I think he ought to know about that, since legally he was the father. Know what I mean?" Celine had asked Jonathan for five hundred dollars to pay for the abortion even though she knew she would be beholding to him. She tried to shake her head, but Jonathan held too tightly. "Open your mouth."

Paralyzed by the cold blade of fear that cut deep into her, she slowly opened her mouth. He forced her head so far back she could hardly breathe.

He leaned over and stuck his tongue in her mouth rolling it over and under her tongue and across all of her teeth. "Just knocking the dust off, sweetheart. You know what to do." Jonathan unbuckled his belt with his right hand but held her hair with his left. "And you better act like you enjoy it."

She remained on the couch and he remained standing. It was the longest five minutes of her life. She had no choice.

In six minutes, he closed Celine's front door and hopped into his pickup. He took a long draw of bourbon, backed out of the driveway and burned rubber.

About a half-mile from his house, Roy Moore swerved his truck to dodge an empty whiskey bottle thrown from a tan pickup by some crazy, drunken redneck. He couldn't wait to get to the safety of his own home where he wouldn't be bothered by idiots like the one he'd just passed.

THIRTY

Spence answered on the fourth ring. In the background the caller could hear Al Michaels on ABC's Monday Night Football vigorously criticizing the Green Bay Packers' defense which had just given up its second touchdown of the first quarter to the Miami Dolphins.

"Mr. Dane?" a deep, male voice asked.

"Yes, this is Spencer Dane." Spence could not hear the caller because of the game. "Pop, turn the sound down a notch."

"Mr. Dane, my name is Gaylord Washington. I am the evening shift supervisor at Graceview Sanitarium in Mobile and I am calling on behalf of a Rebecca Morgan. Do you know her?"

Gaylord, Mable and Rebecca were in Rebecca's new room. Rebecca stood next to Gaylord waiting to talk. New patients were allowed a five-minute access to a telephone each day but they were never told in advance what time of day it would be. They only knew that when a phone was brought to their rooms.

As the seconds crept, Rebecca stared across the ten by twelve room at the single most important thing she'd seen since her arrival, her window. Even though it was barred and looked out over a cracked concrete parking lot, it brought freedom right up to the glass that she could touch.

"Yes. I know Mrs. Morgan."

"Would you have any objection to talking to Mrs. Morgan at this time?" Gaylord asked.

"No. None whatsoever." Spence could hear muffled voices over the phone and then, what sounded like a woman's cackle.

Gaylord handed Rebecca the telephone.

"Mr. Dane," the female voice said, "This is Rebecca Morgan. Can we talk?" she asked in a low voice. Out of the corner of her eye, she watched Mable lead Gaylord by the hand to the bathroom for what she assumed would be Monday night's session of racial harmony. Mable winked at Rebecca and mouthed 'Five Minutes'.

"Mrs. Morgan? Yes, yes we can talk. Did you say you were calling from Mobile?"

"Yes, I am. That's what I want to talk to you about."

"Hold on a second and let me get to another room where I can hear clearly." Spence motioned to his father that he was going into the kitchen to handle the call, prompting his father to order another beer.

As Gaylord walked slowly behind Mable, his ears clung to Rebecca's words. The slight smile that broke his long angular face reflected a great sense of satisfaction, a feeling he had not enjoyed around Graceview in a long while. True enough, he was allowing this one small breach of policy as a favor to Mable but more than that, deep down, he believed Mrs. Morgan was one of those unfortunates who was being railroaded. During his twelve years at Graceview he'd seen the occasional double-team where a lawyer and a psychiatrist collaborated to railroad some poor unsuspecting victim into an involuntary commitment, usually for money. He and Mable had no trouble believing Rebecca when she told them why her daughter had been taken from her and how she was jailed and how she thinks she got to Graceview. It sounded to them like she was fighting big money. And Gaylord knew that anytime you fought big money, big money won.

"Okay, Mrs. Morgan, I can hear better now."

"Mr. Dane, I hope you will help me because you are absolutely the only hope I've got. I can't even call my own family because they, along with my husband, signed papers to commit me. I'm certain he's convinced my parents that I've had some kind of mental breakdown."

"You've been committed?"

"That's what Mr. Washington has helped me find out. He got a quick look at my admission papers and from what he could tell I'm supposed to be suffering from a nervous breakdown. The admitting psychiatrist is some guy I've never even met. A Dr. Sosa. I didn't even know where I was until this morning when one of the patients told me. I've yet to meet with any psychiatrist."

"When was it I saw you last? Was it yesterday? You know... at the jail?" He was thinking, 'How in God's name did all this happen so fast?'

"Yes, it was yesterday. After you left the jail, Jonathan came by and tried to feed me some story about Abi making all this up. He blamed it on some seventeen-year-old kid. We got into a fight... and that's the last I remember. The next thing I know I'm waking up here at Graceview. Four hundred miles from home."

Spence was speechless. Knowing her five minutes would be up soon, Rebecca pressed on. "Mr. Dane, the thing I need for you to do is to put me in contact with my daughter. She needs to know what Jonathan is planning to say in defense of her allegations. She needs all the details. She has no idea how dangerous he can be when he's threatened. If I can tell her what he's done to me, maybe she'll realize what she's up against. Can you help me get in touch with her?"

"Mrs. Morgan, I know where she is, but..." he paused, "but, it would be best if you let me make the contact. You see, foster parents are instructed by the department to disallow early contact between foster children and their parents, in certain cases. And I'm sure the director has designated this as one of those cases. I think if I approach them and let them know what's happened to you, I believe they'll understand."

"Okay, good. Can you tell me who she's with and if she's okay?"

"Yeah. She's fine. She's in the home of Malachi and Clara Nell Peace out in the west end of the county. A great home. He's a preacher and she happens to be one of the best foster mothers this county's ever had. But, I can't really say how Abi's doing though, because I've not talked to her. I was thrown off the case. Remember?"

"Oh, that's right. So they won't let you have anything else to do with Abi?"

"No. Matter of fact there's another reason I won't be the caseworker. This morning I resigned."

"You resigned?"

"Yeah. Long story. Mostly, it's about me and my boss. We've crossed swords ever since I was hired. When we have more time I'll tell you about it. But for now, let me talk with the Peaces. They won't know I no longer work for the department. I think I can work this thing out but it may be in the morning before I can make it happen. That won't be too late will it?"

"No, I don't think so. We called the courthouse and found out that the hearing is not scheduled until 3 P.M. That should work."

I'll call the Peaces after I get off the phone with you and set a time to go see them tomorrow. I'd prefer to talk to them in person so that I can explain your concerns. That okay?"

"That sounds good to me. Listen, Mr. Dane. I really appreciate what you're doing."

"No problem. I've got nothing to do tomorrow anyway," he chuckled.

Rebecca hung up the phone wanting to feel optimistic but cautiously refrained. She consoled herself that at least she had a ray of hope. And that's something she knew she had to keep alive.

She sat on the side of the bed waiting for Mable and Gaylord. Their five minutes had come and gone. She waited five more minutes. Nothing. Worried, she tip-toed to the bathroom door and listened. Nothing. Then, a whisper. A sniffle. She knocked on the door. "Mable, you okay?"

The door slowly opened. Mable sat with her back against the commode while Gaylord lay curled up on the floor, his head in her lap. He had been crying so hard that her scrubs were soaked. The big man kept his eyes closed tight while she stroked his head.

Mable looked up to Rebecca. Her eyes filled. "He told me he was taken from his mother when he was eight. He doesn't know why. It was more than he could take to sit here and listen to you pleading for your child. He just lost it. I ain't never seen him like this. S'it okay if we stay in here till he can move?"

The sight of the broken, motherless man-child and the utter helplessness of her own predicament brought Rebecca to her knees.

***

The telephone rang only once at the home of Judge Morgan. When he picked up he heard the low voice of the head of security at Graceview Sanitarium. Alone in Graceview's secret basement office, the man was surrounded by a wall of mini-TV screens and recording equipment that scoured every square foot of the facility. "Judge, you were right. It's good that we monitored her. She just made a call to someone by the name of Spencer Dane in Lincoln." The man replayed Rebecca's entire conversation for the judge. The judge listened, let out a long breath and hung up. He couldn't let Abi learn about his defense. He needed to catch her totally by surprise, like Nixon said. Stun her. Paralyze her. And blow her away.

THIRTY-ONE

It was a gray day. Cold and blustery with heavy, dark, brooding clouds and winds approaching thirty-miles per hour. Because the heater in his 1989 Volkswagen Beetle was unreliable Spence was layered in insulated long johns, flannel shirt, jeans and his old flight jacket. A small whistle came from the right rear window as it always did when the car reached fifty-miles per hour.

Staring over the steering wheel at the dark ribbon of road ahead, his mind wandered back to a time when a young, energetic caseworker for the Department of Children's Services first traveled this road to the Peace foster home. Idealistic, his passion for his profession was matched only by his naivete. He had no way of knowing, in those early days, the degree to which state bureaucracies stifled individual creativity. He would, like those he worked with, evolve into a technocrat, shuffling paperwork, meeting quotas and learning to speak bureaucrat-ese so that he could regurgitate to his higher-ups, data to reflect that he was doing his job. In reality, he was jumping through their hoops just to keep a job. With the passage of each year he suffocated more and more under the weight of the unyielding, boundless bureaucracy. The colossal empire conceded to no individual whiz-kid. It didn't take long for him to tire of the choke-hold. He also tired of incompetent caseworkers there to only to draw a check under the protection of a union. And he tired of watching vindictive workers tear families apart simply because they could. He did the right thing by resigning, his inner voice assured. It was time for him to go.

Julia had always told him he was not right for this job. She always told him he wouldn't last. As large, heavy drops of rain began to splatter his windshield, he reluctantly conceded she was right.

Like she was about so many things. Like their marriage. She'd never really wanted to marry him and told him, repeatedly, they weren't right for each other. She would have been content to live with him; but marriage, that would be out of the question. He told her that he would prove her wrong; that he would be the best husband womankind had ever known. He was wrong.

It was a day like this when she left. Heavy and dark, windy with rain. He'd gotten her phone call at his office that she had had enough and was leaving. Enough of his drunkenness. Enough of his abuse. And, finally, enough of his indifference. Her parents had tried to convince her to leave him for over a year but she wouldn't listen to them. She didn't want to be a divorced woman. She wanted to prop her marriage up and prove to the world that it could work. But in the end, she could no longer carry the marriage alone. By the time he hung up the phone and rushed home the rain was coming down in sheets. He arrived as she loaded the last of her possessions in her car and slammed the trunk.

Their conversation in the pouring rain was brief, lasting from the garage to the street with him walking beside the car as she slowly backed out. No, she would not stay. And yes, if he changed, they could talk. Maybe. Numb, he stood on the sidewalk and watched her drive away until her tail-lights shrunk to red pinholes in the gray rain. Passersby gawked and honked at the man standing alone in the cold rain for no apparent reason. One stopped and asked if he needed help. He told the man that he guessed it was too late for that.

They'd seen each other only once since that day; at her father's funeral last year in Brewton. He had driven to that small town near the Florida line for her. She was cordial but somewhat distant. Yet, he sensed she still had feelings for him. He didn't get to spend any time alone with her because of her obligations, but he got the feeling she would have been receptive had the opportunity arisen. They'd agreed to stay in touch but had spoken by phone only three times. All three calls made by him.

Deep in thought, Spence didn't see the standard white van with heavily tinted windows pull even with him as he entered a two-lane, tree-lined, isolated straightaway. The passenger window rolled down and a long gray barrel pointed toward his left front tire and fired. At the last second Spence saw the flash on his left and ducked. The sudden spin of the steering wheel burned his hands. The car shot off the road into a green world of thickets and shrubs. Young rain-soaked pines and blackberry bushes slapped at him and slowed the car just enough for him to regain some control of the steering. He felt his head against the roof of the car and a strange weightless feeling rising in the pit his stomach, as he seemed to float out of his seat. The car dove off an embankment, pitched to the right and landed upside down in a ravine, the motor still running. The pain in his ribs spread like fire and was so intense he begged God to pass out.

The driver of the van got out on the side of the road and peered through the rain to see if he could see the Volkswagen. He could not. The slight smile on his pockmarked face told his partner they had done their job well. They celebrated five miles down the road at the first beer joint they came to, buying a round of drinks for everyone in the house. After the first round the man with the pockmarked face telephoned Judge Morgan to inform him that Mr. Dane had been taken care of and would present no further problems today. When they left, a half-hour later, all of their newfound drinking buddies followed them out to their van and gave the boys from Mississippi a rousing good-bye.

***

"Hey! You all right in there?"

The words didn't register with Spence at first.

The man asked again, "You alright in there?"

Spence couldn't see a face. "Not too bad. My... ribs." He spoke as evenly as he could to mask the pain in his ribs.

"Are you able to climb out? The voice grew louder with each word, in order to be heard over the rain.

"I think I'm going to need help." Holding his left arm close to his ribcage for stability, Spence reached for the safety belt release button but couldn't reach it with either hand. He was suspended by the seatbelt like an insect in a spider web. "Can you help me get out? I'm tangled up." Spence yelled.

The car was lying in the muddy ravine almost upside down but tilted to the passenger side. The top of the car was caved in from the impact of the large rocks in the ravine. No other damage was visible.

"Yeah. We're gonna get you outta' there. Hold what you got."

Spence could hear the heavy footsteps above him on the driver's side door. He could not see through the mud-splattered windshield but could hear the voices of the two men planning what to do next. After the talking stopped, there was a long silence. Then, the driver-side door opened and a voice yelled, "I'm coming in."

The two linemen from the Lincoln Power Department had been working on a downed power line about fifty yards from the crash site. They had heard the gunshot and saw the car slicing through the underbrush, but did not see the other vehicle. Together they cut straps, kept his arm stationary and pulled Spence from the car without further injury.

Spence stood ankle-deep in mud, looked up to the sky and gave thanks to the good Lord and Lincoln Power Department. Cold, hard rain never felt so good.

THIRTY-TWO

Clara Nell Peace rarely used the word hate. But on court day she always wore the word out, even if it was in private or under her breath. She hated court day because of what it did to families. Court day made adversaries of mothers and fathers and children. For the record. It was the day battle lines were drawn and strategies unleashed. Words spoken on court day cut deep and had the power to scar forever.

She had seen the devastation that court day inflicted on its victims. She had seen the clashing of legal swords that slashed little hearts and splattered blood on the courtroom floor. She had heard hard words obliterate fragile minds and spirits. Words nowhere near the truth. And more often than not, the truth was too slippery for judges to grasp.

If there was a stronger word than hate to describe her feelings she would use it, but she didn't know what that word would be.

Last night in the dark silence of her bedroom, she never came within reach of sleep. Most of her night was spent offering prayers for Abi to have the strength to endure what was to come. It was about 2:00 A.M. when she tiptoed into Abi's room and sat down in the old pine rocker to watch Abi sleep. As she rocked gently in the dimly lit room, she studied Abi's sweet, peaceful face and longed to hold her in her hands and promise to protect her from whatever it was that brought her here. It hurt Clara most that she was watching a child lose the innocence of childhood. She had seen it so many times before. The simple joys of childhood slipping away never to return. At 2:30 she returned to her bed where she tossed and turned and worried about how tomorrow would shape the rest of Abi's life.

One of the reasons the Peaces were excellent foster parents was their ability to empathize with the children coming in to their home.

It was not their practice to delve into the reasons the children had to leave their families. It was not necessary to probe into the children's family problems during their adjustment period. There would be plenty of time for discussions later, if after the court hearing, the court ordered that the children remain in foster care a while longer.

They were firm believers that children who had been through the trauma of being removed from their homes were better served by simply adjusting. They spent the children's first few days making them feel wanted and loved and trying to put smiles back on little faces.

It was for this reason that the Peaces had no knowledge of the reason that Abi was placed in foster care. They knew that if Abi remained with them, her social worker would apprise them of her family's problems after the hearing.

They had not even asked Abi her parents' names. They felt that if Abi wanted to discuss her family that she would bring them up. They knew of some Morgans around the county but couldn't really say if any of them had a daughter Abi's age. Down deep, they always hoped they didn't know the family.

It was almost lunchtime and Mrs. Peace hadn't heard from Spence. He called last night to say he would be dropping by this morning to talk. Whatever it was, he did not want to discuss it on the phone. She hoped he showed up soon because she planned to surprise Abi with lunch in town. She had always found that taking the kids into town for lunch and a little shopping helped keep their minds occupied so they wouldn't dwell on the hearings.

***

"Clara, can you get the phone?" Reverend Peace's voice echoed out from under the kitchen sink. "I'm still working on this leak." Since the foul weather had prevented him from tending to his daily farm chores, he'd finally gotten around to that worrisome leaky faucet. "Clara Nell, can't you hear the telephone?" he yelled, stretching out every syllable.

Clara rounded the kitchen corner in a semi-trot. "I got it, Malachi. I got it." She shouldered the phone to her ear as she adjusted her just-put-on-dress. "Hello."

"Mrs. Peace?" the male voice asked.

"Yes. This is Mrs. Peace. May I help you?"

"Mrs. Peace, this is Spencer Dane."

"Well, hello, Spencer. I was just about to give up on you."

"Yes ma'am. I don't doubt it." Spencer spoke easier now that the shot had eased his pain. "I was afraid I'd missed you. I had an accident on my way to see you and had to be taken to the hospital. That's where I am now."

"My goodness. Are you alright?"

"I'm going to be fine. I've got a couple of cracked ribs and a slight concussion, but nothing that I'll have to be admitted for."

Clara could hear female voices in the background telling Spence he needed to hang up.

"Listen, Mrs. Peace, I've got to go for one more test, but I wanted to tell you that the reason that I was coming to see you was because Abi's mother called me last night. She needs to talk to Abi. She's got some important things she wants to talk about before the hearing today. And I was hoping you could see to it that Abi called her."

The silence on Clara's end of the line told Spence that she wasn't sure about this.

"Mrs. Peace, Mrs. Morgan told me some things last night that Abi needs to know. These are things that if Abi doesn't know, could devastate her at the hearing."

"Spence, what kind of things are you talking about?" Clara asked, pulling up a chair.

"Well, for one, she told me that Abi's father had her committed to a sanitarium yesterday, in Mobile. She believes he had her committed to keep her away from the hearing today. She's got no memory of how she got there or when. She figures she must have been drugged at the Sheriff's office. Some people she's met have told her that her paperwork states she's had a nervous breakdown."

"Do you believe her?"

"Frankly, Mrs. Peace, I do. I had interviewed Abi and Mrs. Morgan a couple of days ago and got a real feel for the kind of person Mrs. Morgan is and there was absolutely no indication that she was on the verge of a nervous breakdown. She also said something about a seventeen-year-old boy that she needs to tell Abi about. It seems this will be part of her father's defense."

"And you're saying that what you've just told me is going to be addressed at today's hearing?"

"That's the way I understand it," Spence said. After a pause he asked, "Clara, do you know anything about this case?"

"No. I don't," Clara said. "Abi's not mentioned anything about her family. And we've not pressed her to talk about them."

"Clara, I need to let you know a little bit about this situation. It may help you understand the mother's concerns." Spence took as deep a breath as he could and continued. "Do you know Judge Jonathan Morgan?"

"I know who he is. His father and I used to serve on the county school board together." Her fond memory gave way to a growing fear. "Are you telling me that Judge Jonathan Morgan is Abi's father?"

"Yes, he is. Now, you can see this matter has some additional concerns that our usual run-of-the-mill cases don't have. I don't want to get into the details, but… Abi has alleged sexual abuse against her father. He, of course, denies any such thing."

Clara covered her mouth with her hand as Spence continued.

Reverend Peace peered out from under the sink at his wife.

"And, Judge Morgan, as you probably know, is politically well-connected. It's been rumored he'll be running for governor next election. He and his family have every reason to keep this quiet and get Abi back home and in their control. The mother is desperately opposed to this and feels this is why she was taken out of the picture."

The voices in the background told Spence he had to go for his last test.

Spence gave Clara Rebecca's phone number and said he'd get back to her as soon as he could.

Clara still held the phone to her ear after Spence hung up, numbed by what she'd just heard.

Malachi crawled out from under the sink and wiped his hands. "What's the matter Clara? You been told by Ed McMahon you won a million dollars?"

Clara hung the phone up, looked up at Malachi and said, "Malachi… you will not believe what Spence just told me."

Malachi tossed a paper towel in the trashcan, poured them both some coffee and sat down across the table from Clara. "Okay, Clara, what's the problem?"

Clara did her best to remember every word and tell the story as Spence had told it. She prided herself on her accuracy. But as she got into the heart of the story, it became more difficult for her to concentrate on remembering because of the look growing on Malachi's face. His color had grown ashen and his features hung heavy as though gravity had doubled. By the time she had finished he was no longer making eye contact; but staring into his coffee.

"Malachi, are you all right?" she asked, resting her hand on his.

He was slow to raise his head. The pounding in his chest spread to his ears. He looked at Clara but could not force a sound. The rain roared on the tin roof.

The time had come that he hoped he could forever avoid. He weighed his options only to realize what he already knew. He had to tell Clara.

"Clara, I never told you the real reason I felt a call to preach, did I?"

Clara wondered why he asked such a question, now. "You told me you just felt called to do it. I figured a calling was just that. Something out of the blue."

"Well, there was more to it than that." Malachi looked out of the kitchen window past the rumbling clouds to a time forgotten. A time that had mercifully remained buried. Until now. He continued, "Some fourteen years ago before I got the calling, there was some trouble that my baby brother, Josh, had gotten into. I kept it from you because it was such a terrible thing and I figured it was over and done with and nothing would ever come of it. And if it weren't for what you just told me and the fact that we've got Jonathan Morgan's child in our home, I doubt if I would have ever told you."

"Malachi, if you don't feel this is something I need to know, I'll understand."

"No. This is something that needs to come out and come out now. You'll understand when I finish." He brought the cup of coffee to his lips but didn't sip. "Clara, do you remember when Josh was in school at the university?"

"Yes."

"Well, one particular year, I'm not sure if it was his sophomore or his junior year, he and Jonathan Morgan had become close, almost inseparable. They used to carpool back and forth to Tuscaloosa and

I think even shared an apartment together for a couple of months. Anyway, one weekend Josh came home all tore up about something that he and Jonathan had done. Well, it was actually Jonathan that had done it, but Josh, he was there and he was a part of it." Malachi stood up and began pacing and recollecting at a brisk pace. "One afternoon, I think it was around the Christmas break, Josh and Jonathan had been drinking pretty good, hopping around from fraternities to sororities. They ran across this fellow who was dating Rebecca, you know, Abi's mother. He and Jonathan happened to be dating her at the same time. And Jonathan hated him… with a passion. Anyway this fellow was on his way out of Tuscaloosa headed to his relatives in Louisiana for the weekend and Jonathan and Josh decided to follow him. I don't know all of the details but I know that after they got into Mississippi they pulled him over and… somehow got that poor boy out of his car and… and killed him. Jonathan did, I mean. But Josh didn't stop him. It tore Josh up bad. He ain't been the same since. That's why he left here and never came back. He's too ashamed of himself. He knows he could have stopped it." Malachi clenched his jaw. "Josh said they buried the body near some woods. Nobody's ever found it so far as I know." He combed his white hair back with his fingers. "The law treated it as a missing person case, even though his family thought for sure somebody had done something to the poor boy. That family never knew what happened to him. I can't imagine the hurt they've gone through."

Malachi broke down and knelt at Clara's feet crying into her lap. "I had to give myself to the Lord, Clara, it was the only way I could live with myself." Between sobs he said, "And I had to do it for Josh. The Lord needed me to sacrifice myself for Josh's forgiveness. I believe that as sure as I'm drawing breath."

Clara didn't know what to say. She quivered inside thinking about what she had just heard. Jonathan Morgan… a murderer! She could hardly believe it. She tried with all her might to put her shock aside so that she could console her husband. Her tears spilled on his hands as she said, "Malachi, I'm sorry you had to bear this burden all these years alone. I wish you would have allowed me to share your pain." She slowly shook her head. "What you must have gone through."

Malachi needed her mothering. He needed the tender touch of Clara's hand that assured him that she would be with him no matter what and that together they could overcome anything. But being the product of southern raisin', Malachi slowly gathered himself as though his manly pride had taken over and he returned to his seat across the table from Clara.

"Clara, I could have carried that burden to my grave if I'd had to." He looked back down into his coffee. "I don't want you to take this the wrong way but I'm not asking for your forgiveness. It's just time for you to know what I know. I know down deep you would have shouldered some of this burden if I'd let you, but it was mine to bear. Mine and Josh's. Clara, you're as good a woman as any man has right to expect. And I love you for it." The lump in his throat squelched his voice. They reached across the table at the same time and held hands tightly.

Clara thought back to when Malachi gave his life to the Lord. Now, knowing what she did, the selflessness of it made her love for him stronger.

When he could talk he said, "Another reason I told you all this was so that you would know what this man is capable of. For Abi's sake, we need to be prepared for anything. There's nothing he won't do."

A flash of lightning splashed across the kitchen. Drawn by the storm, Malachi stood and walked over to the window to watch the lightning and the pouring rain and was in awe of God's dreadful power. Shreds of jagged lightning ripped across the dark gray and black clouds.

"Malachi, are you the only one who knows this about Judge Morgan, I mean besides Josh?"

"Far as I know," he said with his stare fixed on the speeding clouds.

Malachi turned from the window. "Let's get Abi on the phone with her mother, like Spence asked. It's the right thing to do."

THIRTY-THREE

The expression on Mrs. Peace's face seemed to contradict the good news that they were going to call Abi's mother. As Abi sat down at the kitchen table she watched Mrs. Peace punch in a long series of numbers, which told Abi that these numbers weren't local. Mrs. Peace smiled and held the phone out for Abi. She had not told Abi where her mother was because she thought it best that Abi hear it from her. As Mrs. Peace turned to leave the kitchen she patted Abi on her shoulder and mouthed that she would be in her bedroom. Abi nodded okay.

Gaylord had given Rebecca a spare phone he had stashed away in a supply closet so that she would have a phone in her room no matter what time she got her call. The incoming call would be routed to her room from the switchboard operator, a friend of Gaylord's.

Rebecca shot out of her chair by the window and answered on the first ring. Her nerves were frayed from waiting all morning. "Hello!" she blurted.

"Momma? Is that you?" Abi asked.

Expecting to hear Spence's voice, Abi's caught her off guard. "Abi? Is it really you?"

"Yes, momma. It's me!" Abi shrieked with delight.

"Baby! Oh, how are you?" Rebecca started to cry but cupped her hand over her mouth.

"Momma, I'm fine," Abi said. "Are you okay?"

Rebecca took a moment to compose herself. "Baby, I'm alright… I've missed you so much and I've worried about how you're being treated. It's good to hear your sweet voice."

There was nervous giggling and awkward silences before Rebecca got to the reason for the call. "Mr. Dane and I talked yesterday and he told me you are in a really nice home."

"I am, mom. I really am," Abi said, all the while thinking how wonderful it will be to get back to her own home.

"I'm thankful," Rebecca said. Before Abi could say anything else, she added, "Abi, I had asked Mr. Dane to set this call up because I need to tell you some things... things that aren't good." She paused to get her nerve up. She wished there was a way to sugar-coat this but realized there wasn't. "Honey, I'm going to have to be frank with you. We don't have a lot of time so please pay close attention to everything I tell you."

Abi's stomach tightened. Her mother's tone frightened her.

"Abi, I'm not at home. I'm at a place in Mobile. Your father had me put here yesterday... without my knowledge. He and his attorney filed papers full of lies and said that I'd had a nervous breakdown and needed commitment. But, I want you to know there's nothing to it, sweetie. I'm fine. Except that I'm so far away from you."

"Why would he do that? I don't understand," Abi asked.

"He doesn't want me at the hearing today because he knows I'll object to your returning home."

Abi couldn't believe what she was hearing. She thought back to the conversation that she and her mother had had with Mr. Dane. Everyone was in agreement that she could live at home with certain safeguards in place.

"Abi, I've seen a side of your father in the past twenty-four hours that I never knew existed. He'll do anything to get what he wants even if it means hurting me and you or anyone else that gets in his way. We had a fight yesterday about this... and he knows that I'll never agree to it. As a matter of fact I plan to have an attorney file for your custody. There is no way you or I will ever... ever live with him again."

Abi had been expecting this phone call to be about coming home after the hearing and about all the fun they would have when she got home. She wanted her life to be normal again. She wanted to sleep in her own bed and eat at her own place at the table and lay in her own spot on the sofa in front of the television.

Then it struck her. What if her mom really does need help? What if she's not quite right? It's a wonder any of the family is with all that's gone on these past couple of days. Maybe her father was doing the right thing getting her some professional help. All these thoughts raced through her mind leaving her confused about what to say next. Suddenly, she said what was undeniable. "Momma, I want to go home. I don't want to stay here anymore. Please, let me come home," Abi cried.

It crushed Rebecca to hear Abi's plea. "Abi, if I could give you what you want I would… but I can't. All I need is some more time."

Rebecca was afraid Abi didn't realize the seriousness of the situation. What could she say to get through to her? Although it hurt her to say it, she felt she had no alternative. "Your father cares nothing about you, Abi. He'll do and say anything to make you think he does… but he really doesn't." Trying to stay calm, Rebecca said, "Listen to this, Abi. To show you that he cares nothing about you, let me tell you what he is going to say in court." She took a deep breath. "Your father told me that he has evidence that you made all this up about him so that you and some seventeen-year-old boy could live together and that he planned to present this evidence in court. Does that sound like a father who cares about you?" Rebecca bit her lip.

Abi sat frozen. She could not believe the things her mother was saying.

"Mother! What are you talking about?"

Rebecca had feared Abi would not believe her. Desperate to say something, anything, to keep Abi from wanting to go home, she blurted out the words she thought she would take to her grave. "He's not your real father!" Only breathing could be heard on both ends of the line.

"Abi? Did you hear what I said? Jonathan is not your father. You need to know that. You don't know how I hate telling you this way, but I can't just stand by anymore and let you think he's something he's not."

A heavy sinking feeling in the pit of her stomach began to make Abi sick. Why would she say such a thing? *My mother must be crazy!* She didn't want to believe any of what her mother was saying. She just wanted to leave foster care and live a normal life.

"Abi? Abi? Are you there?"

Abi couldn't take it any longer. Tears burst from her eyes as she threw the phone down and ran from the kitchen, through the den out to the front porch. She was dying to keep on running but the storm wouldn't allow it. She stopped at the steps and screamed with all her might. It ripped through the cold, driving rain and echoed across the pasture.

Mrs. Peace heard the commotion in the kitchen and the front door slam. She pulled the curtain aside in the living room window and saw Abi looking skyward. Her lips were moving as though she was talking to someone, but there was no one there. All Clara could hear was the roar of the rain on the tin roof. She walked back to the kitchen, picked up the over-turned chair and checked it to see if it was broken. Sliding it back under the table, she saw the phone and heard someone yelling on the other end of the line. She picked it up. She could still feel the warmth of Abi's grasp.

"Hello," Clara said.

"Hello," Rebecca shrieked. "Is this Mrs. Peace?"

"Yes, it is."

"Mrs. Peace, this is Abi's mother. She and I were just talking. I heard the phone hit something and then, suddenly, she was no longer on the line. Is she okay?"

"Yes, Mrs. Morgan, she seems to be all right. She's out on the front porch. She looks a little upset but otherwise she seems fine. Is there a problem?" Clara asked.

"I think I really hurt her, Mrs. Peace. I had to tell her something that really upset her. I don't know how much you know about this situation but it's complicated. Did Spence get a chance to talk to you about our family?"

"Yes, some."

Mrs. Peace sat down slowly as Rebecca filled her in.

She reviewed the story about the seventeen-year-old boy and the pictures that Jonathan supposedly had. She told how Jonathan got her committed to Graceview. And then she told that she had to tell Abi that Jonathan is not her father. "Mrs. Peace, I'm afraid that Abi does not believe me. She wants to go home so badly that she does not want to believe any of this. Mrs. Peace, please share with her what I'm getting ready to tell you. I hope it will help convince her that I'm telling the truth." Rebecca took a breath. "Tell her... that her father's name is... Landon Moreau. Tell her that we were in college together and were deeply in love. But one day he left and never returned... it broke my heart. To this day I don't understand why he did that. I had hoped we would marry. Tell her that he knows nothing about her." Rebecca pressed her lips white to keep from crying. "And tell her that after I get out of here, I promise to help her find him. He needs to know what a wonderful daughter he has." Rebecca was quiet for a moment. "I know this has devastated her. Please tell her I am sorry that I had to tell her like I did. But she had to know."

Rebecca couldn't keep from crying. She hung up the phone and walked to the window. The reflection of a mother who'd just shattered her daughter's world stared back at her begging for forgiveness.

"I'll tell her," Clara muttered, shaken by what she had heard. As she hung up the phone, she wanted to find Malachi but she needed to check on Abi first.

***

The blinking red light on Judge Morgan's answering machine denoted that he had missed the call from the head of security of Graceview.

THIRTY-FOUR

Lightning hit a nearby transformer causing the lights to flicker. The split second interruption caused Clara's twenty-year-old refrigerator to vibrate like a jackhammer; something it did every time the power was interrupted. Clara mulled over the conversation she'd just had as she turned the refrigerator off then on to stop its vibrating. Landon Moreau. Landon Moreau. She wondered if that could be the name of the boy Malachi was talking about earlier. She'd ask him after she talked to Abi.

As she headed to the front porch she felt the beginnings of a terrible headache. She peered out of the living room window but couldn't see Abi on either end of the porch. She gathered her knit sweater about her neck, opened the door and stepped outside. Abi was nowhere in sight. She looked down the road and out to the barn. No sign of Abi. She noticed the rain had almost stopped but it was still cold and windy and she was stricken with the fear that as upset as Abi had been, she may have run off.

Clara retreated to the warmth of the living room where upon closing the door she noticed the wet footprints that led from the door to the bathroom. Through the closed bathroom door Clara could hear the shower. She gently knocked. No answer. She knocked a little louder. Again, no answer. She opened the door slightly, liberating steam into the cool hallway from the shower. "Abi, honey? You in here?"

She could hear Abi crying inside the shower. "Honey... I'm right here," she said as she sat down on the toilet seat across from the shower.

Abi was sitting on the shower floor, her back against the shower wall, and her arms around her knees. Streams of hot water and tears puddled at her feet.

"Abi, your mother told me what you all talked about." She could hear Abi clearing her throat as if she might speak. "She wanted me to tell you that she hated the way she had to tell you the things she did, but she didn't feel she had any choice. She loves you more than anything and doesn't want you hurt any more."

Clara didn't speak for a minute. She sensed Abi was thinking. Both were calmed by the rhythmic splashing of the shower and the gray steam that swirled about them.

"I don't feel like talking… I don't feel like anything," Abi muttered.

A long minute passed.

"I don't know what to believe anymore," Abi disclosed in a frustrated tone. "If my mom is telling the truth, I'm not even the person I've always thought I was. How weird is that? If she's not telling the truth, then I really must have a seriously mentally ill mother. In either case, I have a father who is either a sexual abuser or one who is so sorry that he walked out on my mother when she was pregnant with me."

Before Abi could mire herself in self-pity, Clara said, "Abi, listen. Sometimes life presents us with challenges that we think are impossible to handle. This is one of those times. But believe me when I tell you you'll get through this. It may not be easy, but you will be fine. And believe it or not, there will be more of these as time goes by; some more difficult than this. And you'll get through those too. They're something we all have to go through. They're as much a part of living as drawing breath. The trick is to never, ever give in. And, sweetie, from what I know about you, you're a fighter. A real survivor. And that's the kind of person you have to be in this old world. Believe me I know," Clara said as she thought back to her two miscarriages and the death of their daughter during delivery. Even now, twenty-two years later, that memory of death at birth still tears at Clara. She remembered how proud of herself she was for finally taking a pregnancy to term. But she is forever scarred with the horrible memory of faceless nurses with prying hands pulling little Amanda out of her arms. They said it had something to do with her umbilical cord. So what if she wasn't breathing, she was still mine, she thought. Amanda was my flesh and blood. My only child.

Returning to herself, Clara said, "Abi, I want you to know that I believe your mother. I know some things about your family… that lead me to believe she is telling you the truth about your father."

"Oh, yeah? Which one?" Abi retorted.

"Your real father," Clara said. "Your mother said that she wanted me to be sure to tell you that his name is... Landon Moreau." Clara spoke slowly. "They were in college together and deeply in love. For some reason that your mother doesn't know, he stopped all contact with her, never even returning to school. It broke her heart. 'Cause she had hoped they would marry. She said that he doesn't even know about you. And although she has not had any contact with him since college, she wants to help you find him so that he can know what a wonderful daughter he has."

Abi let the weight of Mrs. Peace's words sink in and settle the part of her that was angry and confused. A growing sadness crept in and moved all of her other feelings aside. It saddened her to think about her mother being hurt by someone she loved enough to marry. She wished she could hold her right now and tell her how much she loved her and make that hurt of long ago go away.

With the hearing only about an hour and a half away Clara knew that she needed to get Abi up and moving as soon as she could. "Sweetheart, I think I'll go make you and me some hot cocoa. How does that sound?"

Abi did not reply.

As she stood, Clara said, "Honey, how's about you coming on in the kitchen as soon as you can and we'll try to get ourselves in a little better mood with a little hot cocoa. Okay?" It was hard for her to push like this. She would much rather spend all afternoon doting over Abi insulating her from these hurtful realities.

"Okay."

Clara closed the bathroom door behind her and headed for the bedroom to find Malachi. He was at his desk reading scripture, which always helped him find his way in difficult times.

"Malachi. She and her mother talked," Clara whispered as she shut the door.

He peered over his reading glasses. "How did it go?"

"About as well as could be expected given all that her family has gone through. Abi's upset." She placed her hand on his shoulder. "Malachi... does the name Landon Moreau mean anything to you?"

She could see it in his eyes.

"That's him! That's the name of the boy that Jonathan killed. I couldn't call it when I was telling you about him earlier but I knew I'd know if I heard it." He thought for a second. "How did you know that?" He was still sitting at an awkward angle with his head turned, waiting for Clara's response.

"Mrs. Morgan told me… and she told Abi… that Jonathan was not her father… that Landon Moreau was." Her hand slid from his shoulder as she sat down on the side of the bed.

Malachi's eyes widened as he stood up and gripped his worn Bible and pointed it at Clara. "He's Abi's father?" It was more of a statement than a question, born of relief. "Well I ain't surprised. It all adds up, now." The words hung in the air never completely ending until he blurted out, "Did she say anything about his death?"

She shook her head. "No. Not a word. I don't think she knows what happened to him." She began to talk fast and nervous wanting to bring Malachi up to where she was on the matter. "'Cause she told us that when they were in college he left her and never spoke to her again. It broke her heart, she said. She, to this day, has no clue why he did that. And Malachi, here's the saddest part. She told me that as soon as she can she wants to help Abi find her father." Clara's chin quivered, "So he can know what a wonderful daughter he has. I just about died when she told me that."

Malachi heard Abi coming down the hall to her bedroom and put a forefinger to his lips. "Shhh." He nodded towards the hall and Clara knew to be quiet. Neither wanted Abi to learn of this now. Especially just before her hearing. She didn't need to be any more upset than she already was.

"I've got to go make her some hot cocoa," Clara said. "We've got to get her spirits up as much as we can before the hearing this afternoon. You know we've got to meet Ms. Waddle at the courthouse at three o'clock."

Malachi nodded, deep in thought about what he just learned.

Clara whispered, "Give me a couple of minutes to make the cocoa; then you come on in to the kitchen with us and we'll see if we can't make her feel a bit better. I don't know how she's going to do it but she's got to get herself ready to face all those folks at the courthouse. Given what she's been through, I just don't know how in the world she's going to do it. I just don't know how."

THIRTY-SIX

The silver-domed courthouse came into view when Clara turned the pickup on to Main Street. Even from three blocks away Abi could see the steps beneath the three-storied columns from which she and her grandfather used to watch Christmas and Veterans' Day parades. Closing her eyes she could almost hear the high school band's rendition of *Winter Wonderland* and feel the nippy December gusts biting her cheeks. She could almost smell the wonderful concoction of inebriating scents swirling about from candy, popcorn, pine and holly and the horses, cars and fireworks.

The pickup stopped abruptly in the parking space on the north side of the courthouse marked FOR SHERRIFF'S DEPARTMENT ONLY. The Department of Children's Services always instructed Clara to use the space for court hearings. It was closer to the side exit and more private than either the east or west entrances.

Abi's nostalgia did not mix well with the growing knot in the pit of her stomach. She was dizzy with apprehension.

Clara sensed Abi was in no mood to talk. She helped her up on to the curb and into the courthouse where they climbed the private stairs to the second floor law library. From there, Clara walked one step ahead of Abi as she led her by the hand to a small room on the east side of the building. Abi felt claustrophobic in the eight-by-twelve room.

Crammed into the room were a caramel colored Naugahyde love seat, two orange plastic chairs donated by an elementary school and a ten-year-old Xerox copying machine. There was nothing on the gray walls. At least the room had a view of Main Street and the east lawn. And it had a bathroom, which Clara knew from experience was a necessity due to the long waits involved with these matters.

Abi noticed two things when she sat on the love seat. That the Naugahyde was cracked and that 'Buddy loves daddy.' It was carved into the wooden armrest.

Clara showed Abi where the bathroom and the magazines were and told her to settle in, to get as comfortable as she could because waiting was half the ordeal. Then, she went downstairs to the snack bar for cold drinks and aspirin. As Clara patted Abi on her shoulder, Abi noticed Clara's pale, blue-veined wrist and how old and frail she looked. She seemed to have aged years these past two days.

By three-thirty the cokes were gone and half the magazines had been flipped through with still no word from the judge or the lawyers. The tension of the past half-hour had mercifully numbed Abi to a state of semi-consciousness allowing her to lose herself in an article about spelunking in Alabama caves. Every now and then Clara would notice Abi's finger staying on one word of the article as though she couldn't keep her mind on what she was reading.

Clara stepped halfway out in the hallway after coming from the bathroom to see if she could see anyone. She heard male and female laughter coming from Judge Vincent's office and knew, then, that the attorneys were in the judge's office telling jokes and catching up on the latest gossip. She returned to her seat next to Abi who did not look up from her magazine.

Another twenty minutes had passed when a soft knock was followed by the entrance of a grinning Trudy Waddle. Trailing Waddle was Abi's court-appointed attorney, Richard Hill, a short, pudgy, twenty-five-year-old who had just passed the bar exam. Because of inexperience, he hadn't earned a reputation of any sort.

"Abi, I'd like you to meet your attorney, Mr. Richard Hill," Waddle said, with as grand a sweeping gesture as the room would allow.

Hill stepped over to where Abi sat, wiped the cracker crumbs off his fat little fingers and extended his hand which Abi shook. "Hello, Abi, it's very nice to meet you," he said, as his tongue shoved a bite of cracker to one side of his mouth.

Clara watched as Abi attempted to stand and force a smile in an attempt at being brave.

"Oh, please, be seated," he said, swallowing the last bite.

"Abi, Mr. Hill needs to spend a few minutes with you to go over your case. Okay?" Waddle turned to Clara. "Judge Vincent is in court now on another matter and has two delinquency cases scheduled after that. Since our case is a last minute addition to her docket she wants the attorneys to get together in the conference room shortly to see if an agreement can be reached by all parties. So, let's you and I leave these two alone for a few minutes, shall we?" Waddle held the door for Clara then left her, saying she had some other business on the first floor she had to attend to. Clara walked to the main hall where she sat down on one of the two long oak benches. Next to her was the family of one of the two delinquency cases that Judge Vincent would be hearing. She listened and shook her head in disbelief as the fourteen-year-old daughter threatened to cut her mother if she didn't testify as she told her to.

Mr. Hill sat in one of the orange chairs across from Abi and opened a folder containing an inch thick stack of papers. He shuffled and yanked papers until he found what he was looking for.

"Well now, let's see here," he said, pulling out a long stretch of stapled sheets. "I've read over the petition here and let's see... and the report to the court from the Department of Children's Services by a Mr. Dane." He flipped to the last page of Dane's report, shot a quizzical glance at Abi and returned his gaze to the papers in his lap.

He wrinkled his meaty brow and licked his thumb to turn another page. "It says here that... uh, that, you... have alleged that," he cleared his throat, not quite able to speak the words. "That your father has been... having sex... with you. Is that right?" His eyes couldn't bear to look at her. They clung to the pile of paper in his lap.

"Yes, sir," Abi said, incapable of embarrassment any longer. She found herself feeling sorry for Mr. Hill whose hands trembled as he drew little boxes on his stack of paper. She could tell he was not used to this. It made her wonder about him.

"Why don't I let you take a look at this report and that way... that way you can see if everything in there is what you, uh, actually said." He thrust the department's report into Abi's hand and leaned back to gather himself, relieved that he could stop talking about the uncomfortable subject.

Abi looked at the pages. They contained a written account of her conversation with Mr. Dane. After scanning the first paragraph she was certain of the accuracy of the report. Since she had no desire to revisit those feelings she had during the interview, she let her eyes slide blindly over the remaining text.

"Yes, sir, this is what I said," Abi said, returning the papers to Hill.

"Okay," Hill nodded. "There's really no need for me to go into every detail as long as I know what you're alleging." He collected all of his papers and crammed them back into his folder. "All right, Abi, I'm going to go out there and sit down with those other attorneys and tell them this report is the truth. And that you've not made any of this up, right?"

Her eyes shot up.

He regretted asking that as soon as it came out. "I'm sorry, Abi. I don't want you to think I don't believe you. It's just that this is such a serious matter that I need to be real sure." He leaned forward, elbows on knees and let out a heavy breath. "Listen… this is the first case like this I've ever been associated with and well, it's made me a little apprehensive." The perspiration on his upper lip verified his words.

Hill closed his folder, patted the top of her head and stood. "Well, I need to go on in there with the other lawyers and see what happens. I'm sure we can hammer something out." He turned quickly and left. Abi wondered what he meant.

THIRTY-SEVEN

J. Wendell Nixon had instructed Judge Morgan to maintain his usual Monday workday schedule. Therefore, the judge had been in his office on the second floor since 8:00 A.M. His secretary, Melinda, had brought his coffee and schedule by 8:15. He had shot the bull with some of the district attorney's staff about the weekend's football games and scheduled a lunch for tomorrow with the probate judge. He could tell by everyone's expressions and behavior that no one had any knowledge of his hearing today. He had Melinda postpone the two divorce cases he had slated for today. His only job-related responsibilities were sorting his mail and returning phone calls from Friday.

Juvenile proceedings are closed to the public and strictly confidential. Judge Morgan was thankful. Any violation of this confidentiality is a crime and punishable by law.

Melinda had brought his lunch from the Victory Café while he was in the law library researching the Alabama statutes under which juvenile court judges and the Department of Children's Services operate. He was specifically interested in the section of the Code of Alabama in which the law defined child abuse and dependency and the section that addresses the department's responsibilities in removing children from parental custody, particularly without a hearing.

By two o'clock he had learned of Judge Vincent's full docket. By two-thirty, he had reviewed case strategy with Nixon. Both were pleased with the caliber of the opposition's attorneys.

Three o'clock found Nixon and Judge Morgan in an almost celebratory mood.

At three-fifteen, Judge Morgan received his father and grandfather into his office. They would be sitting with him in court in Mrs.

Morgan's absence. An impressive and forceful show of family support.

A phone call was made to Mr. Ward at the seventeen-year-old's home where he and the kid were on stand-by. Ward said they could be at the courthouse in twenty minutes if the judge wanted the kid's testimony.

Melinda served hot tea and the wait began in earnest. By four-fifteen ties were loosened and every head wondered what the future held.

THIRTY-EIGHT

Abi tried to take herself to another place. To think would drive her crazy. She went to the window and looked out to the front lawn at the stretching shadow of the courthouse as twilight signaled darkness was closing in. Her eyes held a flat stare as her thoughts locked. She thought neither of what had been nor what was to come.

A sudden movement caught her eye. From high up on an old pin oak near the flagpole, a young red-tailed hawk swooped down with blurring speed to clench its last meal of the day. A defenseless, unsuspecting mouse had strayed too far from the safe confines of the courthouse basement. Abi watched as the mouse tried to turn and run back to the basement. It was too late. Its little legs found only air to run on as it ascended higher and higher. Finally, on the highest branch of the pin oak that could sustain the hawk's weight, nature took its course. Her hand shot to her mouth as she gasped at the sight of the young hawk tearing into the mouse-flesh. She clenched her eyes and held a scream in her throat.

As the minutes passed she grew calmer. A realization descended upon her that was as clear a lesson as she had ever been taught. This lesson she would never forget. Only the strong survive. The weak are doomed.

The silver twilight was losing its battle to the approaching darkness, giving Abi a chill of cold finality. She sensed that the end of this day could signal the end of her life as she has known it.

THIRTY-NINE

J. Wendell Nixon did not have cracker crumbs or old food stains on the lapels of his tailored gray, pinstriped, double-breasted suit, but he relished the opportunity to do battle with lawyers who did. That, coupled with the fact that neither of the opposing attorneys attempted to maintain even minimal eye contact with him, signaled a quick kill.

The three attorneys were led by the judge's secretary to a small conference room adjacent to Judge Vincent's chambers. She explained that the judge remained engaged in court but would recess to issue an order if an agreement could be reached. The room was small and contained no windows, which contributed to the strong odor of stale coffee and musty law texts.

Robert Kingsley, the attorney for the Department of Children's Services led off by stating his client's position. He was a frail, thin, slick bald, fifty-year-old widower who was thankful he had the department as a regular client. Neither his appearance nor his demeanor bestowed confidence in prospective clientele. He spoke with the voice of a choir-girl when calm but like a stepped-on cat when excited. With all of his exterior deficits, he could, however, be a crafty and skilled lawyer. He leaned back into his chair forcing the loose skin of his little chicken-neck to ride over his too tight collar and said, "The department remains firm in the position that the girl should remain in foster care at this time with absolutely no parental contact." Adjusting his bifocals, he continued. "I would like to refer you to the copy of the forensic interview by the department, which you were both given. If you will note, the interview was conducted when the girl was in the hospital. And it was conducted without any duress whatsoever. It is the department's belief that this representation by the child is truthful and that any deviation from our position would place this poor child at risk of continued abuse."

It did not go un-noticed by Kingsley that when he talked, Nixon maintained a Cheshire cat-like grin. "Furthermore, my client believes that neither parent deserves to have custody of this child at this time. The mother, although not the direct perpetrator, is indeed, a perpetrator just as much as the father, because of her failure to prevent this depravity from occurring." He reached to flip a page of his notes when Nixon broke in.

A handsome man, Nixon still had the appearance of easy living and hard drinking. His wavy, gray hair, always meticulously cut and styled, had been fortified with transplants over last three years. His reddened face, chiseled by the south's best plastic surgeon, maintained the classic Greek profile, with the exception of a slightly sagging turkey neck, a testament to the opulence to which he was accustomed. His easy smile was disarming and belied his ruthlessness, which he could tell wouldn't even be needed today.

"Gentlemen," Nixon said, clasping his hands atop the stack of papers before him. "Would you permit me a moment?" His raised eyebrows were intended to be a sign of courtesy that he hoped his over-matched opponents would recognize. The southern male ego being what it was, Nixon decided not to provoke but to seek the path of least resistance. Without wielding too heavy a sword he hoped these two could be led to the point where they would logically conclude that the girl was not telling the truth. He believed if he waged war, they would dig in their heels and prolong this battle to no telling what end.

"If you'll permit me, I would like to share with you the evidence that I have, which I believe will help clear this little matter up for everybody and we'll be able to get on home before supper gets cold. You fellows amenable to that?" The Cheshire grin grew.

Kingsley and Hill were eager to hear such evidence if any existed and if the truth were known, were just as eager to align themselves, in such a serious matter, with the great Birmingham barrister. They looked at each other, nodded and shared expressions that said, 'Why not?'

"Gentlemen. It is not insignificant who the alleged perpetrator is in this matter." Nixon had a certain pace he maintained when he spoke that allowed him to gauge the impact of his words. His smooth velvet tone mesmerized his audience. "The accused in this matter is a good and decent man. He is not only a wonderful father to his own children, he is also a father-figure to every child in Rutherford County. He is the single driving force behind the proposed construction of the county's children's advocacy center designed to help the county's abused and neglected children. This is not a man who could behave as alleged."

"Robert? May I call you Robert?" Nixon asked.

Kingsley nodded.

"Robert, let me pull this together for you. Here's what you've got." Nixon leaned into the table towards Kingsley. "Your client has one single statement of one teenaged girl. No witnesses and no corroborative evidence. What do we have? We have indisputable evidence that proves without a doubt that my client is totally innocent of these scurrilous charges. Not only does the evidence that we have exonerate my client, it provides the court with the identity of the individual responsible for the initiation of the allegations. We have a signed statement from the teenaged boy with whom this girl has been sexually active, stating that he put her up to making these allegations so that she could leave home to go live with him. In addition, we have a signed statement from the boy's aunt with whom he lives stating that she knew about it. As if we needed any additional corroborating evidence, we have actual photographs of the girl and this kid engaged in sexual activity that represents numerous occasions. And, we have signed statements from the girl's grandfather and great-grandfather, both of whom are ex-judges here in Rutherford County, stating that they were aware that the girl and her parents had been having problems, relating to the aforementioned behavior." Only now did Nixon draw a breath.

Kingsley and Hill sat motionless.

"Robert, I know of no other way to say this, but you have no case. Please understand, I say this with the utmost respect for you. You are merely acting in good faith on behalf of your client, as any attorney would. But, it is crystal clear to me that your client provided you with only limited information born of an incomplete investigation. Hell, your people haven't even interviewed the child's father, the so-called perpetrator."

Although Kingsley was taken aback by Nixon's presentation, he gamely offered a retort. "Well, let's not overlook the significance of the social worker's forensic interview and subsequent assessment."

"Ha!" Nixon shot back. "That is worth absolutely nothing and Robert, I know that you know that." The Cheshire grin. "Hell, boys… all he did was write down what the girl was willing to tell him. You think that's substantive? You boys must be used to getting your way around here, if you think that dog's gonna hunt." His face reddened and his brows furrowed as he scowled, "I must tell you, in all seriousness, my client has a lot to lose in this matter; an awful lot. He didn't hire me to do but one thing. Win. And I can assure both of you that I plan to do just that. If either of you have any desire to go to the mat on this, I am ready."

Kingsley and Hill flipped through the stacks of paper before them looking for anything that could bolster their arguments, thankful for the opportunity to avoid Nixon's glare.

"By the way, Robert, even if that social worker's assessment was worth the paper it was written on, the son-of-a-bitch has been fired. You don't even have him for testimony." Nixon leaned his full weight back in his chair. "Pretty shoddy work boys. Pretty damn shoddy."

Hill sat spellbound at Nixon's rapid-fire delivery before he realized that Nixon and Kingsley were waiting on him to make a comment. He put his hand over his mouth and coughed, stalling for a second or two and said, "Well, now, I reviewed the allegations in the petition with the girl and she reassured me that everything in there is true and that…"

Nixon cut him off. "Mr. Hill did you really expect her to come in here today and suddenly say that it was all a pack of lies. Get a grip, man. Of course, she's going to say it's true. She's not an idiot. But, Mr. Hill, it all boils down to evidence." He scooted closer to the table. "We've got it and you don't." Nixon let those words settle in. "Look, don't y'all remember how it was to be a teenager? Man, I sure do. I've got stories I can't tell even now because the statute of limitations hasn't expired on some of them," he laughed, as did the others, knowing that that was their cue. "What we've got here is a teenaged girl with raging hormones who's got the hots for some young stud and daddy won't have any part of it."

Kingsley and Hill nodded their heads as they sorted through the statements of the seventeen-year-old kid, his aunt and the girl's relatives. The names on the affidavits were Ty Harper, age seventeen and Rose Tarleton, age forty-three. It did seem like the girl lied in light of all of the evidence.

Hill asked, "And you say you've got photographs?" His raised eyebrows pleaded for a tempered response from Nixon.

Nixon had saved the photos for last. The coup de grace. His well-manicured right hand extended four black and white three by five's of a couple in the front seat of a car at night. The girl's back is to the camera but the side of her face was exposed. It looked just like Abi. The four photos depicted the couple in two separate sexual positions. The first, with the girl in the boy's lap facing him, her back to the windshield. And the second, with them facing each other, their sides to the windshield.

Kingsley and Hill were appalled. Both jotted quick notes for their files. They passed the pictures between them and shook their heads.

When they laid the photos down in the center of the table, Nixon closed his file and tossed it onto the heap.

"God almighty," Kingsley exclaimed, feeling betrayed by the incompetence of the department. "Why can't they do their jobs down there?" he muttered to himself getting up from his seat.

"Game, set and match!" said Nixon.

Hill fell in line with Kingsley. "Teenagers! What are you gonna do?"

"Yeah, what are you going to do?" Nixon replied.

Nixon seized the moment. "All right, gentlemen. Can we agree, now, that since you know what I know, my client gets his daughter back tonight?"

Cocked eyebrows all around.

"No problem here," Hill said, checking his watch, thinking about supper.

Kingsley and Hill left the room to discuss the status of the case with their respective clients. Kingsley found Waddle coming from the downstairs snack bar and pulled her to a nearby corner where he informed her of Nixon's evidence.

"I can't believe this. You're telling me that Abi has been having a thing with some delinquent from Dalton County and that they came up with these allegations so she could go live with him?" Waddle asked, an octave higher than normal.

"Nixon said that her daddy could have told y'all all of this if you had just interviewed him. Why didn't you do that?"

"It wasn't my case at that time. It was Spencer Dane's. I just get cases after they come into foster care. So don't get huffy with me," Waddle retorted.

"Well, no matter whose case it was, it's an embarrassment to me and I really don't appreciate being hung out to dry like this."

"What did the girl's lawyer have to say about this?" Waddle asked.

"What could he say? He's like me. He thinks that all this could have been avoided if you all had done a better job with your investigation. He and I just sat there like two knots on a log listening to all of the evidence piling up against us. It was damned embarrassing. They even have pictures." He pointed a skinny little finger at Waddle. "It's so over it's not even arguable."

"So where are we in all this?"

"The girl's lawyer is meeting with her now; then we'll all get together in the conference room before we sit down with the judge. The only question now is when the girl will return home."

The lawyers' words hung in his ears as Hill hurried down the hall to talk to Abi. 'Don't take any of her lip. Be firm. Let her know that we know the truth.'

Hill knocked once and entered. He was surprised to see that Mrs. Peace had returned. "Uh, ma'am, do you mind if I speak to Abi alone? You know, attorney/client privilege kind of stuff?"

Clara wasn't surprised. She had seen all this before and she knew the routine.

He offered Abi a cracker, which she declined. "Abi, some things came out during our discussion that don't look too favorable for you regarding those allegations against your father." He cleared his throat and wiggled his pen between his meaty right thumb and index finger.

Abi scooted upright in her seat. "What do you mean?"

"Well, we all now know about your boyfriend and all the trouble he has caused your parents." Hill avoided eye contact, choosing, instead, to talk to the legal papers in his lap.

"What boyfriend?"

"Now, Abi, it's okay, you don't have to keep on with this charade. We've seen his signed statement that he put you up to all of this and well, we have seen pictures of you and him together."

Stunned, Abi remembered that her mother had warned her about this. And she was right... her father would do anything to save his own neck.

"Look, Abi, the evidence against you is overwhelming. If we'd had a full hearing today you would have been decimated. The attorneys have agreed, in principle that it is best that you go on back home. The only thing on the table now is when."

Abi's head started spinning and she was getting that heavy sickening feeling in her stomach.

Hill sped on. "Your father's attorney wants you to go on home tonight. But I was thinking maybe tomorrow night, you know, say, twenty-four hours from now. That way you and the foster parents will have plenty of time to say goodbye and all that stuff." Before he could say another word, Abi bolted for the bathroom.

He stood outside the bathroom door and listened as Abi expelled the contents of her stomach. "Well, I can see you're not feeling too well, so if you don't have any objection, I'll suggest tomorrow night about this time, okay?"

Another splash.

"Okay, then. I'll head on out and run this by the others. Hope you get to feeling better. There's a lot of stuff going around, you know."

FORTY

An agreement had been reached. The lawyers had assembled in Judge Vincent's courtroom after she recessed the delinquency hearing that had been in progress. The attorneys stood as Judge Vincent returned from her chambers where she had reviewed the case.

"Please be seated," the judge directed. At six-one, two-hundred and forty pounds, Judge Gwendolyn Vincent was a black-robed mountain of a woman. At thirty-five, she had not yet earned the graying of her jet-black hair that distinguished many of her profession. She liked things simple and to the point. She detested repeating herself, didn't suffer showmanship and was yet to be intimidated by any attorney. She, unlike Judge Morgan, was in the middle of her second term of office and was very popular throughout the entire county.

Even though she supported Judge Morgan's opponent during the last election, she took no comfort in seeing him before her. The fact that he was in her courtroom told her only one thing… that Judge Morgan had a serious family problem. She'd seen enough cases to realize that not everything alleged in petitions was gospel. Filed allegations weren't always true but they always, at the very least, signaled a serious family problem. Objectivity was her forte.

To her right sat Judge Morgan and J. Wendell Nixon at the respondent's table. Behind them in the first pew sat Jonathan's father and grandfather.

To her left sat Robert Kingsley and Trudy Waddle at the petitioner's table.

Abi's attorney, Richard Hill, sat alone in front of the judge.

Judge Vincent scribbled a note to herself then peered over her bifocals at Mr. Kingsley. "Are the parties here?"

"Yes, your honor, all of the parties are here today," he replied.

"I don't see a child," Judge Vincent said after a cursory glance around the room. "Mr. Kingsley, do you see a child anywhere in this courtroom?"

"Your honor, the girl, that is to say, my client is not feeling well. She's, uh, in the bathroom," Hill blurted.

Jonathan was relieved. He hoped to avoid a face to face confrontation with Abi.

"Is she sick?" asked the judge, pulling off her glasses.

"Yeah, she's pretty… I mean yes, your honor, she's sick at her stomach… I heard her… I mean it sounded like she was throwing up."

"And you left her there by herself in that condition?"

"Well, her foster mother was heading right back in. See, we'd already talked. We were through with everything and I was leaving anyway. She's knows what I'm going to say in here, you know, as far as recommendations and such." Hill nodded, shaking newly formed sweat beads down his collar.

"Are you saying that your client has absolutely no objection to the agreement that's been reached?"

Hill began to squirm ever so slightly in his chair. "Well, your honor, she clearly understands the reason for the agreement." He swallowed hard. "And voiced no objection."

The judge returned her glasses to her prominent nose, as she clicked on the recorder. Before I proceed I must inquire as to the identity of the two gentlemen sitting behind the respondent."

"Your honor, these gentlemen are the father and grandfather of my client," Nixon explained.

"I must ask the gentlemen to please step out of the courtroom as they are not parties in this matter." The judge nodded to the gentlemen as they left.

"Let the record show that the Juvenile Court of Rutherford County is in session regarding the matter of Virginia Abigail Morgan, a minor, styled Rutherford County Department of Children's Services, petitioner, versus Jonathan and Rebecca Morgan, respondents, case number JU 1999-912.01. The record will show that the respondents are represented by the Honorable J. Wendell Nixon, the petitioners, by the Honorable Robert Kingsley and the Honorable

Richard Hill, is serving as the guardian ad litem." The judge took a quick sip of water.

"The Court understands that an agreement has been reached by all parties. Is this correct?"

Kingsley spoke first. "Yes, your honor. The department is in agreement with respondent's attorney and the guardian ad litem that the child should return home. We have been made aware of evidence, heretofore unknown by the department that significantly alters the department's previous position. Therefore we have no objection to the child returning home."

Nixon buttoned his coat as he stood to say, "Your honor, my client, Judge Jonathan Morgan, has maintained all along that the Department of Children's Services made a grievous error when they failed to conduct a thorough investigation that obviously should have involved him and…"

"Please sit down Mr. Nixon," said the judge, not even bothering to offer him a glance. "We are not taking testimony here so please do not attempt to inject any." Judge Vincent eased her entire weight back into her leather chair casting her gaze at the empty pews in the rear of the courtroom. "It was my understanding that we are gathered here only to agree or disagree on a resolution of this matter. Is the Court suffering under an illusion?" The corners of the judge's mouth dripped with disdain.

Nixon returned to his seat and said, "No, your honor. The Court is under no illusion."

"Good. Now, Mr. Nixon, I want a yes or a no from you. Does your client want his daughter to return to his home?"

"Yes, your honor, he does."

"Thank you, Mr. Nixon."

"Now, Mr. Hill. Does your client have any objection in returning home? Yes or no?"

"No, your honor, she realizes the evidence against her is…"

The judge leaned over her desk. "Mr. Hill. Yes or no? Those are your only choices. I don't require anything else."

"Uh, no, your honor."

"Good. Now," she folded her hands, "the only remaining issue is when the agreed upon resolution should take place. Am I correct?" the judge asked.

Clara held the door open for Abi. Having nothing left to throw up, Abi wanted to leave the room to find her attorney to tell him about her mother. She needed to tell him what had happened to her and that she wants to seek sole custody of her. Clara walked slightly behind Abi so that Abi could not see her watery eyes. It had broken Clara's heart to listen to Abi's anguish as she described what her attorney had told her. And now to see her struggling down the hallway, bent over from nausea, was more than Clara could take.

When they saw the green and white *In Session* sign illuminated over the doorway to Judge Vincent's courtroom they knew where Mr. Hill was. But Clara knew that no one barged into court when it was in session. She sat Abi down on the end of the bench, made her as comfortable as possible and headed to the judge's office to ask the secretary if the judge would be taking a break soon.

Waiting had taken its toll on Abi. She had been waiting ever since she arrived nearly two hours ago and was becoming more irritable and impatient by the minute.

Why do I have to wait and wait and wait? she yelled in her head. I can't take this any more! A flashback blurred her mind. Again. It was the swooping hawk. Only the strong survive, she remembered. She began to nod her head. That's right. Only the strong survive. Only the strong survive! She willed herself to act. I can do this. I can do this. She put her hands down on the bench and pushed herself up. She took a step. I can do this. She walked toward the courtroom door. She swelled with determination. Only the strong survive. She felt chills going down her back. Head up. She remembered what her mother said as the elevator doors closed on them at the hospital. Be strong, Abi. Be strong.

The heavy eight-foot oak door slammed behind Abi echoing off the dark oak-paneled walls, as she took in the sight before her. She had tried to envision this scene before. She had played in her grandfather's courtroom when she was much younger but she had never seen a courtroom in session.

She was struck by the size of the black-robed woman sitting above everyone, flanked by the American and Alabama flags. The great seal of the state of Alabama was directly over her huge head like a halo of authority.

She saw Trudy Waddle, her mouth agape, and a man who must be her attorney at a table to her right. Her father sat frozen next to a man who must be his attorney at a table to her left. And she saw her attorney all alone sitting in a chair equal distance between the others, directly in front of the judge, his head turned all the way around facing her. No one spoke. All eyes were on her.

Unrestrained fear shot through Judge Morgan. The unpredictability of what Abi might do froze his mind.

Abi sensed the absolute power that she possessed at that moment. "I will not live with that man!" Abi yelled at the top of her lungs, pointing a finger at Judge Morgan. "I will not live with him!" She fed off of the adrenaline coursing through her body. "He is not even my father!" With that she began to walk toward Jonathan. Her creased and reddened face clenched with anger. Then she ran. The slapping of her shoes on the tile floor echoed around all four walls as pews flew past her on either side. Part of her seemed to be in slow motion and part of her raced out of control. She did not know how this would end but she didn't need to know. Instinct took over. Her will to survive exploded raising her spirit from the depths of despair.

"Bailiff," Judge Vincent yelled. "Stop that girl!"

The sixty-six-year-old bailiff shot out of his chair and stepped in front of Judge Morgan at the same time Clara opened the door looking for Abi. She gasped at the scene before her. The bailiff grabbed Abi, pinned her arms to her side and attempted to inch her towards the exit.

Abi cried out, "No! Let me go. You don't understand. My mother should be here. This is not fair." She twisted and strained but the bailiff held tight. She was too weak from being sick to put up a fight.

"Mr. Hill, is this your client?" asked Judge Vincent, seeking a quick resolution to this predicament.

Mr. Hill was struck dumb by the sight of Abi scuffling with the bailiff.

"This man hid my mother away so she couldn't be here!"

"Bailiff, remove this young lady from the courtroom. Ms. Waddle, isn't there a foster parent assigned to her during these proceedings?" the judge asked.

Before a shaken Waddle could answer, Clara stepped inside the courtroom and said, "I'm her foster mother, I'll take care of her."

The judge had some questions that needed answers. And they needed answers now. "I need to see the attorneys in my chambers. The court is in recess for ten minutes." As she was getting out of her chair, the judge noticed that Mr. Hill remained frozen. "Now, Mr. Hill. Now!"

"Yes, your honor," Hill muttered, fumbling with his papers.

Clara put her arm around a spent Abi and led her out to the hallway and back to their waiting room.

Since there were only two chairs in the judge's chambers, Mr. Hill stood against the bookcase. The judge leaned back in her chair and lit a cigarette. "Okay, gentlemen, what's going on? I need some straight answers." She inhaled deeply, threw her head back and blew a gray column toward the ceiling vent.

Nixon led off. "Judge, after that display in there, I guess you can see, now, what my client has had to endure these past few months. This girl is completely out of control. She's incorrigible. I should like to address the girl's comment about her mother being hidden away." He pulled on his cuff links for a dramatic pause. "The fact of the matter is that Mrs. Morgan is receiving in-patient treatment at a facility in Mobile. Graceview Sanitarium. The family, which includes her own father, agreed that she needed some psychiatric treatment due to the excessive amount of stress she has been under due to the child's behavior. Look, the poor woman had a nervous breakdown. How many of us here could go through what she's gone through and not have one."

Flicking ashes in the just-made paper ashtray, the judge asked, "Who's the admitting psychiatrist?"

"Dr. Emanuel Sosa."

"Don't believe I'm familiar with him," the judge said.

"I'd be surprised if you were. Dr. Sosa's from the Mobile area. Actually Pritchard."

"How'd you all come to use someone so far removed from here?"

"Dr. Sosa is considered a leader in his field and Judge Morgan wanted the best treatment his wife could get," said Nixon.

"The other comment the girl made, the one about his not being her father. What is that about?" asked the judge.

"Don't have a clue on that, judge. My guess is that she hates him so much she just wants to disown him. You know; typical teenage reaction. Look judge, we've got overwhelming evidence here that would, no doubt, convince you of my client's innocence. And to tell you the truth, I'm beginning to believe that it might be in everyone's best interest to go ahead and have a full hearing and take testimony in order to protect not only my client, but everyone, including the court." Nixon raised an eyebrow to the judge. "For appeals purposes and such, you understand."

The judge looked at Kingsley. "What do you think Robert? You've been awfully quiet."

"Judge, to tell you the truth, I don't see the need in a hearing, especially since we are in complete agreement on the resolution in this matter. There is no way we can win this case given the evidence that the respondent has produced. To go through with a full hearing would be a total waste of taxpayers' money, not to mention the utter waste of the department's time and resources. The strain of direct testimony and cross-examinations on the mother and father and especially the child would be catastrophic. If we can resolve this thing without a hearing, I'm for it."

She turned to Hill. "Mr. Hill, based on what we all just witnessed your client doesn't seem to be in agreement with the proposed resolution as we had been led to believe." The judge removed her glasses to pinch between her eyes, weary from a full day of hearings. "Would you say that's a fair assessment?"

"Yes, your honor," Hill said, silently promising himself he would never accept another dependency case from the court.

She adjusted her glasses atop her nose as another column of gray spiraled to the ceiling. "Mr. Hill, how do you feel about a full hearing?"

Inexperience written all over his face, Hill said, "I honestly don't know, judge. I don't know who to believe." He shifted his weight from his left to his right foot. "But I do know this. The evidence in this matter is overwhelmingly in favor of the respondent. It would not be a pretty sight to try to fight through everything that they have. I really don't think that my client could take the stress of a full blown hearing."

The judge sat upright; grabbed a pen and was about to speak when Hill added, "But if my client wants me to fight this thing, then I guess I have no choice. I work for her."

The judge drove her cigarette butt into the paper ashtray as she honed her thoughts. "Gentlemen, let's do this. Mr. Nixon, can you get me a copy of the mother's psychological assessment that includes the reason for her admission, her present state and her prognosis?"

"Yes, your honor. We can do that."

"I need it by tomorrow afternoon. Check with my secretary before you leave and she'll give you our fax numbers."

"You'll have it," Nixon responded.

"Mr. Hill. I want you to find out from your client what's behind those comments she made today. And if after talking with her, you think she needs any type of counseling or psychological assessment, make that recommendation to the court when we reconvene. Got it?"

"Yes, your honor."

"Robert, the only thing you really need to do is to inform your client that the girl will remain in the department's foster home until we reconvene forty-eight hours from now. At that time I will make a decision on whether or not to proceed with a full hearing." The judge finished her notes, looked up and asked, "Any questions?"

Nixon had no questions. He had all the answers. Kingsley had no questions. He was tired and ready to leave. And Hill had no questions. He was intimidated by all he had seen and heard. The judge buzzed her secretary to inform the parties of the delinquency hearing that the hearing would reconvene in five minutes. Time for one more cigarette.

FORTY-ONE

"Where in the hell did all that come from?" Nixon shouted, slamming Jonathan's office door behind him. He pointed a finger at Jonathan and said, "That little scene out there may end up costing you. We almost had this settled. If we don't satisfy the judge's curiosity about that little outburst, you can get ready for a full-fledged hearing." He finally drew a breath. "And after seeing how unpredictable your daughter is, if I'm you, I don't ever want her on the stand."

Nixon threw his briefcase on the conference table. "And how in God's name did she know about Mobile?"

Jonathan stood up from his chair with a long face of exasperation. "I don't know." He shook his head. "As far as I know, the only person that could have told her is Rebecca. But I don't know how she could have possibly gotten to Abi without us knowing." He thought for a second. "Our man at Graceview would have called me before her phone had a chance to cool. The only time he's reported in was when that social worker was about to cause us some trouble."

"Well, how about you following up on that and let me know what you find out. Now, tell me what she meant by that comment about you not being her father."

Jonathan had hoped he wouldn't have to go into that. It was history he'd hoped he could keep forever secret. "I don't know. Maybe she's throwing all the mud she can just to see what sticks."

Nixon noticed Jonathan's hesitation in answering. "Look, as your attorney, I have got to know everything you know. I am the one who decides what is and what is not relevant in this case. You know that. I sure as hell don't want to be blind-sided again." Nixon sat down on the corner of the judge's desk, leaned forward and said,

"Listen, I don't give a rat's ass if you're this kid's father or not. But, you'd better tell me if there's something here that could cause a problem. If you're going to withhold information from me, I'll walk out now. I'm history. Do you understand me?"

Jonathan sat back down in his chair and folded his hands on his desk. "Okay." He collected himself. "When Rebecca and I were in college, she dated another guy at the same time she was dating me. To make a long story short, he got her pregnant and left her. She never heard from him again. He was a real low-life. Anyway, I loved Rebecca so much I married her right after that. Seven months later, Abi was born. She's not my child, but I love her like my own. I'm the only father she's ever known." Jonathan stared at Nixon and could sense he was pleased with the story. Damn convincing. "There; you happy?"

Relieved to hear this, Nixon replied, "Big damn deal! Happens all the time. You should have told me earlier, and you know it." Nixon stood to gather his overcoat. "Has the girl known this all along?"

"No. I mean her mother and I promised never to tell her. And up until now I didn't think she had a clue."

"Well now we know differently, don't we? As soon as you get home, get in touch with our man at Graceview and see if there's a leak. And if there is tell him I said plug it."

"I'll let you know."

"This is still our case to win. It's ninety percent in the bag. We have all the evidence and we need to keep it that way. And Jonathan, no more surprises."

"Right." Jonathan nodded as his thoughts turned to Graceview.

FORTY-TWO

Malachi tossed a change of clothes, toiletries and his Bible in the old, worn Samsonite. "It's the only way, Clara. The only way." His jaw firmly set, she knew there was no chance of changing his mind. She sat on the edge of the bed teary-eyed and helpless listening to him explain why this had to be done. They kept their voices low. "Clara, you and I both know that Judge Morgan and his high-priced lawyer ain't about to lose this court case. We've got one shot at stopping this man and we've got to take it."

She knew he was right and hated it. She was afraid for her husband.

The telephone rang and Clara left Malachi with his packing.

It was Spence.

"Spence. I am so glad you called."

"Mrs. Peace, I wanted to check on Abi and see how the hearing went. Did she do okay?"

"It didn't go well, Spence. She's pretty torn up. She went to bed as soon as we got home. Didn't even want no supper."

"Did she have to testify?"

"No. She didn't get a chance to. The judge wanted all of the attorneys to get together to see if an agreement could be reached. And as I understand it they reached one but Abi just about changed all that. Spence you should have seen it. It was awful."

"What happened?"

Clara told every detail of Abi's outburst in the courtroom and how proud she was of her, a little girl up against all those lawyers fighting for what she knew was right. "Even though she shouldn't have busted in there, it was the only reason the judge ordered a continuance," Clara said.

"There's a continuance?" Spence asked.

"We're to return in two days. Thursday afternoon."

"Clara, did the judge elaborate on the basis of the continuance?"

"From what I know, it was because Abi told her that Judge Morgan placed his wife at the sanitarium. The judge wants to find out why she was admitted."

"All that means is Judge Morgan's lawyer will instruct his hired psychiatrist to say what they tell him to say."

"I know. Malachi and I have been talking about that. We don't see any way that Abi can win this case. Do you?"

Before he could answer, Clara lowered her voice and said, "Spence, Malachi is as upset as I've ever seen him. He's talking about doing something that scares me to death."

"What do you mean?"

"He says there is only one way to stop Jonathan Morgan."

She let out a long breath. "Do you remember that boy that Rebecca Morgan claimed was Abi's real daddy?"

"Yeah. She did mention that Jonathan wasn't Abi's father."

"His name was Moreau. Landon Moreau. Anyway, Malachi's brother, Josh, knew about Landon because Josh and Jonathan were friends when they attended the university. Jonathan hated this boy. Spence, a long time ago Josh told Malachi that Jonathan killed him."

Spence interrupted, "He what?"

"He killed him, Spence. Thirteen or fourteen years ago. Josh told Malachi right after it happened. He and Jonathan followed the boy going home to relatives in Louisiana, pulled him over somewhere in Mississippi and Jonathan killed him. It tore Josh up so bad he left here and never returned."

Spence listened dumbfounded.

"Malachi wants to go find Josh. He's packing right now."

"I can't believe this."

"We've looked through some of Josh's old letters and the last one we received was over a year ago from a town called Navarre Beach, Florida. Malachi thinks he's probably still there. It's somewhere in the panhandle, near Pensacola. He thinks it's about a six or seven-hour trip. Anyway, Malachi wants to get Josh to take him to where Moreau was buried. He figures if he can find the gravesite, the authorities can identify the body. And with Josh's testimony put

Jonathan Morgan away for the rest of his life. That way Abi will forever be free from ever having to live with that man."

"This is incredible," Spence said, his mind racing. "And you say Malachi is getting ready to leave now?"

"Yes. I reckon he'll be leaving in the next half hour or so."

"Clara, do you think he'd let me go with him?"

"Oh, Spence would you? I'd forever be grateful. Can you hold and let me go ask him?"

"Sure." Spence welcomed the opportunity to help Abi and her mother since things had gone so terribly wrong for them. It's not like he'd miss any work.

"Spence. He said he'd come by and pick you up on the way out of town in about forty-five minutes. Okay?"

"That'll be good. Gives me enough time."

"Malachi asked about your ribs. Are they taped up?"

"Yeah. I'm taped up. The doc said there's nothing could be done for cracked ribs. Just grin and bear it."

"Spence, I really do appreciate you doing this. I'll rest a lot easier knowing you're with him."

"Glad I can help, Clara. And listen, we'll be fine. You don't need to worry about a thing. Oh, by the way Clara, Rebecca will be giving you a call later today."

***

The second phone call Clara received was the one she dreaded most.

"She's in bed asleep," Clara whispered into the phone, hoping it hadn't wakened Abi. "She went to bed as soon as we got home from the hearing. Said she wasn't feeling well. I really don't think we ought to wake her." Clara hated sharing bad news, especially when she felt as though she had no choice.

Rebecca's heart sank as Clara talked about what happened at the courthouse. Her face reddened with anger and her voice quivered as she told of Abi's incompetent attorney and how he caved in to Jonathan's lawyer. "But you would have been real proud of her," Clara added, as she told how Abi fought the only way she could for what she thought was right.

Rebecca tried to picture little Abi fighting all those lawyers. But, the image was too heartbreaking to imagine. She shook her head trying to remove the picture from her mind. For the moment, she preferred the only sight before her, a single street light outside her window. God, she hated Jonathan.

"There's a continuance until Thursday," Clara said. "The judge wants to hear from the psychiatrist regarding his reason for admitting you."

"We all know what that'll be worth," said Rebecca.

Neither spoke for a moment. Rebecca was thinking about how she could get to the hearing on Thursday while Clara was thinking whether or not to tell her about Malachi's plan.

Clara said a silent prayer for strength and guidance. Then, she said, "Mrs. Morgan, there's something I need to tell you."

"What is it?" Rebecca asked.

"Malachi and Spence left about a half hour ago for the gulf coast to look for Malachi's brother, Josh." A deep breath. "Do you remember him?"

"The name sounds familiar. Wasn't he a friend of Jonathan's?"

"Yes, that's what Malachi told me. As a matter of fact, he was at the university at the same time as you and Jonathan."

"Why do they need to find Josh?" Rebecca asked.

Clara was filled with dread as she continued. "Well, Josh left here about thirteen years ago and has never…"

"Why do I need to know this?" Rebecca asked.

"Mrs. Morgan, Josh knew Landon Moreau."

Even after all these years the mere sound of his name did something to her. Before she realized, she asked, "Does he know where Landon is?"

"Mrs. Morgan, what I'm about to tell you is not easy for me. I know it's going to hurt you and I hope you will forgive me."

Clara barely forced the words out. "Josh… witnessed Jonathan … kill Landon Moreau."

The reality that these words were meant to convey did not register with Rebecca. She'd heard the words. But they were such horrible words. They couldn't be referring to the two most important men in her life. "What?"

"Mrs. Morgan, I know this is not the best way to tell you, but you need to know, especially now."

"Jonathan killed Landon? Is that what you said?"

"Please don't make me say it again," Clara pleaded. She wished she could stop and hang up but she knew she had to keep going. She had to say all of this while she could. "Josh knows where Landon's body is buried and Malachi plans to get Josh to show the authorities where it is. He figures this is the only way Jonathan can be put away."

Landon. Dead! Killed by Jonathan. Her head began to swim as she remembered how devastated she felt when she thought he'd abandoned her. She remembered their talks about marriage and their plans to take a trip to Martinique to meet his parents. She remembered his sweet smile, his deep blue eyes and his tender touch. He was such a gentle and compassionate man. Her thoughts sprang back to the present. "Landon's dead? Is that what you are saying?"

"Mrs. Morgan, I know this is a lot for you to handle right now, but you have to know this because of how all of this plays into what we're planning to do to help Abi."

"My God. I can't believe this!"

"I know, Mrs. Morgan, I know."

"How and when did your husband find out?" Rebecca asked.

"Malachi said that Josh told him right after it happened, thirteen or fourteen years ago. He said that Josh and Jonathan had followed Landon into Mississippi as he was headed to Baton Rouge to visit his folks. I think he said it was during Christmas break. They pulled him over somewhere in Mississippi and Jonathan killed him. That's about all Josh told him. He left here and never came back. Hadn't been the same since."

Rebecca's mind shut down.

"Mrs. Morgan, are you okay?"

Rebecca could not force a response. She felt dizzy.

"I know this was a terrible thing to tell you but I think it would have been worse had we not. We thought you needed to know that this may be the only chance we have to help Abi, especially since she probably can't win in court."

Hearing no response, Clara continued. "When they locate Josh, which'll probably be in the morning, they'll head out to Mississippi by mid-day. Malachi figures that if they don't have to travel too far into Mississippi, they could locate the burial site by tomorrow afternoon. He's going to be checking in with me, so if you can call me tomorrow, I'll let you know what they've found. Okay?"

Rebecca heard herself whisper, "Okay."

"Mrs. Morgan, I want you to know Abi is okay. We're taking real good care of her. Don't you worry about her. Just pray all this works out."

"Yes... I will," said Rebecca. She hung up and lay down in a curl on her bed, facing the wall. She squeezed her eyes tight trying to hold back the tears. It was futile.

***

The telephone rang at the Morgan residence and the head of security at Graceview briefed Judge Morgan on Rebecca's phone call. He, then, replayed the conversation in its entirety at the judge's insistence.

Five minutes later, an oily, pasty, pockmarked face in Mississippi hugged a thin, black flip-phone and listened as Judge Morgan gave detailed instructions regarding a gravesite in a Civil War cemetery near the DeSoto National Forrest, between Laurel and Hattiesburg.

FORTY-THREE

After several hours on the interstate and sparse conversation the hum of Malachi's pickup had put Spence to sleep. It was just as well, for Malachi was not a talkative man. To him, conversation should be used only to impart significant thoughts. Idle conversation was of no interest to him.

Alone with his thoughts, Malachi recalled that Josh had called him only five or six times in the past ten years. Every time he was drunk. He knew demons chased his little brother. And he knew his brother would cave to the bottle or anything else that would numb his mind.

Josh had lived in Florida ever since he left although he never stayed in one place long. He'd lived in Fort Lauderdale for thirteen months, the longest in any one town.

He never had trouble finding work because he could do anything; a genuine jack-of-all-trades. Carpentry, plumbing and most electrical work. He could operate a bulldozer and a backhoe. But none of these satisfied anything in him outside of paying his bills.

Malachi was not sure how long Josh had been in Navarre but he guessed twelve or thirteen months. In his last letter, he said he had a little sailboat that he chartered that kept him busy during the tourist season. He called it home.

In the silence Spence dozed. He woke once to see past his reflection in the window. The starlit blackness reminded him of late night trips he and Julia took to her parents in Brewton. It was during these trips that she would complain that he never talked to her. She whined incessantly about his drinking and his pot smoking. He offered no excuses. Never one to possess an unspoken thought, she pontificated that his was the type of personality that needed a crutch, because, down deep he had no confidence in himself. She didn't stop there. She was convinced that his job with its horrors involving abused children contributed to his dependency on getting high every day. She was probably right.

What she did not know was that he needed to be high in order to maintain his relationship with her. He had never known how to be intimate. It scared him. Being high helped lower his anxiety and allowed him to risk being close to her. He had been brought up in a home by parents who were not affectionate to each other or to him. Not once did he see his parents hug or kiss or say 'I love you' to each other. The older he got the more comfortable he became in maintaining distance in his family relationships and later, his dating relationships. It was the role he was taught. Distance provided safety. You only got hurt when you got close. He never told Julia about this. He couldn't bring himself to hurt her more than he had.

"Looks like we got a stroke of good luck," Malachi said, as his slamming door woke Spence. Malachi tossed Spence a bag of sausage and biscuits and said, "The gas station attendant said we're about thirty minutes from Navarre and there ain't but one sailboat charter he knows of. It's in the sound just across the toll bridge."

"Great," Spence yawned. He sat up and un-wrapped a sausage and biscuit. "Got coffee?"

"Yeah, it's around here somewhere." Shaking his head, Malachi remembered. "Coffee's on the roof. Would you grab 'em while I fix my biscuit?"

"No problem," Spence said, "can't hardly make it in the mornings without coffee."

Twenty-nine miles and two biscuits later Malachi dropped two quarters in the toll-booth and drove across the three-quarter mile bridge to the island of Navarre. On their left the sun shot an orange streak down the channel, past a lone pelican on a concrete buttress. Santa Rosa Sound lay to their right in a silver stillness blanketed by a dense fog. They passed a couple of thatched-roofed bars where the locals mingled at happy hour three hundred and sixty-five days a year. The fog was so thick they could see only a couple of hundred-feet out into the sound. No sailboat was in sight.

A half-mile farther where the road dead-ended, they turned east towards Pensacola Beach looking for anything that was open.

Finally, at a twenty-four hour convenience store the nineteen-year-old clerk with green streaks in her blonde hair confirmed what the gas station attendant had said. There was only one sailboat charter operating out of Santa Rosa Sound and she happened to know Victor O'Fate, the man who ran it. Malachi and Spence swapped bored looks as she raved on about O'Fate before mercifully giving them directions. They learned that he'd take in strangers who had no place to stay. That he'd find employment for them or send them on their way with some of his money in their pockets. That he'd helped re-build homes damaged by hurricanes. And that he took in stray or injured animals. Some he'd raise; some he would find homes.

"Sounds like quite a fellow," Malachi said to her, turning to leave. "Thanks for the information."

"No problem," said the clerk. "Tell him Baby says hello!"

"Okay," Malachi said, grinning at Spence.

"I'll tell him."

They returned to the thatched-roofed bars and parked near a thirty-foot pier with a dinghy tied to it and waited for the fog to lift. The sailboat was supposed to be moored in the middle of the sound, according to Green-Streaks, whom, they figured, was quite familiar with it.

"You getting nervous?" Spence asked, noticing Malachi's jumpy right leg. Waiting for the slow-to-come-answer, he rolled down his window to take in the salt air.

"A little," Malachi confessed. "It's been a long time." Malachi's silence told Spence he was worried about what he might find. "I hope this O'Fate fellow can give us some leads. We don't have a lot of time."

The silvery fog was reluctant to dissipate, but ever so slowly offered a ghostly outline of a sailboat approximately two hundred yards directly west of them. They wasted no time in borrowing the dinghy tied to the pier, figuring the owner would not be needing it in the next hour or so. Malachi proclaimed that no commandments or laws would be broken if they'd leave a note to the owner accompanied by a small user's fee.

Spence, being the smaller of the two assumed the position in the bow. After a few minutes of un-synchronized rowing they finally got the hang of each other's rhythm and were soon making good time.

They sliced through the mirror-like water so effortlessly that the only sounds were from the oars and the bow splitting new-cut water.

As they drew closer to the thirty-two foot Catalina they heard music and singing. It sounded familiar to Spence. "Does Josh sing?" he asked.

"Not that I ever knew," Malachi said.

With each stroke of their oars, the music became clearer.

Yes, I am a pirate. Two hundred years too late.
The cannons don't thunder, there's nothing to plunder,
I'm an over-forty victim of fate.
Arriving too late. Arriving too late.

Spence recognized it as a Jimmy Buffett song. "Hey, Malachi, it's a tape or CD. Nobody's singing." Spence knew Buffett's music well. He and Julia used to sing along with his songs all the time, especially when they went to the beach. They'd even managed to attend the *Parrothead Concert* in Key West, Buffett's adopted hometown, back in '89.

The song had repeated itself before they got to the boat, giving Spence and Malachi the impression that it played all night long. As they pulled alongside the sailboat Malachi yelled, "Mr. O'Fate?" There was no answer. After yelling two more times and receiving no answer they climbed aboard.

Spence was nervous about trespassing on another man's boat. He knew men had been shot for less. "He must be down below," he said.

Malachi yelled over the music to the cabin. "Mr. O'Fate!"

Still no answer.

With an approving nod from Spence, Malachi stepped down to the cabin entrance and knocked. "Mr. O'Fate, are you in there?" He looked back at Spence when there was no answer with a 'what- do-I-do-now look?'

The music stopped. Malachi could hear movement inside the cabin.

"Gimme a minute," a tired male voice answered.

Malachi stepped back up, next to Spence.

The cabin door swung open and out of the cabin's darkness stepped a frail, deeply tanned, leathery-skinned little man wearing cut-off jeans and sandals. His gray hair was swept back into a tight ponytail that stopped right between his shoulder blades. The long ponytail made his five-foot nine-inch frame seem shorter. His left hand held a just-lit Marlboro while his right cupped over his eyes in an effort to shield the morning sun. Squinting his eyes so tight he could barely see the men he was talking to, he blew a gray spiral and asked, "Can I help you fellas?"

Spence saw that Malachi was taken aback, so he asked, "Mr. O'Fate?"

"Yeah. I'm Victor O'Fate. Who're you?" he said, taking a second long drag on his cigarette.

A sleepy female voice oozed out from the depths of the dark cabin. "Victor... is somebody there?"

O'Fate glanced quickly over his shoulder to the direction of the voice and said, as he headed back into the cabin, "Excuse me a minute fellas, be right back." As he turned, his ponytail swung around revealing a bright red parrot head tattoo centered squarely between his tanned shoulder blades. A joint dangled loosely from the parrot's beak.

"Quite a character," Spence said, trying to gauge Malachi's take on their host. "Do you think he knows where Josh is?"

Malachi ever so slowly shook his head, walked up to Spence and whispered, "*He is* Josh."

Spence looked up at Malachi from the folding chair he'd just found and sat down in and said, "That guy? That's Josh?"

"Not much left of him, is there?" Malachi turned and stared out over the sound toward the sun. The fog had risen to where he could see the toll bridge that they'd crossed. Traffic was picking up. "Yep, that's definitely him." Malachi was shocked at the sight of his brother. Josh was so thin he was almost unrecognizable. Malachi had noticed the slight trembling in his brother's hands and knew that his fear that Josh was slowly killing himself with drugs and alcohol might be founded.

Before Spence could ask another question, Josh opened the cabin door and said, "Okay, fellas, where were we?"

Spence studied Josh. He saw the deep wrinkles that had been chiseled into his eyes by years of salt water, wind and sun. And now he could see the resemblance in the two brothers. The same high cheekbones and square jaws. The same full head of hair, although

Malachi's had whitened much sooner. And the same kind dark brown eyes.

Because Malachi had positioned himself to the south side of the deck, Josh could now clearly see him without having to squint.

Malachi and Spence did not speak. They watched as Josh's eyes cut from Spence to Malachi then back to Spence then back to Malachi. They watched Josh as he cocked his head to the right and sized up his intruders.

After a quick drag on his cigarette he flashed a crooked half-smile at Malachi, flicked his cigarette over the rail and walked up to Spence. With his back to Malachi he leaned over until his face was inches from Spence's and whispered, "Man, you don't care who in the hell you hang around with, do you?"

The whites of Spence's eyes widened. He glanced at Josh's hands looking for the weapon he knew Josh held.

The look of pure fear on Spence's face was more than Josh could take. He raised up and threw back his head and laughed with such force that every vein under his leathery face and neck stood out like blue lightning. Through tears of laughter he turned and walked towards Malachi. He held out both arms and when he caught his breath said, "Mal, how the hell are you?"

Josh's familiar laugh took Malachi back to a simpler time when two brothers, the sons of Raymond and Margaret Peace, were carefree, mischievous and the holy terrors of the west-end of Trinity, Alabama.

Malachi stepped forward and hugged his brother alarmed at the strange feeling of Josh's bony mass and afraid to squeeze too hard. He stepped one step back still holding Josh's shoulders and smiled. "Josh, I've missed you. How are you?"

"Mal, I'm doing okay," Josh said, with a half-smile that was not convincing. He nervously stroked the side of his head reaching for his ponytail and pulled it over his shoulder, where he continued to stroke it every few seconds.

The brothers were at an emotional standstill attempting to recover from the mutual shock of standing before the other after so many years. Both were flashing back to the time they last saw one another when a very bad thing had happened.

Spence offered an icebreaker. "Josh, is… uh, Mr. O'Fate real or just a name you use?" Then realizing that he hadn't introduced himself, Spence added, "I'm Spencer Dane, a friend of your brother's." He held out his hand.

Josh turned to Spence, shook his hand and said, "Good to meet 'cha Spencer Dane. And yeah, Mr. O'Fate is real. You're looking at him. And he's as real as real can get." Josh cracked a devilish grin, winking at his brother, as though Mal would understand simply because they were brothers.

"Sweetie," the female voice crooned again from down below.

Trying unsuccessfully to be cool about it, Josh said, "Boys, gotta check on my friend. Be right back," as he disappeared into the warm darkness of the cabin.

Spence and Malachi stared at each other, then broke into smiles.

Malachi nodded for Spence to take a seat in the folding chair. "As soon as he returns I'll get to the point. Until then we might as well make ourselves comfortable. He could be a while," he said, as he walked towards the bow, taking in a deep breath of warm salt air. He wondered if every morning was like this for Josh. Loud music. Women. Most likely liquor and drugs. What was Josh really like now? Had the demons of his past followed him only to rob him of what little happiness a nomad could find? Malachi's thoughts were interrupted by the sounds of Josh stumbling up the steps, closing the cabin door behind. This time he held a drink. Malachi looked at Spence. The drink was not a good sign.

"Okay boys, where were we?" Josh began as he took a long sip. "Oh, yeah, Spence, you were asking about O'Fate. Hey," looking down at his drink, "would either of you like a drink? It's Puerto Rico's finest?" After both said no, he continued, "Well I took that name, O'Fate, when I lived in Key West. You know, Jimmy Buffet territory." Spence nodded. "Anyway, I got the idea from one of his songs. You know the one that has the phrase, *I'm an over-forty victim of fate?*" Josh raised his eyebrows seeking any sign that either recognized what he was talking about. He glanced at Mal, then Spence. Malachi did not know the song but Spence did.

"Isn't that what was playing when we pulled up to your boat?" Spence asked.

"Could have been," Josh nodded quickly, giving the impression of strained thought, as though he could remember anything from last night's haze of cocaine and rum. "Yeah, sure could have been. I had

Buffet on all night." Another sip. "Well, anyway, I went crazy over Buffet when I lived in the Keys and that song just nailed itself to my soul. Like it was written about me. So, I thought hey, you know, why not? *I'm the real* victim of fate. If anybody deserves that name, I told myself, it's me. Victor O'Fate is the real me." He flashed a wide grin at them both. "Y'all do get it don't you. *Victim of fate.* Victor O'Fate. You do get it... right?"

"We get it," Malachi said. Offering his brother a crumb of approval, he added, "It fits, Josh, it really does."

Josh smiled and leaned back on the rail basking in the warmth of big brother's endorsement. He needed to keep talking, but couldn't think of anything to say. He wanted to stay in control of the conversation because he was afraid of what Mal and Spence had come for. He knew it had to be serious. But he couldn't bring himself to ask what it was.

Time was beginning to slip away and Malachi knew he had to get to the reason that they came. He hated to dredge up the thing that Josh had spent most of his life running from but he had no other choice.

Malachi began, "Josh, we need your help." He looked over at Spence. "Spence and I are trying to help a young girl who is in a desperate situation back home."

Josh's eyes cut to Spence as he took another drink.

"How do you boys figure I can help some little girl back home?" Josh asked, shaking the ice cubes in his glass.

"Well," Malachi said, "we think you can help us because you know her mamma and daddy."

Horizontal lines grew across Josh's forehead. "Yeah? Who are they?"

With no hesitation, Malachi looked Josh dead in the eyes and said, "Jonathan and Rebecca Morgan," and waited.

FORTY-FOUR

The Colonial Bread truck eased through a light early morning mist to the east gate of Graceview Sanitarium. It sat for the 6 A.M. weekly delivery. At 6:01 the rusty, ten-foot high electric gate slid open to allow the truck to proceed to the loading dock at the mandated five-miles per hour pace. As he passed through, the driver, in his starched, all white uniform and cap, smiled and extended a sleepy half-wave to the guard like he has every week for the past year and a half. When the truck reached its destination the driver cut the engine. Had it not been for a lone screech owl in the woods that bordered a third of the facility there would have been complete silence. The trustees had not yet arrived at the loading dock.

Every week the head of Graceview's kitchen was provided six trustees, handpicked by security, to unload crates of bread, flour and cornmeal. The inmates considered being selected for this 'kitchen detail' a reward. It was a plum they all sought.

At 6:10 the driver could see in his rearview mirror, the heavy metal door slide open and a guard leading the trustees through the doorway towards the rear of the truck. The trustees were not allowed to talk but they were allowed to work at a less than brisk pace in order to enjoy as much time as they could outdoors. Even though the unloading rarely took over an hour, they were permitted a fifteen minute break.

Today the truck-bed was stacked three-quarters full with seven rows of eighteen-inch crates, six feet high, weighing no more than twenty pounds each. Each crate could be lifted easily by most of the trustees, even the women. The protocol called for two trustees in the truck-bed to unload the crates from their stacked positions to rear of the truck-bed. From there a line of four trustees would form a 'bucket brigade', as they liked to call it, to move the crates to their final destination, the heavy wooden skids that would be moved by dolly to the kitchen's entrance.

Five minutes before the break, the short female trustee with the shock of red hair cried out in pain as she fell to the ground thrashing about in convulsions. With her eyes closed, her mouth shut tight and her arms flapping against the ground like a wounded bird, she repeatedly slammed the back of her head in the dew-covered grass. Her fellow trustees froze in their tracks, some holding crates, others staring helplessly at the guard for him to do something.

One of the two trustees working in the truck-bed, Gladys Parvillion, a Lorcet addict, jumped down and ran past the small circle of on-lookers to the kitchen to telephone the nurses' station for assistance. The second trustee quickly grabbed the rear-door strap and pulled the sliding metal door shut. She pulled out the pocket flashlight taped to her right calve and made her way to the seventh row of crates that bordered the cab of the truck. There, in the driver-side corner, she located the sack containing the clothes she had worn when she arrived at Graceview. She crouched down in the space that had been arranged for her and waited. Slowly the truck began to move. No one paid any attention. The driver smiled and tossed up his usual half-wave as he passed the guard at the electric gate, whose eyes were glued to the commotion at the loading dock.

Before a nurse could arrive, Gaylord Washington, the evening shift manager, who had uncharacteristically requested to work overtime, rushed to the rescue of the convulsing trustee. Scooping her up in his powerful arms, he ran with her to the nurses' station, with the on-lookers following behind them. Keeping her eyes shut, the red-haired little munchkin whispered, "Piece of cake, Gaylord, piece of cake." Looking down to the bobbing head cradled in his arms, he saw a faint grin starting to grow and said, "Don't blow it now, Mable. Wipe that stupid grin off your face." She did. But he could not restrain the one growing on his.

The shifting of the old truck's worn gears told Rebecca that they were picking up speed. She couldn't believe they were actually pulling this off. She found herself holding her breath with every shift of the gears. When the driver reached the last of the gears, she exhaled and told herself to relax. They'd be lost in Mobile's traffic soon. The mellow rumble of the truck's engine soon delivered an unexpected tranquility. During a ten-minute stretch of highway, she almost dozed.

Never had Rebecca been consumed with revenge and hatred for another human being as she was for Jonathan. She ached to feel her hands around his throat. She wanted to bring him to the edge of death. She wanted to see the fear in his eyes only the dying possess. She wanted to hear him beg for mercy. And she wanted to tell him, 'Go to hell you bastard.'

The truck geared down and Rebecca could hear echoing of the engine as though they were in a cave. The truck slowed, then the driver killed the engine. A door opened and closed and footsteps came down the side of the truck to the rear door. The rear door raised and light flooded the truck-bed. Even sitting behind the crates hidden from view, Rebecca was blinded by the new light.

"Lady, we're where we're supposed to be," a deep voice said. "I'm gonna pull the door down halfway. You can change into the clothes we left for you. Any questions?"

"No," Rebecca said, from behind the crates. "No questions."

The door slid halfway down and she began to change.

After her eyes adjusted she changed clothes and stuffed her hospital clothes into the corner of the crate. She crawled past the stacks of cornmeal, stood, then knocked twice on the door and said, "Can I come out now?"

A big black hand in a starched white sleeve shoved the door all the way up. Rebecca stared into the smiling face of Leonardo Dejon Washington, first cousin of Gaylord. "Hope your trip wasn't too rough," he said, offering her his hand.

Taking it she jumped down to a concrete floor. "No, it wasn't bad at all," she said, taking in her surroundings.

"Gaylord said for me not to talk to you much. He said the less we talk, the less we'll have to lie about, later, in case we're ever questioned about any of this. And I reckon he's right." Leonardo talked like he had water in his mouth, always keeping his lower lip in a kind of semi-circle, like something was on the verge of spilling out.

Rebecca nodded in agreement as she turned three hundred and sixty degrees studying the old abandoned warehouse. Two rows of windows spanned all four sides about ten feet from the ceiling.

Leonardo extended his right hand dangling a set of car keys. He nodded in the direction of the northeast door of the warehouse and said, "Outside that door sits a white Ford Bronco. It's all gassed up and there's a map in the front seat, in case you need to know how to get out of Mobile. There's also forty-five dollars in the glove compartment for more gas and a little something to eat."

She was overwhelmed. "But how did you all…"

Leonardo shook his head. "Don't ask no questions, ma'am. Gaylord said to take it as far as you need to. But when you get to where you're going, leave it somewhere else. Do you understand?"

She nodded. "I don't know what to say, I…"

"Ma'am, time's a wastin'. Just say 'thanks' and get on out of here."

She looked gratefully into his eyes. "Okay. Thanks." She snatched the keys from his hands and headed for the door. The feeling of exhilaration flooded her body making her legs feel light as feathers and she broke into a run.

Leonardo's deep voice boomed off the walls. "You be careful, now, ya' heah! Ain't no need to be meetin' Jesus on the road."

She never turned, but raised her right arm giving him a thumbs-up.

As she slammed the Bronco's door she pulled her hair back with both hands and took a deep breath. She turned the ignition and started the engine. "Hang on, Abi. Momma's on her way."

FORTY-FIVE

Troubled minds do not let tired bodies sleep. Clara's night had been fitful. Until she had brainwashed herself into believing that everything would turn out fine with Malachi and Spence, she had not been able to come close to sleep. She was up with the sun and glad of it. She put the coffee on and buttered some bread before putting it in the oven.

She tiptoed down the hall to tell Abi that breakfast would be ready soon. Opening the door she saw that the covers were folded back on the bed. She opened the door all the way. No Abi. Everything looked normal. Teddy was in his place on her pillows. Nikes were at the foot of the bed. And her clothes still in the closet. But Clara had an unsettled feeling. Years of caring for children had honed her instincts. She'd not heard Abi get up. In this small house almost every move could be heard. She scanned every foot of the room then turned to go out the door to check the bathroom when she saw it. Taped to the back of the door was a note. Pulling it off the door she read. *I've got something I have to do. Don't worry about me. If all goes well, I'll call you tonight. Love, Abi.*

Clara tried to read the note a second time but her shaking hands prevented it. She stepped back on unsteady legs to sit down on the bed. She buried her face into her hands. What is Abi thinking? And why hadn't she confided in me?

She'd always felt responsible for the failures and problems of others. Years ago, a therapist told her even as an adult she was still the little girl she used to be. Always striving for approval; never getting enough. Always doing for everyone else; making all the sacrifices and feeling guilty if she didn't. He said she would probably go to her grave not feeling worthy because no amount of doing for others could ever reap enough approval for her. She remembered laughing at him when he said that. But that was just her way of covering up the sadness of the truth he'd spoken. Nowadays, though, she had come to be at peace with who she was… a woman trying to give children what she never had. A mother's unconditional love.

As the hall clock struck seven the smell of burning toast brought Clara back to reality. She ran out of the bedroom, slipped on the hall rug, hitting her head on the door facing. She was stunned for a second but quickly regained her composure. Finally getting to the kitchen she pulled the flaming toast out of the oven and slung it into the sink. She turned on the faucet with her right hand while feeling the growing knot on her forehead with her left. Smoke mushroomed across the ceiling as the last piece of toast was drenched and the flames extinguished.

"What else could go wrong?" she said, as she opened the back door to draw out the smoke. She pulled on the sweater that hung on the backdoor coat rack and sat down with a cup of coffee to think about what she should do next. She knew she was supposed to call Children's Services to report Abi missing. But down deep she didn't think that would be what Abi would want. At least not yet. She wished she could talk to Malachi but she had no way of reaching him. She'd have to wait until he called. And she dared not call Abi's mother. The poor woman wouldn't be able to take the news that her daughter's whereabouts were unknown.

It finally settled on her that she couldn't even go looking for Abi because Abi told her in the note that she would be calling at some point later today. Resigned to her in-house confinement she picked up the note and read it again. *If all goes well.* Was she doing something dangerous? *If all goes well?* That part of the note gave Clara a chill.

FORTY-SIX

Spence and Malachi exchanged glances when Josh pulled his third beer from the worn brown leather doctor's bag between his feet on the floorboard. He'd told them when they'd left Navarre that he'd packed a few necessities. He said it was his lucky bag. He'd discovered it on the roof of his apartment in Key West after a tropical storm and knew it was an omen boding good fortune. Malachi and Spence were not certain of the contents of the doctor's bag but they knew it clinked. Although Malachi didn't like the drinking, he decided that if it'd help Josh make the trip, he wouldn't say anything. They couldn't do what they needed to do without him.

Josh had told them the body was buried in a Civil War cemetery in Poplar Town, Mississippi, on the eastern edge of the DeSoto National Forest just across the Alabama line. It is the only Civil War cemetery for black soldiers in the state. The plan was to see if Josh could locate the burial site and if he could, Malachi and Spence would fetch law enforcement while Josh stayed at the site.

About noon Malachi pulled off Highway 45 ten miles from Citronelle to an old, tin-roofed country store and bought Vienna sausages, crackers and cold drinks. He and Josh double-checked his map and saw that they'd be taking Highway 45 into Mississippi until he got to Greene County. There he'd have to depend on Josh to get them to the cemetery.

Cumulus shadows dotted the highway as Malachi's fixed gaze watched the highway's white stripes shoot underneath his truck. Both windows were rolled down because of the rising temperature. Josh closed his eyes and leaned his head back, his ponytail swishing slightly from the wind that blew beer-scented air around the cab. The morning's drinking had begun to numb his mind when he said, "Yeah, we had Viennas and crackers that day, too." He popped a whole cracker in his mouth and followed it with a short pull on his beer. "Didn't have no appetite that day, either... after what I'd seen."

Neither Malachi nor Spence spoke.

Josh drained his can, tossed it into his bag and pulled out another. Spence noticed that the beer, which no longer dripped with condensation, was as warm as the day.

Josh kept his head laid back and his eyes closed as he talked about the day he and Jonathan followed Landon Moreau from Tuscaloosa. It was dusk when they pulled in behind Moreau's white Camaro at the only Amoco service station in Laurel, Mississippi. He remembered it like it was yesterday. Moreau had finished pumping gas and had gone in to pay the cashier. There was no one else in the station. Jonathan walked into the station grabbed a couple of cans of Vienna sausages and said, "They don't sell no black gas here."

"You know," Josh said slowly, "it didn't even faze Moreau. He just turned his head to the right to get a look at Jonathan, paid for his gas and walked out the door. Looking back on it, I don't think he even knew who Jonathan was. I'll never forget the wide-eyed look on that cashier's face. He thought something real bad was getting ready to go down. I could tell it pissed Jonathan off that he wasn't able to get a rise out of him."

"By the time Moreau drove off we'd paid the cashier and jumped into Jonathan's car. Man, was he steamed. He yelled at me to get his pistol out of the glove compartment. Even grabbed me by the collar. But I wouldn't do it. I told him how crazy that was. I hadn't ever seen him like that. I don't guess I ever knew how much he hated the guy. I shoved another beer in his hand instead. About ten miles out of Laurel on a straight stretch of road, we caught up with Moreau and ran him off the road into a ditch. He had hit his head on the windshield or something and for the rest of the night was in and out of consciousness. Jonathan pulled him from his car and threw him in our backseat and we took off. About five miles down the road, Jonathan suddenly pulled off on the shoulder of the road and said we were going back. I remember just staring at him and him staring back at me. He was like, you know, consumed with crazy hate. I know now, what I didn't know then. At that moment, Jonathan knew he was going to kill Moreau. We went back to that gas station, got five gallons of gas in a can and headed back to Moreau's car. Jonathan took the car tag off, soaked the car with gas and set it on fire. Moreau was still out of it in our backseat; he didn't know what was going on. After Jonathan made sure the car was engulfed in flames, we hauled ass. East. Back toward the Alabama line, away from the direction Moreau was headed. We ended up at the edge of DeSoto National Forest. And that's where it happened."

Malachi detected the emotion growing in his brother's voice.

The blood drained from Josh's face when he said, "Jonathan grabbed an arm and a leg and I grabbed an arm and a leg and we dragged Moreau out of the car and into that cemetery. We had to prop him up against the trunk of a tree 'cause he couldn't even lift his head, much less stand up. I remember it was a cedar tree." Josh took a long drink. "It was pitch black that night. No moon. Nothing. After we propped him up where he wouldn't fall over, Jonathan walked back to his car and left me with Moreau. His eyes were barely open and there was a trickle of blood coming from his left ear. I told him he was in big trouble and that he needed to run off... I wouldn't stop him. But he couldn't hear me. He was out of it. Jonathan returned carrying a flashlight, a pocketknife and a piece of rope. When I saw the knife, I told Jonathan this had gone way too far. Wasn't no sense in doing nothing else. He laughed and told me to go get in the car if I wasn't man enough to take it."

He tied Moreau's arms behind his back, cussing him the whole time, then leaned him back against the tree. He was out cold then. I couldn't take it. I headed for the car but I tripped over something and almost fell down. When I turned to see what it was, Jonathan flashed the light where I had stepped. I'd knocked the top off an anthill and ants were running everywhere. He grinned and I could tell he was thinking something bad. Then, he returned the light to Moreau's face. That's when I saw him carving his initials into Moreau's forehead. Blood was running into Moreau's eyes and down his face. I remember thinking that must be what Jesus looked like with that crown of thorns on his head. Then Jonathan scooped up a handful of the anthill and shoved it into Moreau's mouth and up his nose. He took off one of his socks and gagged him with it. I froze. Ants were crawling out of his nose and ears. He was dead in ten minutes. Suffocated. I don't think he was conscious through any of it. Just jerked a little bit there at the end. We buried him and got the hell out of there."

Josh turned his head into the wind and took a deep breath of warm air. His eyes watered. "You know what that son-of-a-bitch said when we got back in the car? He said, 'How 'bout some Vienna sausages and crackers?' " Josh's voice cracked as he repeated it. "How 'bout some Vienna sausages and crackers! Do you believe it?" He finished his beer, reached for another and shoved the Viennas and crackers away. "You boys can have 'em." He wiped his runny nose and said, "I got what I need."

Forty-five minutes later the cemetery's crumbling sandstone archway came into view. According to the bronze plaque underneath it, one hundred and ninety-three unidentified Negro soldiers who fought valiantly and gave their lives for the Confederacy were buried here.

The pounding of Josh's heart filled his ears and muted the crunch of the gravel drive as the shadow of the archway slid across the truck. The sight of the cemetery shot a current of fear through his body. He heard the thud. Again. THUD! It kept getting louder. He closed his eyes tight. It wouldn't stop. He took a long pull from his beer, opened, then shut his eyes tight. But the vision that had haunted him for so many years had returned. Moreau, bound and gagged, his body twitching and jerking out its final seconds of life; his head slamming backward into the tree, splattering blood in every direction. Thud! Thud! Thud! Josh shook his head and opened his eyes.

His forehead dotted with sweat, Josh blurted, "Let me out. I'm gonna do this alone. You guys stay here." Malachi and Spence looked at each other and nodded in agreement.

The cemetery was designed in a perfect square encircled by the dusty chert drive and a four-foot high sandstone wall. Four fifty-year-old magnolias, one in each corner, lent stately respect to the unnamed occupants. The lone cedar stood across the chert drive in the northeast corner of the cemetery, about fifty yards from where they were. Josh slammed the door and headed straight for it as he began to hum *The Star Spangled Banner*. As young boys their dad had told them in times of trouble they could always find the bravery and courage they needed in the national anthem. He'd told them that song had helped untold numbers of Americans who stood for good and fought evil. And anytime he or Malachi were afraid or in a real bad situation, all they would have to do is hum that song and they would instantly feel the surge of bravery that that song gave to all Americans, past and present.

Malachi cut the engine and watched his little brother walk away. Just a shell of the man he used to be. "What time you got?" he asked Spence.

"Two thirty-five," Spence said.

"I imagine he needs a little time to be alone to make his peace. Let's give him five or ten minutes before we follow. Think that's enough?" Malachi opened his door to let the breeze in.

"Yeah, that'll do." Spence reached in the paper bag for the last of the Vienna sausages and offered them to Malachi, who said no thanks. "You think all this is going to work out?"

"Yeah, I do. I don't see any way it won't." He swatted a fly off the steering wheel. "Soon as Josh locates the gravesite, we'll go get the sheriff and let Josh explain the whole story. Then, we'll bring him back here, so he can do all the official things he has to do to make this a formal investigation, you know exhume the remains and all that stuff."

Spence swallowed a sausage and asked the question that had been on his mind the whole trip. "When they dig up the remains and identify Moreau, won't this all boil down to Josh's word against Jonathan's? I mean all Jonathan's got to say is that Josh did it and then it's his word against Josh's. Right?"

Malachi let out a deep breath. He knew Spence was right but wouldn't concede the point. "I've thought about that. Even before we left home I knew this wasn't clear-cut. But I couldn't *not* do this just because it would be difficult to prove." Deep down, Malachi knew this was risky for Josh. He knew fingers could be pointed at Josh just as easily as at Jonathan.

A loud crack splintered the air. Blackbirds scattered from all four magnolias.

"What was that?" asked Spence.

"Sounded like a limb broke… or a gunshot," said Malachi.

They couldn't determine which direction the sound came from. The cemetery was bordered by the DeSoto National Forrest on the northern and western edges and the sound ricocheted off the trees from several different directions.

They bolted from the truck and headed towards the cedar. "Can you see Josh?" Malachi yelled, his voice shaking from running.

"Not yet."

Spence got to the huge cedar first.

Josh was on his back next to a freshly dug grave staring sightless to the heavens with a .22 caliber bullet-hole in his right temple. The pistol was in his right hand. It had erased, for all time, the memories of Jonathan Morgan. A six-inch ribbon of blood snaked through the grass into the empty grave.

Spence turned and grabbed Malachi before he could see Josh. "Mal, it's..."

"What is it? What happened?" Malachi yelled, then shoved Spence out of the way.

His eyes fell on his little brother. A sob caught in his throat and his knees buckled. Spence caught him. Words could not be found. Disbelief gave way to reality and Malachi cried out.

Spence stepped around Malachi and checked Josh's pulse. There was none. He reached over the oozing wound and closed the eyelids.

Malachi cried that it was his fault; his selfishness had taken his brother's life. He raised his head and a fist to the heavens and wailed, "My God, how could you let this happen?"

Spence saw a piece of paper clutched in Josh's left hand. "Mal, there's something in his hand. We need to see what it is."

Malachi's watery bloodshot eyes stared at Spence. He threw his head back again and cursed his God with all the anger his body could evoke.

Spence reached for Josh's left hand and pulled the warm wadded up paper from it. He held it out for Malachi to take but Malachi wouldn't end his fight with God. Spence un-wadded the wrinkled white paper and read, *Long time no see, Josh. The scavenger hunt is over. You lose.*

***

Jonathan Morgan's answering machine clicked on and recorded the voice of a pockmarked-faced man driving away from the DeSoto National Forrest in a standard white van with heavily tinted windows.

His low smoker's voice informed that the job had been completed and the next call would come from Biloxi, where a boat had been chartered to Deer Island to make the appropriate disposal of the remains of Landon Moreau deep in the Gulf of Mexico.

FORTY-SEVEN

Abi slammed the dented backdoor of the 1999 sky-blue Jeep Cherokee saying thanks as she watched it drive off. An hour earlier, she had been afraid to hitch a ride with J. Ray Jessup and his girlfriend, Mona Leesa Coltrane, but the gold cross hanging from J. Ray's neck convinced her she would be okay.

It wasn't until they'd gone about five miles that she'd noticed the pistol in the floorboard next to what appeared to have been twenty or more cartons of Marlboro cigarettes. J. Ray and Mona didn't comment on them. Neither did Abi. They said they were from Texas but the Jeep had Louisiana plates. Again, Abi asked no questions.

For almost the entire hour she was with them, Abi watched J. Ray's eyes in the rear-view mirror. His dark deep-set eyes and his low simian forehead gave him a menacing appearance that belied the true gentleness of his personality. He spoke softly, almost effeminately, when he asked Abi where she was going and why she was hitching a ride. He seemed to be afraid of Mona who was the more aggressive of the two. Her personality matched her coarse rock star looks with her spiked, jet-black hair, heavy makeup and studded black leather jacket. Her black, high-gloss fingernails stood in sharp contrast to the lily-white Marlboros she kept sticking in J. Ray's lips every time he finished one.

Abi didn't tell them the whole truth about her troubles at home, only that she had some. Mona had laughed at her and told her that she didn't have no kind of troubles compared to hers. Between lighting J. Ray's cigarettes, she'd told how her own mother took her to court to take her three children away from her. She didn't look old enough to have three children but she said she'd had all three in eleven months, the last being twins. She told Abi she couldn't understand why a judge would take her children away if she'd never done anything to hurt them. They'd never done without anything. They didn't have much, she'd said, but they had what they needed. She'd told the judge how much she loved her children and how much they loved her, but that wasn't enough. So what if their fathers were not around. The judge had told her when her hallucinations stopped; she could try to get them back. She'd asked Abi over and over how that judge thought her hallucinations had hurt her kids. Abi shook her head and said she didn't know. "The judge couldn't tell me either," she'd said, "but that didn't keep him from taking them." Mona had always thought she'd been born with a special gift of being able to see people and hear voices that others couldn't see and hear. Turns out, she'd said, it wasn't no gift at all. It was a damned curse.

A cold wind whipped Abi's hair as she stood and watched the Jeep shrink in the distance. The last thing she saw was Mona leaning over to feed J. Ray another cigarette.

A sudden tug on her jeans broke her thoughts. She looked down into the bright blue sparkling eyes of a perfectly round, rosy-cheeked dirty face. "Hi," said the little girl who couldn't possibly see at the moment because the wind had blown her stringy blonde hair completely over her eyes. She couldn't have been more than two. "Hi," she repeated. That must be the one word she knows, Abi thought. Abi smiled and knelt down until her face was level with the little girl's. "Hi. What's your name?"

"Hi!" the little girl sung as she held out the remains of a buttered biscuit molded by the fist of her warm little fingers. Abi politely took the offering and acted as though she took a bite. "Ummm, good. Thank you," Abi said, handing the biscuit back to her. She was dressed in a dirty white T-shirt, pampers and pink rubber sandals. It couldn't be more than forty-five degrees, Abi thought. She needed to find this girl's home. Abi took the girl's empty hand and said, "Let's go find your mommy. Okay?" Together they walked past the aluminum sign at the asphalt entrance to the trailer park that read *Blocton City Line Trailer Park, Dalton County's Finest.* Abi remembered the name of the trailer park from the paperwork her attorney had shown her the day he reviewed her case with her at the courthouse. Ty Harper and his aunt, Rose Tarleton were supposed to live here. The trailer park was laid out in five separate lanes with two rows of fifteen trailers on either side. Abi had never seen so many trailers. She felt like she was entering a small city. Most of the homes looked alike, tan with brown trim. Abi wondered if the tenants ever mistakenly entered the wrong home.

When they passed the fourth home the little girl pointed to the right and said, "Mommy!" She pulled Abi past a new emerald-green Firebird parked next to the front stoop and pointed to the door.

"Is this where you live?" Abi asked.

She and Abi stepped up three steps onto the stoop where she then pointed at the doorknob and said, "Mommy!"

"Is your mommy inside?"

The little girl just grinned and pointed directly at the doorknob and repeated, "Mommy!" Her eyes never left the doorknob. She seemed to expect it to turn at the sound of her voice. Abi knocked lightly. They waited a minute. There was no answer.

Abi leaned over. "Are you sure this is where you mother is?"

Again, the little girl grinned, pointed at the doorknob and said, "Mommy!" her eyes never leaving the shiny brass doorknob.

"Okay," Abi said. She knocked again but louder. She pulled the little girl up against her legs to shield her from the whipping wind as they waited. Suddenly the door swung open and a short, fat, balding red-faced man opened the door as he shouted something to the back of the trailer. He tucked his shirttail in his pants, stormed out and yelled, "And if you can't keep her out any longer than that I won't be coming back and I believe you know what that means." He stood on the stoop buckling his belt and asked Abi, "You any kin to her?" his head nodding toward the inside of the trailer.

Abi stammered, "N-No sir."

"Good for you honey. That means you ain't likely to be as crazy as she is." He reached for Abi to steady himself but she jumped inside pushing the little girl ahead of her. She slammed the door and locked it. When she turned around it was too dark to see; she then realized the little girl was no longer beside her.

She slid her hand along the wall until she found the light switch. When her eyes adjusted she could see that all of the windows were covered with cardboard and aluminum foil. A velvet Elvis flanked by a velvet matador hung over a worn Naugahyde sofa. A kerosene heater sat in the center of the room tilting ever so slightly because of the sagging floor beneath the worn and stained shag carpet. Incense was burning next to a lava lamp on the coffee table. The mixture of the incense and kerosene began to make her nauseous.

A short, attractive blonde in a tattered green terry-cloth robe strode into the room with the little girl holding on to her hem. Not until she grabbed her Pall Malls and beat one out of the pack did she look up at Abi. "Want one?" she asked, as she combed her hair back out of her face with her left hand.

Abi shook her head.

The blonde then walked to the kitchen, turned the front burner on and stepped up to the sink to drink water from the faucet. She swirled it about in her mouth and spit it out, then, cupped her hands and splashed her face with the cold water. She dried her face on the sleeve of her robe, leaned over to the red-hot eye, lit her cigarette and took a deep draw before blowing a gray tunnel to the ceiling. All the while the little girl held tightly to her hem.

"You bring Charlsie home?" the blonde asked, nodding down to the little girl.

"Yes. Well, she really brought me," Abi smiled.

"Well, it wasn't time for her to come in. Next time you grab somebody's kid and take it upon yourself to stick your nose where it don't belong, you might want to think about it a little longer."

"I'm sorry," Abi said. "I thought she might have gotten out on her own, you know, without you knowing. And anyway, like I said, she brought me here."

"If you hadn't been nosing around out there, she'd never have brought you here. Who are you anyway and what do you want?" She cut the eye off and reached into the oven and grabbed a biscuit for Charlsie. Charlsie took it eagerly and smiled at Abi as she took a bite.

"My name is Abi... and I'm looking for someone."

"Ain't we all, honey? You just goin' to have to get in line with the rest of us." She took a long drag on the cigarette. "You see that man that just left?"

Abi nodded.

"Well, at this point in my life he's the best thing I've found. I know this ain't the best situation for Charlsie but for now, it'll have to do. He pays my rent and my car payment and when I need him to, he'll even buy us some groceries. My job at the chicken plant barely keeps us in food and clothes." The blonde looked Abi up and down. "You got any idea how much that man means to us? Don't bother answering. I can see you don't have a clue. We can't afford to lose him. If I lose him, Charlsie and I'll be back in the streets." Her voice began to quiver as she asked, "You ever been where you don't know where your next meal is coming from or where you'll lay your head at night? Charlsie and I don't have much, but what we do have is this. We know tonight we're gonna have cornbread, greens and potatoes. After that we'll be laying our heads down together in the same bed. And I'm here to tell you, Missy, that's pretty damn good." She brought a trembling cigarette to her lips. "I reckon you're too young to realize this but, in time you will. Being with the ones you love is all that's really important in this world. It don't matter where and it don't matter what kind of stuff you got," she said, looking around the room.

Abi nodded slowly. "Yes, ma'am. I know what you mean."

"You do, do you?" the blonde retorted with a cock of her head. "Well, why don't you just tell me how you know so much at your age. I might learn something," she snickered. She grabbed for the Pall Malls and beat another one out. "The floor's all yours."

For the next half-hour Abi talked about the abuse, the court, the foster home, her mother, her father and her real father and her last ditch effort to find Ty Harper and get him to tell the truth. When she finished she learned she and Charlsie's mother, Lisa Jett, had something in common. Lisa's younger sister, Sonya, was the girl who lived with Reverend and Mrs. Peace before Abi arrived. Lisa confirmed that Mrs. Peace's assumption that Sonya had run off with the Elrod boy was correct. They had eloped to Iuka, Mississippi, but now live in Jackson. He has a steady job at the tire plant there and she has a good man she can count on. Neither Lisa nor Sonya had heard from their mother since she took off for California to be in the movies.

A half-hour later, Abi hugged Lisa and Charlsie goodbye and promised to stay in touch after everything was settled in court. The sun broke through the scattered clouds and helped warm the cold wind on her face. She headed toward the address Lisa had given her for Rose Tarleton and Ty Harper. Lisa had said she knew of them. Rose, because of her trafficking prescription drugs and Ty, because of his hell-raising.

Abi didn't need to turn around to know Lisa and Charlsie were still standing on their stoop watching her walk away. She could feel their presence. She felt how much they really wanted her to get her life back on track. In a sense they were in the same boat. Abi didn't think bad of Lisa for doing what she had to do to take care of Charlsie. Like Lisa said, it's called *survival.*

Within ten minutes, Abi stood in front of a brand new blue and white double-wide mobile home with an Alabama Crimson Tide mailbox that read, Rose Tarelton, Lot 77, Blocton City Line Trailer Park. Begonias bordered a wooden wheelchair ramp to the front door.

Abi took a deep breath and knocked on the door. She heard a woman yell, "Get the front door, Ty. Get the door." Then she heard what she thought was a drawer slam. "I got it, I got it," a male voice called out.

The door opened and the sunlight shone into the smiling face of seventeen-year-old, Ty Harper. He was wearing a white t-shirt and jeans with a bath towel slung over his shoulder. His black hair was still wet from his shower. "Can I help you?" he asked.

Abi sank into his dark brown eyes.

"Are you here to see my aunt?"

"Uh, no. I'm looking for someone and I don't know if this is the right place or not." She blushed.

"Well, who are you looking for?" he said, with a trace of impatience.

"Uh, Harper. Ty Harper," she managed to say.

"You're lookin' at him," he said, as he opened the door for Abi to enter. "Come on in."

Abi couldn't believe the home was so well decorated. The furnishings reminded her of some of the furniture in her own home. Two beautiful *Frace* prints adorned the walls above the side by side leather recliners that sat on either side of a huge leather sectional. Across the room was a mahogany armoire that contained the entertainment center.

"Who is it, Ty?" the woman yelled from another room.

Ty smiled and leaned closer to Abi. "Who is it?"

"My name is Abi. Abi Morgan."

The name didn't ring a bell. "Do we know each other?" he asked.

"We sort of do."

Ty's blank stare began to fade when Abi said, "I'm from Lincoln. You and I have never met but I think you know my father." She paused. She could see he had not yet made the connection. "Do you know Judge Jonathan Morgan?"

She could see the realization spread across his face but he held back and said nothing.

"I think you know who I'm talking about," Abi said. "Either he or someone representing him came to see you and your aunt recently." She raised her eyebrows soliciting his selective memory.

"I think I know who you're talking about," Ty said. "Did he send you to see me?"

Abi shook her head and flashed a grin. "No. Actually you're probably the last person on earth he'd want me talking to right now."

Ty squeezed his eyes shut and clenched his teeth, as he remembered the things he agreed to say that he and Abi had done. "Oh, man." He shook his head and reached for a chair. He sat down, grabbed the towel off his shoulder and began twisting it, trying to think of what he should say. He looked up. "So you're the one I testified about? I mean, not in court, you know, but on paper?"

"That's me," she said coldly.

He raised both of his hands. "Listen, I had to do it. I had no choice."

Abi stood above him. "You had to do it? You had to lie about me?" Her voice filled with the frustrations of the past few days. "Do you have any idea what your lying has done?"

"Who is it, Ty?" yelled the female voice from the rear of the trailer.

Ty turned in the direction of the voice and said, "I've got to go see about her. I'll be right back." Before he left the room he grabbed the remote control and turned the television on to prevent Abi from being able to hear him and his aunt talking.

Abi had a sinking feeling things weren't going to go as she had hoped. She couldn't afford to make him angry. She realized she needed to change the tone of their discussion. Be less confrontational, she thought. After all, what was done was done.

In a couple of minutes she could see his silhouette coming down the dark hallway carrying something in his arms. He appeared to be looking down at it and she thought she could see his lips moving. Entering the room, Ty smiled and said, "Hey, do you like babies?" He looked back down into the bundle in his arms then back at her and beamed, "This is my boy." The baby nuzzled up against the side of the bottle's nipple and Ty moved it into his mouth. "Ty Gene Harper, Jr. Ain't another one like him on the whole planet," he bragged.

Abi was dumbfounded. Seventeen-year-old Ty Harper had a child? He was a father?

"I never thought I'd like kids, but you know, when you have one of your own, things change. You know, it's a piece of you, something that, oh, I don't know, something you've given to the world." Ty caught himself before he went on and on, "I get so carried away when I talk about him, sometimes, I can't stop."

"I can tell you're proud of him," Abi said.

"You want to hold him?" Ty asked.

"I probably shouldn't, I…"

"Oh, go ahead. There ain't nothing to it. He won't break," Ty said. "Here, sit down in the recliner. He really likes it." He moved the newspaper from the seat and Abi sat down.

She opened her arms and Ty handed him to her. "Now, start rocking," said Ty.

As Abi began to rock, she could feel the baby's warmth as he molded himself to her arms. He smelled like baby powder and his dark brown hair was a fine as air. He looked straight into Abi's eyes as his long fingers gripped his bottle and he made sucking sounds that melted her heart. She looked up at Ty and asked, "How old is he?"

"Ten months," he said. Ty leaned over Abi and said, "Watch this." He touched his son's hand with his forefinger and just like he knew he would, the baby grabbed it. "Look how strong he is. I can almost lift him out of your arms. What a grip he's got!" Ty smiled. "He's gonna be some kind of athlete, I figure. Probably football or baseball."

Abi could see the pride all over Ty's face and knew he loved his son.

Ty snapped back to the moment, remembering some manners. "Hey, can I get you anything? Something to drink?"

"No. Thank you, though," Abi said, never letting her eyes leave the baby's as they rocked as one.

Ty pulled up an ottoman next to Abi and sat down. He combed back his damp hair with his fingers and said, "You know, I never met your father. Never even talked to him. The guy I talked to was a lawyer, I think or maybe he worked for a lawyer, I'm not sure." He looked into the eyes of the person he knew he must have hurt and said, "I guess you're here to find out why I said what I did."

"Don't you think I deserve to know why you said those things?"

Ty was silent as he stared at the floor for a minute. "I don't know how they found me and I don't know the reason they wanted me to do those things, but it was the best thing that's happened to me in my whole life." He stood and walked to the refrigerator, pulled out a Coke and raised it toward Abi.

"No thanks," she said. She rocked in rhythm to the baby's muffled sucking sounds as Ty began to pace.

He popped the can's top. "My probation officer called me and told me a man wanted to meet me. He said the man had some work for me and that I would be paid very well. Looking back, I guess my PO got his cut too." He walked over to a picture on the wall above the sofa and pointed. "See this?" He carefully took it off the wall and handed it to Abi.

It was a picture of a young woman holding a baby who bore a strong resemblance to the one she was rocking. "That's my momma. She's standing on the steps of the Dalton County Hospital two days after I was born. That's me she's holding. My aunt took the picture." Ty felt his throat closing up. "My daddy wasn't even there; he was out on a week-long drunk somewhere." Ty sat down on the ottoman and looked into Abi's eyes. "That was the last time my momma held me. That night my father shot her. Said I was a bastard child; not even his. My aunt said he came in crazy drunk, called my momma a whore, pulled a pistol out of his pants pocket and shot her in the heart. Then he turned and pointed the pistol at my crib but my aunt threw herself in front of me. She caught the bullet in her back and has been paralyzed from the waist down ever since.

Abi remembered the wheelchair ramp outside.

"My uncle finally got the pistol away from him and called the police. My daddy ran off before the police got there and we hadn't heard from him since. Don't know if he's dead or alive. And don't care." Ty cleared his throat. "They took momma to the hospital but she didn't make it through the night. She died on the operating table."

Abi could barely see the baby through her watering eyes.

"Three years later my uncle died and since then, my aunt raised me all by herself. I owe my life to her. Can you imagine being in a wheelchair and raising a kid? Her disability check couldn't even pay the rent and keep us in groceries. Never the same house more than a couple of months at a time. It got so bad she'd sell her pain medication so I could have a new pair of shoes or a gallon of milk. It's been like that all my life. That is, until that man came to see us." Ty stood and walked to the center of the room. "Look around. We've never had it so good. You ask me why I did it?" He set his jaw and said, "I did it to for the woman who ruined her life so I could have one. I did it to keep her in one place for a change. So she won't have to sell her own medicine for me to have a shirt or a winter coat. I did it to give her what she never had. Something that resembled a life! I owe her." He swallowed hard. "And up until this week, the court was about to take my boy from me because we didn't have a safe place to live. But, since that man came to see us, they say my home is plenty good enough to take care of him, now."

"I'm sorry, Abi said." She took a deep breath. "Has he been with you since he was born?" Abi asked.

"He was with his mother across town until about two months ago. She left him on the doorstep late one night with a note that said he wanted to get to know his daddy. Hadn't seen hide nor hair of her since. She must be related to my daddy." Ty tossed the empty can in the garbage. "He's gonna have a life with me; a fighting chance. And if I have to give it to him by lying on a sheet of paper to some stranger then, by God, I'm gonna do it."

Abi and the baby rocked as one as the room fell silent.

Ty ached with the sadness of past hurts and was embarrassed for shedding a tear in front of a stranger. Especially a girl. He wiped his nose on his sleeve and took a deep breath. "You didn't just come here to ask me why I lied, did you?"

Abi knew she could not, in good conscience, ask Ty to tell the judge he had lied. She could not live with the thought of him losing all he had gained; especially his son. She replied, "I just wanted to know why you did it. That's all." She averted his gaze.

"I don't believe you," he said. "You want something else. What is it?" His face reddened and his voice rose. "Don't you pity me! Tell me the truth! Don't you think I can take it? Tell me what the hell you came here for!"

Abi's frustration erupted. "Okay, you're right. I came here for the one thing you can't afford to do for me… tell the truth. I wanted you to go with me back to Lincoln to tell the judge why you said those things about me."

Red-faced, Ty leaned over and grabbed his son from Abi's arms. He walked to the sink to leave the baby's bottle. Then, he disappeared down the hall.

He returned without the baby. "You're right," Ty said emphatically. "I can't give you what you came for. The man told me if I ever told what really happened he'd see that my probation would be revoked and I'd go to prison. My aunt is still on probation for selling her medicine and he said he'd do the same to her. If that happens, you know where that leaves my son. My hands are tied."

"Ty, I know. I realize that now. If I'd known…"

Ty began to think. "And even if I muddied the waters with an about-face, there's no guarantee the judge will believe the truth… which wouldn't even be under oath like the original testimony," he said.

Abi covered her face with her hands. Ty had been her only chance and now, that chance was gone. Time was running out.

"There's got to be a way that judge can learn the truth," Ty said.

Abi looked up. "Well, if neither you nor your aunt can step forward, there's really no one who can. The man that came here was the only other person who knew about the deal right?"

A thought bubbled to the surface. "Wrong. There is someone else," Ty said. Abi could see the wheels of his mind spinning. He pointed at Abi and said, "Stay where you are, I'll be right back. I've got an idea." He headed down the hallway. She could hear drawers being opened and closed and then he yelled, "Can you drive?"

"Sort of," she replied, "I'm almost fourteen."

"It's time you learned," Ty said, emerging from the hallway dangling the keys to his Chevy S-10 in his right hand and holding something black in his left.

FORTY-EIGHT

Rebecca closed the door to the telephone booth and counted the mice pellets on the two-foot square concrete floor until Clara answered on the sixth ring.

"Hello," Clara gasped, out of breath.

"Mrs. Peace? Is that you?" She turned away from the onlookers inside the Quick Mart and faced the parking lot.

"Yes," said Clara, bringing her breathing under control. "I was outside getting the mail and ran to catch the phone. I thought you were Ab… I mean I thought you were Alice," Clara said, hoping Rebecca didn't hear her clearly.

"Did you say you thought I was Abi?"

"Well, I thought … you see… I really didn't know," Clara floundered. She couldn't hide this. And now she knew she shouldn't even try. "Well, yes. That is what I said. I thought you might be Abi."

"Do you mean to tell me she is not there… with you?" Rebecca asked.

"Mrs. Morgan, I must be honest with you. I really don't know where she… I mean…"

"What do you mean, you don't know where she is? How can you not know?" Rebecca's free hand rolled instinctively into a hard fist.

"Let me explain, Mrs. Morgan. Please…" Clara begged.

Rebecca leaned her head back against the dusty glass booth and listened as Clara told of Abi's note. Her eyes closed tight and her heart sank as she shook her head at the words she heard. Clara begged for forgiveness, but Rebecca could not hear her plea. She was trying to think where Abi could be. Clara talked a minute longer and they hung up with Rebecca never saying another word. She needed to put herself in Abi's place. What would motivate her to leave the house? Where would she go? There was only one place.

***

At dusk Rebecca had parked the Bronco somewhere other than her destination, as instructed by Leonardo. Fifteen minutes earlier she had driven past her home and saw no signs of life. She knew if Abi was in the house she wouldn't risk turning any lights on. Jonathan's car was nowhere in sight. He always left his car in the driveway on the side nearest the kitchen door. Rebecca had circled the home twice, for good measure, then parked five blocks away and walked quickly through the growing darkness. As far as she could tell, no one recognized her. Her plan was simple. Get Abi and get out. Don't worry about clothes or anything. Then get a lawyer. She didn't care what time of day or night it was, she needed a lawyer.

She walked to the back entrance that led to the kitchen and peeked in. She could see no lights anywhere. The green glow of the oven clock was the only illumination in the kitchen. She grabbed the door handle and turned. It was unlocked. She stepped in. That familiar good-to-be-home feeling washed over her. Everything looked the same, smelled the same. She looked past the kitchen toward the dining room. Total darkness. Maybe Abi wasn't here after all. She started to turn on the overhead light but thought better of it. She grabbed a flashlight from the kitchen closet. If Abi wasn't here, she'd just get a change of clothes, her checkbook and get out before Jonathan returned. She shined the flashlight on the black and white tile floor and followed it through the den to the stairs. They seemed so much longer and steeper than she remembered. She chalked it up to stress. At the top of the stairs she tiptoed to Abi's room. Standing in the doorway, she swept the room with the light finding no sign Abi had been there.

She tiptoed from room to room. No sign of Abi.

A wave of fear swept through her as she entered the master bedroom. It used to be her favorite room in the entire house. It was the room where she shared herself with the man she grew to love, at least early in their marriage. After all, it was where Thomas and Sara Beth were conceived. But as years went by, it came to symbolize everything that was wrong with their relationship. It became the room where she went through the motions of being a wife leaving her passion for love and life in empty bottles under the bed. It was the room where the realization of lost love haunted her. And it was within these four walls that she deteriorated into a reclusive alcoholic depression.

She pulled an overnight bag from the top of the closet and tossed it on the paisley comforter of their un-made bed. She heard the lighted numerals of the clock radio on the nightstand flip to 6:06 P.M. and it dawned on her that she couldn't ever remember hearing that before. It was so quiet. Too quiet. Then, it occurred to her. Where was Boomer? No one ever entered the house without Boomer barking. Something was wrong. She needed to get what she came for and get out.

Rebecca opened the drawer to her nightstand to get her checkbook. It was not there. She threw a pair of slacks and a blouse in her bag and headed down the stairs to the study where checkbooks were secured in the safety deposit box.

She followed the disk of light across the study's hardwood floor to the roll top desk, where she rested the flashlight, aiming the beam in the direction of the safe behind the Renoir.

"Like a moth to flame," a male voice boomed in the dark.

Rebecca screamed and clutched her throat.

Across the room, with Boomer in his lap and a drink in his hand, Jonathan flicked on a lamp. Rebecca's eyes shot from Jonathan's *I've-got-you-now* smile, to Boomer's wagging stub of a tail, to the .45 that rested under the lamp.

"You know, Rebecca, if you weren't so damn predictable, you'd have no redeeming qualities whatsoever." He raised his glass as if in a toast to her, and then took a sip. "Rather endearing, actually." He pointed to where he wanted her to sit on the sofa next to the recliner and said, "Please, won't you have a seat and join me in a drink. You must be exhausted from your little break-away." Boomer jumped from Jonathan's lap onto the sofa next to Rebecca begging for affection.

She sat quickly and said, "No, I don't think so," stroking Boomer's head, trying to calm herself. "I'm not staying."

"Oh, but, I insist," he said, reaching for the decanter. "I know how you must have missed *Jack* while you were away." He poured two fingers of Jack Daniels into a crystal tumbler and handed it to her.

She took the drink and held it in her lap, with no intention of drinking. She needed to keep her wits about her.

"Drink up, my dear; you mustn't be rude to your host."

She didn't know how confrontational she could be because she had no way of knowing how long he'd been drinking. When he got drunk he could be unpredictable. "Jonathan, if you don't mind, I'd rather not…"

"Oh, what a terrible host I am," he grinned. "We must have a toast. To what shall we toast, my love? Hummm?" His face had the look of playful control, like a cat toying with a mouse. "I've got it!" He raised his eyebrows and placed a hand over his heart. "To *love*," he laughed. "It's what makes the world go round. Isn't that right, sweetheart?" He looked down at her glass. "Rebecca, please. Don't be a rude guest. Raise your glass and toast with me."

Rebecca's heart pounded. She raised her glass. It must've weighed five pounds. She brought it to her lips, but could go no further.

"Rebecca," he said, picking up the .45 and pointing it directly at her suddenly pale face. "Now, take your drink like a good little girl." She did.

It burned more than she ever remembered. The taste of bourbon was as horrible as the bitter memories it brought back.

"That's my girl," he said, with a wide smile. "Now, drink the rest of it and I'll give you another." He waved the pistol as though he was leading an orchestra.

She drained her glass and he smiled, again.

"Now, wasn't that good? I can't imagine how much you've missed that," he said, as he stood to pour her another. He laid the pistol on the end table, took her glass from her hand and reached for the decanter. She thought about diving for the pistol but in a split second her nerve and the opportunity vanished. He handed her half-full glass back to her. "Rebecca," he said, sitting back down and taking the pistol in his hand. "Do you know you're a fugitive?"

"Is that right?" she asked, playing along.

"Why, yes. My friends at the Sheriff's office tell me you've almost attained outlaw status," he howled. "And, get this. This is the best part... you're considered dangerous!" He laughed until tears shot from his eyes. Restraining himself, he said, "That's right. You are an escapee from the looney bin. A threat to yourself and the public." He took a long sip and waved the pistol for her to do the same.

She brought the glass to her lips and faked a swallow.

"I've got to hand it to you, Rebecca. I don't know how you got out of that place, with all the surveillance we had and all the phone calls we recorded. I am impressed. My hat's off to you." He pointed again to her drink and again she faked it. This time he caught it. "Rebecca, take a swallow of your drink." She did. "Now, take another." She did. "Thank you." He looked at his watch as if he had a schedule. "Someday, I'd be real interested in learning how you pulled that off. But, I don't have the time right now. You see I've got things to do tonight. Like, oh, you know, defending myself from my crazy, drunken wife who broke out of the hospital to kill me." He smiled. "You know, Rebecca, crazy people do crazy things." He enunciated his words with measured assuredness to let her know he had thoroughly planned this out and was in complete control.

Her drink was beginning to take the edge off, but she would not let herself relax. "That's quite a little scenario you've conjured up. Did you come up with that all by yourself or did daddy and granddaddy help you with that?"

He couldn't control the twitch that shot through his right eyelid and Rebecca knew she had hit a nerve. She faked another drink. Her mind was blurred with outrageous things she could say or do but she knew one thing, she needed to stay smart. He was in control. "Sorry, to disappoint you, Jonathan, but I have no weapon. Therefore, you see, you have nothing to defend yourself against." She smiled. "I'm just a little ole wife returning to her little ole home."

"Ah, but you do have a weapon, my dear." He reached across the end table behind the picture of them in Tahiti on their seventh wedding anniversary and pulled out a .22 caliber pistol in a plastic baggie. "Voila! Your weapon, madam." He bowed from the waist, pleased with his performance to his captive audience.

The sight of the second pistol unnerved her, but she fought for composure. "So let me see if I've got this right. You plan to claim self-defense because your mentally ill wife broke out of her hospital in order to, what, kill you? Jonathan, why, would I want to kill you?

You are the concerned husband who sought psychiatric help for his troubled wife. Why would I kill the one person trying to get me help? Hummm?"

"Ah, but you see. You're one of those poor troubled souls who didn't think you needed help. They are really the most disturbed, you know. And I've got some fine upstanding witnesses at the Sheriff's office who will testify to your previous violence towards me and how hostile to treatment you actually were." He took his glass from the coaster and waved it as he talked. "Typical reaction of the mentally unstable, really. Retaliation aimed at those responsible for their commitment. Face it, you hated my guts for it. And now, you want me dead for it."

Rebecca realized her chances of getting out of this rested in her ability to keep the conversation going and Jonathan drinking. "And since you will assert self-defense, do you plan to actually kill me or do you plan to just wound me, so that your cronies can return me to Mobile?" She brought her glass to her lips.

His eyes brightened. "Good question, Rebecca. I'm thrilled you're paying attention. Because this is the part I'm having trouble with." He glanced at her glass and frowned. "I'm afraid you're not keeping up your end of the drinking." He pointed the .45. "Now, bottoms up," he sang. She slowly slid the bourbon to the back of her throat, swallowed hard and returned to the conversation.

"Jonathan, I do see your problem. On one hand, you're so very close to getting rid of me forever, which has, I'm sure, an almost indescribable deliciousness to it. But, on the other hand, you would forever be known as the man who killed his wife, the mother of your children. And I don't believe anyone has ever climbed into the governor's chair with that kind of baggage. Do you?" She looked down at Boomer as she stroked his head. "However, if you chose not to kill your poor deranged wife but simply injured her, in an attempt to subdue her, why, my goodness, you could ensure that she continued to receive the treatment she so desperately deserves. You'd practically be a hero. The mental health and women's rights advocates alone would bestow sainthood upon you. Yes, Jonathan, I do see your dilemma."

He delighted in her willingness to joust with him, especially when all of the odds were against her. He'd always admired her spitfire spirit. "It's a tough call, isn't it?" he said.

She smiled and nodded.

FORTY-NINE

Abi saw no lights in the house as she eased Ty's pickup into the driveway. She quickly cut the engine, slid out of the truck and gently pressed the door shut with the heels of her palms. Tiptoeing to the closed garage door, her stomach tightened thinking Boomer would erupt any second from inside the house. She knelt down and peeked underneath. In the darkness she could see the four tires of her father's BMW against the shiny concrete floor.

As she stood, a gentle breeze tossed a strand of hair across her face. She looked up at the starless sky to see dark clouds marching steadily from south to north. For a split second they parted allowing a beam of moonlight to bathe the backdoor. As she reached for the doorknob, she looked in the door window, past the kitchen to the faint glow on the dining room floor. It had to be a light from the study across the hallway. A shadow moved across the glow and she knew he was home. Good, she thought. She wanted him to be here. She turned the knob ever so slowly so as not to alert Boomer. Deep down, it really didn't matter to her whether her father heard her entering or not, because she was going to see him one way or another. But at this moment the element of total surprise appealed to her need to control this situation. Closing the door behind her, she removed her shoes and stepped softly across the kitchen tile floor towards the dining room. She heard his voice coming from the other end of the house. With each step, it sounded as though he was talking to someone. Then, she heard a female's voice. He laughed. There was soft music in the background, Sinatra, and clinking sounds, like ice cubes in glasses.

"See how this appeals to you," Jonathan said, draining his glass. "My poor crazy wife, mad as a hatter and out for revenge arrives at my house rip-roaring drunk. Somewhere between here and Mobile, she obtained a cheap .22 pistol with intentions of blowing my brains out. Of course, being warned by the sanitarium that she'd broken out, I was prepared and had all the doors locked. When she finally arrives, she's so drunk she can barely walk from door to door trying to get in. Through the front door, I attempt to talk some sense into her but she rants and raves and actually says she's here to kill me. Suddenly, she shoots the front door lock and enters, firing twice at me, as I turn for the study. The next shot hits me in the thigh as I finally get to the .45 I keep in the roll top desk. I turn and fire one lucky shot as she fires her last and it catches her right between her beautiful hazel eyes." Proud of his story, he flashes a toothy grin, raises his glass to her, nods and takes a sip.

"Quite a plot, Jonathan," Rebecca said, offering applause worthy of the performance. "It's clear to me now why you became a lawyer. It's because you're so full of bullshit." They both laughed. He, because she was right and she, because she was afraid not to.

As Abi stepped onto the dining room's Oriental rug, she could clearly make out her father's voice, but couldn't identify the female voice. Her softer voice was farther away and muffled by Sinatra and his orchestra.

"So," Rebecca said, trying her best to prolong the conversation and delay the inevitable, "I get to shoot you in your thigh?"

Abi stepped to the entrance of the dining room where she was finally able to hear the lady's voice. And what she heard sounded like her mother. But how could that be? Abi froze straining to hear more.

"Now, Rebecca, do you think I'm actually going to hand you that pistol and expect you to just shoot me in my leg?" He choked off a laugh. "My dear, you've not been reading enough mystery novels. Here's the deal. You get the bullet between the eyes first. Cuts down on a lot of problems, you understand. I mean, come on, put yourself in my position." He grinned. "Then with gloved hands I take the .22 from the plastic baggie and shoot the front door lock a couple of times. I return to the foyer where I fire two shots into the wall of the study, then, a third into the fleshy part of my thigh. At this point, I place the .22 in your hand, making sure to get the necessary fingerprints. Case closed. Crazy bitch dead. Wounded judge pitied. It's a beautiful thing."

Abi threw a hand over her mouth. Her heart pounded in her head stifling any thoughts of what she should do. Should she say something now or wait? Her mother doesn't seem upset. Maybe she should follow her mother's lead for the moment.

Keeping her eyes on the .45, Rebecca said, "Well thought out, Jonathan. But tell me, what do you plan to do about Abi?"

Jonathan dropped his grin and cut his eyes to her. "You still don't believe me, do you, Rebecca? Even though that seventeen-year-old punk signed an affidavit admitting he put Abi up to saying all those things, you still don't believe it?" He paced and rattled his ice. "How can you not believe that? With pictures and everything!" he asked, holding his arms out. "How can you not believe all of that evidence?"

"I talked with Abi," Rebecca's voice shook with rising anger. "And I know my daughter. She does not lie." She drew a long breath. "I also talked with her foster parent and…"

"I know damn well who you've talked to and when you've talked to them. There hasn't been one thing you've done in that place that I didn't know about." His face reddened with the anger he had kept in check.

"I got out without you knowing it!" she shot back.

He took a long sip; shot her a sneer that almost smiled. "Yeah, I'll have to give you that one. Had a little help, did you?" His smile peeled back to reveal hatred and clenched teeth. He pointed the .45 right between her eyes and glared down the sight of the barrel. "Drink up, my dear. I need for you to be, at least, legally drunk."

She took a small sip trying to think of anything to prolong the conversation. Then, it hit her. She coolly said, "I heard a nasty rumor that you had something to do with the disappearance of Landon Moreau."

Swirling his drink, Jonathan drove his eyes into hers and said, "Rebecca, will you ever be able to turn loose of that old nigger boyfriend of yours? Can't you get it through your thick skull that all he ever wanted was a little white tail? Is that too hard for you to grasp? And to prove I'm right, once he got it, he was gone. Am I right?"

Rebecca ignored his parry and pressed on. "Word is that you and Josh Peace ran him down somewhere in Mississippi and killed him. I don't guess you know anything about that." She took a small sip to satisfy him. She could see the veins in his neck were beginning to show and his eyes were shrinking to slits.

Abi stood riveted by what she was hearing.

He needed another drink. He laid the pistol down, stood, glared down at her and reached for the decanter. A slight wobble shot a rush of adrenaline through her. Maybe, just maybe. She thought about grabbing the pistol but opted to keep the conversation moving. The drunker he is, the better.

He poured almost to the brim, leaned over and sloshed a couple of shots into hers. "You know, Rebecca, you're not helping your situation here by talking about your old boyfriend. I don't think that's where you want this conversation to go." He picked up the pistol with his right hand. She watched as his knuckles whitened around the cold steel as he set the decanter down with his shaky left. A row of sweat beads lined his upper lip and the vertical vein in his forehead told Rebecca to beware.

Abi could no longer restrain her emotions. She couldn't stand listening to hateful words any longer. "Stop it!" she yelled, as she stepped out from behind the dining room wall. "Stop it!"

She saw the flash from her father's right hand and the look of horror frozen on his face. In excruciatingly slow motion she saw her mother cover her mouth with both hands, her scream drowned out by Boomer's howl. She felt a kick in her left side and before the room turned upside down, saw her mother coming toward her. Facing the ceiling, the vibrations of hurried footsteps on the hardwood floor jarred her back, as real time returned.

She heard her mother's voice, far off at first, then, felt her mother's hand lift her head. Being shot was not what she had imagined. No pain at all really. She couldn't feel a thing. Except the fear of dying. She didn't really think she was dying, but how could she know? She knew one thing. She was going to do what she came to do.

Rebecca looked back at Jonathan, his right arm dangling by his thigh, the pistol barely hanging by his forefinger, the betrayer. The color drained from his face; water filling his eyes. "Don't just stand there. Call an ambulance! And hurry!" He stood rigid. "Jonathan," she yelled at the top of her lungs, "grab the telephone and call the hospital and I mean right now!" Blood poured from the hole in Abi's sweatshirt and at that moment Rebecca knew she was going to watch her daughter die.

He blinked and moved catatonically to the phone and pushed 911.

Rebecca knelt beside Abi. Their eyes locked. She kissed Abi on her cheek and stroked her hair. "Baby, everything's going to be all right. Your daddy's called for help and they're on their way." Rebecca forced a smile for Abi while she pressed gently with her right hand against the growing red stain in the sweatshirt. In the background, she heard Jonathan tell the operator what had happened and where they lived.

By now, feeling was returning and Abi felt a fire growing to the left of her stomach. She clenched her teeth as it caught her breath. Then, the pain subsided as quickly as it had come. "I ... feel okay... mom." Abi returned a smile. "Really, I don't... feel too bad." Again, the pain streaked across her side taking her breath with it. Through clenched teeth, Abi said, "Mom... I have to... talk to dad." The pain subsided. "I came to do something and... I need to do it... now. Please call him over here." Rebecca's puzzled expression dissolved into eagerness to do whatever Abi asked. She didn't understand what this was about but it didn't matter. It was what Abi wanted. Time was, now, more precious than ever. "And... mom, whatever happens... promise me you will not... not file any charges. Okay? This... was an accident. You know it... and I know it." Rebecca could not bring herself to make such a promise but she nodded, quickly turning to Jonathan. "Jonathan, get over here. She wants you!"

Jonathan could not force himself to raise his head and look at what he had done. "Lay the gun down and get over here!" Rebecca yelled. "Do it, now!"

He leaned over and dropped the pistol in his chair, turned and looked through water across the room at the blurred image of his daughter prone on the dining room floor.

"And bring a pillow from the couch!" Rebecca yelled.

He could not take one step. He fell to his knees, a sobbing heap of remorse and shame.

Rebecca could barely control her rage at the repugnant sight of his self-pitying breakdown. She shot across the room, grabbed him by the collar of his shirt and dragged him, on his knees, across the hardwood to Abi. "You get over there and talk to her!" Rebecca said, straining with her grip. "For some unknown reason she wants you, now. And, by God, I'm going to make sure she gets you." She left him on his knees beside Abi and went to the front door to watch for the ambulance.

He could not bring himself to raise his head and look into her eyes. All he could see was the growing red stain. He sobbed until he couldn't breathe. Then, he felt Abi's warm hand on his.

"Daddy," she said, "I... want to come home." The pain wasn't bad now. "Look at me, daddy. Please!"

He brought his breathing under control and raised his eyes to hers. She put both her hands around his.

"Daddy... you know what I mean."

He could find no words but nodded.

The pain shot across her side. Through pursed, drying lips, she said, "Promise me. No more."

He could not force a word.

She squeezed his hand. "Promise me... daddy. The sex... no more!" She gasped for more air.

His tears began a new stain on her shirt. The words were slow and heavy but they finally came. "I promise... I promise, Abi. No more."

A smile spread across her face. "Thank you, daddy. I'm ready to come home, now."

The wail of the ambulance in the distance was growing stronger. "They're almost here," said Rebecca, opening the front door wide.

"I... need to talk... to mom, now," Abi said.

Jonathan got to his feet and turned to Rebecca. "She wants you," he said, wiping his nose on his sleeve.

"Jonathan, stand in the doorway and direct them in," said Rebecca as she knelt by Abi.

Abi's breathing was steady, now, as the pain had subsided. "Mom... lean closer," Abi whispered. She reached under her sweatshirt and tugged at something until it came loose and pulled out a mini-cassette recorder. She put it in Rebecca's hand and said, "You can turn it off, now. I got what I came for." A bolt of pain, the worst yet, streaked across her side. Abi grimaced and a tear raced down her temple into her hair. "I got... the truth. Put it... in your pocket. Give it… to Chief Bush." Abi squeezed both eyes tight. "The pain's… real bad," Abi whispered.

Rebecca slid the recorder in her pocket as the paramedics bolted through the front door. One took Abi's pulse while the other prepared an IV. They reached their arms underneath her and gently lifted her onto the stretcher and then onto the gurney. Rebecca was told she could not accompany Abi in the ambulance but could follow them at whatever speed necessary.

The paramedics gently laid two safety straps across Abi tightening them until they were snug, steadying her for departure. Abi turned her head to her mother, mouthed *I love you* and closed her eyes.

The metal brackets on the gurney rattled as the two paramedics hurried the limp body down the front steps and into the rear of the ambulance. Rebecca watched as the ambulance's double rear doors slammed shut and sped away, splashing all of the darkness with its rotating red light. She began to cry as the siren softened in the distance. The thought of Abi dying and the robbery of all that could have been was more than she could bear. "No," she said, shaking her head hard. She didn't have time for self-indulgence. She had to be strong. And she needed to get to the hospital for Abi's sake.

Behind her, Jonathan's sniveling broke her concentration. The mere thought of having to turn around and face him made her sick to her stomach. She took a deep breath, closed the front door, locked it and turned around. He sat, motionless on the sofa, elbows on knees, face in hands, a puddle of tears and drool between his feet. She took a step towards him. And Sinatra sang on.

EPILOGUE

The pastor's trembling blue lips failed him miserably as hundreds of heavily-clothed mourners huddled at the graveside service beneath rolling gray skies seeking comfort in his words. Friends, dignitaries and curiosity seekers braved intolerable weather to pay their respects to the Morgan family in their moment of tragedy.

Shifting winds tossed the pastor's words about the crowd, no one section hearing a complete sentence. "In times like these," he said, "we always ask ourselves, 'Why?'" His frozen lips could barely form words. "Why, oh, Lord, why? Death… is always tragic. But, never more so than this." He swallowed hard and ran his tongue across his lips to warm them. "Such a promising future. So much untapped potential. So young." The blustery wind forced coat collars up as coattails flapped a stilted cadence with his words. Hats were pulled down and the remainder of the eulogy fell upon muffled ears.

The Morgan family sat motionless underneath the burgundy canopy in their cold metal folding chairs staring at the closed mahogany casket sprinkled with the first drops of rain. The only sounds, the soft whimpers of Thomas and Sara Beth, huddled underneath Rebecca's arms.

At the conclusion of the service, mother and children were escorted back to the Sullivan's black Cadillac. Friends and on-lookers kept their proper distance showing respect for the family. Heads shook in bewilderment at how such a terrible tragedy could happen to such a good family. Throughout the crowd, gossip- mongers swapped whispers about what they thought really happened. "I can't believe a man as young and vibrant as Jonathan Morgan would take his own life. It's just hard to believe," one said. "It just doesn't add up," agreed another.

It confounded many that two pistols were involved in the

tragedy. The .45 that shot Abi and the other, a .22 that the judge used on himself.

But when it was all said and done, the consensus was that Judge Jonathan Morgan, with the best years of his life ahead of him was so distraught over the accidental shooting of his daughter that he just snapped. Put a bullet in his temple. Hard to believe for most. But not for some. Chief Joe Lee Bush had assured everyone the evidence was undeniable. The prints on the .22 belonged to the judge. Facts don't lie, he'd said.

Rebecca's gloved hand reached out from underneath the umbrella for the back door handle of the Cadillac. She turned her head and took one last look through the gray rain at the huddled mass of blank faces. Underneath the black widow's veil, the corners of her tight, bright red lips turned up as she slid into the backseat and closed the door. Raising the black veil over her head she said, "Take us to the hospital, father. The doctors are releasing Abi at two and she's ready to come home."